The Last Battle

Tamar Anolic

CONTENTS

ACKNOWLEDGMENTS

Many people have helped make this book a reality. First, a thank you to my beta readers: Jennifer Romanski, MSW, your comments on my early drafts were invaluable and your work with veterans is equally important. I commend you for everything. Thanks also go to Melissa Rubin, who provided a second set of comments that helped shaped the final manuscript.

Thanks also to Melissa and my father, for accompanying me on a tour of West Point, when I was sure that neither of you would be interested in going.

I would also like to thank Bob Rubin for the cover artwork and design of the entire outside of the book, front and back. Bob, your energy and enthusiasm pushed this project forward. I can only hope people judge this book by its cover.

Thanks to the women and men who have served in the United States' armed forces in Iraq, Afghanistan and beyond. I have been engrossed in tales of your service since I started on the journey that resulted in this book, and I still have more to learn.

CHAPTER 1

Colonel Zac Madison clenched her teeth and stared at the computer screen in front of her. Her email's empty inbox taunted her. She took a deep breath and could smell the Iraqi desert through the walls of the Forward Operating Base. *There's no way we're going to get the supplies we need,* she thought. *We're running low on armor and bullets, and no one gives a shit.*

She stared at the laptop for a second longer before slamming the screen down. *Fuck this shit,* she thought. *We'll just have to capture those terrorists and be done with it.*

She shut off the lights in the makeshift room she called her office and headed outside. As she walked, she rubbed her head long enough to make sure that her blond hair was still short enough to comply with Army regulations. Her blue eyes scanned the night's darkness, and her hand rested on the machine gun at her side. *This is my third deployment already, and my second here in Iraq,* she thought. *It's a miracle I'm still alive.*

Zac looked up and could see the stars. The sky had an orange tint from the nearby fires that burned huge piles of trash. *I don't think I've had a clean breath of fresh air since I got here. It could be the only thing I miss about growing up on the farm.* The taste of the desert was also pervasive, a sandy taste that Zac knew she wouldn't forget.

1

It was quiet, *but that won't last,* Zac thought. Anxiety hung in the air around her, as heavy as the armor she was wearing. When she turned back towards her unit's living quarters, she saw Lt. Colonel Matthew Edwards coming towards her. He snapped into a salute.

"At ease," Zac said.

"Ma'am, the men and the vehicles are ready for our mission at 0300."

"And what about you? Are you ready?"

"Ready to catch a bunch of terrorists and maybe end these wars?" Matt asked with a grin. "You bet!"

"Good," Zac replied, smiling in return.

Half an hour later, she was driving the second of four Humvees that exited the base. *Our intelligence better be right,* Zac thought as the base disappeared from her rearview mirror. *Searching an abandoned factory in the middle of the night begs for trouble. But Matt's right- these guys are supposed to be among the few terrorist leaders we haven't gotten yet. If we catch them, we may end this thing.*

Zac eyed the Humvee in front of her. *Matt's driving that one,* she thought. She felt her heart race with anticipation, even as a feeling of dread seemed to emanate from the empty desert around them.

Suddenly, a loud explosion ripped through the air. "Shit!" Zac yelped, instinctively slamming on the brakes. The soldiers in her Humvee grabbed their weapons more tightly, their teeth clenching. The Humvee in front of them lifted into the air, landed upside down, and burst into flames.

"Matt!" Zac yelled, knowing there was no way he could have survived an IED of that force. "Radio it into the base," she cried to the soldier next to her. She hit the accelerator and swerved around the burning Humvee, trying to get out of there as fast as possible. "See if you can get air support and a bird. We're still pretty close to the base. Tell them to hurry up!"

Gunfire erupted all around them. In a second, Zac's Humvee slammed into the ground, and she knew her tires had been blown out. Out of nowhere, she could suddenly see enemy soldiers materializing from the desert, wearing black

2

clothing, their faces covered in masks. A few carried grenades and other explosives, and they all carried machine guns. From the light of a distant fire, Zac could also see a rocket launcher. "We have to get out of this vehicle!" she cried.

Diving out of the Humvee, Zac quickly fired her machine gun. To her satisfaction, her initial shots felled a number of the enemy. Several more shots did the same. Just behind her, the exploded Humvee continued burning, and Zac could feel its heat. All around, she could hear firing and cries of pain. The sound was deafening.

Suddenly, right nearby, a grenade exploded, sending Zac flying several feet with the force of the explosion. Searing pain covered her body, and Zac had no doubt that she'd been burned. At the same time, she felt an intense pain in her leg. Looking down, she saw an open wound with blood pouring out of it. *Fuck!* she thought. *I've been hit!*

Angrily, Zac fired several more times, and took several more casualties. But a minute later, even she succumbed to the intense pain all over her body. As she passed out, Zac prayed that the American troops succeeded in pushing back their enemies.

When she awoke, Zac saw nothing but a sea of white. Panicking, she thrashed against whatever was holding her down.

"Relax, relax, you're safe now," said a quiet voice next to her.

Zac's heart continued to race. She swallowed and looked around. She was in a hospital, and a medic in a U.S. Army uniform was standing next to her. Her name band said Rodriguez. "Where am I?" Zac croaked.

"At the American Army hospital in Landstuhl, Germany," Sergeant Rodriguez replied. "We had to airlift you away from the fighting."

"Ah, Colonel, you're awake," said another voice from the

doorway. Zac looked over and saw Brigadier General Jim Conrad, her direct superior officer. "I was beginning to wonder whether you would make it," Conrad continued when he realized he had her attention.

Sergeant Rodriguez snapped into a salute.

"At ease, Sergeant. Would you give us a minute?"

"Yes, sir!" Sergeant Rodriguez briskly exited the room.

Conrad came over to Zac's bedside and sat down.

"What happened to me?" Zac asked.

"Well, what do you remember?" Conrad said.

Zac took a deep breath and described as much as she could.

"You kept firing after you got thrown by the grenade?" Conrad asked, incredulous.

Zac nodded.

Conrad shook his head in disbelief. He was silent for a moment. "Well, your men pushed back the enemy. Killed most of them, but took a few prisoners as well and have been questioning them ever since. Last I heard, the hostages broke down and told where their base of operations was. You did well, Zac. I think the end of the war is in sight, and I didn't think that last week."

"But what about me?" Zac asked.

"You're pretty badly burned on your left side and back as a result of the grenade."

Zac turned, trying to get a look at the burns, but most of her body was wrapped in white bandages. "I don't feel anything," she said.

"The doctors have been pumping you full of painkillers. You wouldn't be alive without them. They also had to change your dressings several times while you were out."

Zac's face crinkled in disgust.

"Truly," Conrad said. "But frankly, I'm surprised you survived as intact as you are. All the other men near that grenade were either killed or are missing limbs. Sorry," he said as Zac winced. "I guess you were far enough away to avoid that."

"What-" Zac's voice faltered. She swallowed, and found

that her throat was very dry. "What about the soldiers in the Humvee in front of me?"

"Why don't you get some rest?" Conrad replied.

"Dammit, Jim, I need to know!"

Conrad heaved a breath. "The driver was killed immediately," he said. "The rest didn't last much longer."

"Matt was one of my best officers," Zac said.

"I'm sorry," Conrad said.

Zac reached for the glass of water on the table next to her bed, hoping Conrad didn't see the tears coming down her face. *I should have been the one driving that first Humvee,* she thought. *I was the superior officer and in charge of the mission.* After she had drunk half the glass of water, she looked back at Conrad and asked, "What about my leg?"

"The bullets shattered your femur. You've been through two surgeries already, and you'll probably need another. You'll be in that cast for several weeks, but after that, you'll walk. With a limp, in all probability, but you'll walk."

"What about active service?"

Conrad looked away for a moment before shaking his head. "Your wounds are pretty bad, Zac. You're not going to fight again."

"What do you mean, I can't fight again?" Zac yelled. "Where's my gun?"

Sergeant Rodriguez reappeared in a hurry. "Sir, perhaps this isn't the best time to have this conversation," she said to Conrad.

"I'm sorry," Conrad said to Zac. He stood. "I'll come by later."

Zac glared at him as he disappeared. *Don't leave me here!* she wanted to yell, but she felt herself start to drift off. As her eyes closed, she noticed that Sergeant Rodriguez had hooked up her IV again.

When Zac awoke again, Conrad was sitting next to her bed,

and instantly, she regretted yelling at him. *He's going to discharge me for insubordination,* she thought. "I'm sorry, sir," she said. "I was totally out of line."

Conrad heaved a breath. "It's not easy news to get," he said.

"Please tell me it isn't true," Zac said, feeling heat rise in her face.

"I wish it weren't. You're one of the Army's best officers. But you'll get decorated several times over and receive an honorable discharge and a disability retirement."

"I'm not disabled!" Zac snapped.

A doctor, dressed in scrubs, hovered at the doorway for a minute before hearing the tenor of the conversation and disappearing.

"Let's see how you heal," Conrad said.

"Jim, I'm thirty-four years old. What am I going to do with the rest of my life?"

"You could teach at any of America's military institutions. You could write a book."

"A book, sir? About what?"

"Yourself. The war. It'll sell if we win, and it looks like we're going to. Listen, Zac, you'll still have your disability checks. You don't have to decide anything immediately. You need to let your wounds heal anyway."

There was a silence. Zac glared at Conrad, who looked away, eying the white walls that surrounded them. Zac took a breath and smelled disinfectant and blood.

Finally, Conrad asked, "do you have family you can stay with, at least until you've healed?"

"No way," Zac replied. "I went to West Point to get away from my parents."

"Was it that bad?"

Zac nodded. "They were assholes. I'm lucky I survived." She tugged uncomfortably on the white sheets that pinned her to the bed. "But my grandfather died recently, and he left me his house and the several acres of land it sat on. I'd say that's my only option at this point."

Conrad nodded. "Where is that?"

"A little outside of Tulsa, Oklahoma."

"Just don't disappear off the face of the Earth. There's already talk of Congressional inquiries into how we're fighting these wars, and the Army itself may need to perform an inquiry if any of those rumors about Victor Rice are true."

"Yeah, I've been hearing a lot about that." *People have been saying that Victor disappeared from one of our bases and may be fraternizing with the enemy. I can't believe that's true. Victor treated me like family when I was running away from my parents and everything else. But he was also one of the wars' biggest critics- even if his complaints were based on real things, like our lack of supplies. I don't know what to think anymore.*

"We definitely have a few facts to clear up," Conrad admitted. "But you did know the guy, so you'll be expected to testify at his trial if the matter goes that far."

It was more than a week later before the hospital staff was comfortable putting Zac on a plane home. As she was wheeled out to the aircraft, still in her hospital bed, Zac's left side remained immobilized- her leg by the heavy-duty cast that was still on it, and her arm and torso by the bandages in which they were wrapped. So, Zac put her right hand around the bed's cold metal rail as she was wheeled outside.

When she got outside, she used her right hand to shield her eyes from the sunlight, the first direct sunlight she had seen since getting to the hospital. As Sergeant Rodriguez, who was wheeling her out of the hospital, slowed to a stop, Zac raised herself up to see what the delay was about. In front of her, other wounded soldiers were being loaded onto the medical plane on the tarmac.

"Lie back, ma'am," Sergeant Rodriguez said.

Zac complied, and a minute later, she was being wheeled over to the plane and up a ramp into the cabin. *This isn't too different from the plane I flew out in when I was deployed,* Zac thought.

Only then I was wearing full armor. Here, everyone's lying down.

After awhile, Zac could hear the plane door being closed. The plane slowly turned and headed for the runway. Then it moved faster and faster until Zac could feel it lifting off into the air. She twisted so that she could see out a window. The ground, which she could only see at an angle, was growing smaller and smaller.

"Lie down for awhile, Colonel," said one of the medics.

Zac complied again, and when she did, she could feel herself drifting off to sleep. When she awoke, the plane had stopped moving. Glancing around, Zac could see that no one was watching her, and she took the opportunity to sit up and look out the window. Outside, she recognized John F. Kennedy Airport in New York City from the times she had flown in and out of there while attending West Point. *I'm home,* Zac thought, and felt tears running down her face.

She spent two days at a hospital in New York before being cleared to be moved to Reynolds Army Hospital in Fort Sill, Oklahoma. *I'm looking forward to seeing Grandpa's house again,* she thought as the plane landed in Oklahoma. *I hope it's in livable condition.* She spent two weeks at Reynolds, enduring another surgery on her leg in the process. But once that was over, her discharge date approached.

"Do you have someone coming that can help you get home?" asked Nick Taylor, the doctor who had been overseeing Zac's care since she had arrived at Fort Sill.

Zac nodded. "My younger brother is coming to pick me up," she said.

"The one that visited a couple of times and is still in college?" Dr. Taylor asked. Zac nodded. Taylor smiled. "He looks like you. No one else in your family can make it, though?"

Zac shook her head. *No one else wants to,* she thought. A half an hour later, she was relieved to see her brother Ben standing in the doorway to her hospital room. "Ready to go?" she asked.

"Ready when you are," he replied.

Zac grabbed her crutches and stood up. Ben moved to help her. "I got it," Zac said.

Dr. Taylor reappeared in the doorway. "Please be careful," he said as Zac hobbled toward him, her left side still bandaged and her left leg sticking out as she maneuvered with her crutches.

"I will," Zac replied, noticing that Ben looked nervous too.

"Don't forget your follow-up appointment next week," Taylor said.

"I won't," Zac said as she and Ben made it out into the hallway. Outside the hospital, Zac waited in the warm sunlight as Ben drove his car around to the front of the hospital. *Spring has definitely arrived*, Zac thought as she heard a bird start singing nearby.

When Ben pulled the car up to where his sister was waiting, he hopped out and moved the front passenger seat all the way back. Then he put Zac's suitcases in the trunk. Zac tossed her Army ruck, with its varying green camouflage colors, over the passenger seat and into the back. Then she maneuvered into the front seat.

"That was relatively graceful," Ben said as he closed the door behind her. "I'm impressed."

"Me too," Zac replied as Ben got into the driver's seat and started the car. *I wasn't sure I could do it.*

In a few minutes, they were out of the hospital complex and heading towards the highway. "Have you been to Grandpa's place at all since he died?" Zac asked.

"Only in the days after the funeral," Ben said. "The inside looked okay, but the outside was pretty overgrown. Abe and I spent a couple of days mowing the lawn and that kind of stuff before we went home," he added of their older brother.

"That was months ago."

"I know. It might be a mess again when we get there."

"Great," Zac said. "It has all those acres in back, too."

Ben nodded. "Abe and I tried to harvest as much of the crops as we could, but Grandpa had been using all that land as a farm. There was no way we could run the whole place in the short time we were there." He maneuvered the car onto the highway.

"This car is getting awfully close to us," Zac said, pointing out the window as the car to their right accelerated and came closer.

Ben shrugged. "As long as he stays in his lane, we should be fine."

Zac shook her head vehemently as the car got closer. "Watch out!" she exclaimed, unconsciously grabbing one of her crutches as if it were an M-16.

Ben put a hand on his sister's shoulder, even as his other hand remained on the steering wheel. "Relax," he said. "We're in Oklahoma, not Iraq. That's a bad driver, not a suicide bomber."

"Can't you drive any faster?"

"I'm already going ten miles an hour over the speed limit. Besides, I've gotten two speeding tickets in the last three months. I don't want any more."

"Dammit."

Ben inhaled deeply as he eyed the road in front of them. "What about all of that anti-anxiety medication they gave you at the hospital?" he asked. "Maybe you want to make use of that?"

Zac shook her head. "No way. The guys I served with who got out before me all turned into walking pharmacies-medication for anxiety, medication for the pain, medication to sleep, medication for the nightmares."

"It sounds like the military hospitals are a little overwhelmed."

"If they would hire more doctors, including more doctors who actually gave a shit, maybe they'd have less of problem."

"Dr. Taylor seems okay, though," Ben said.

"Yeah, he is," Zac admitted. "But they need more like him."

They rode in silence for awhile. Zac stared out of the window to the flat land speeding by outside the car, trying to get her heart rate to slow down. Then Ben asked, "have you heard from Ma and Pa at all?"

"A couple of times," Zac said. "They called when I first got to Reynolds, and maybe once after that."

"That's it?" Ben asked. "They never visited?"

"Nope. Neither did Abe or Melanie," Zac said of their older siblings.

"That's incredible," Ben said.

Zac shrugged. "I was trying to get away from all of them when I went to West Point. I guess it worked."

Ben swallowed, but he kept his eyes on the road.

"Sorry," Zac said. "But our family is tough. You and Clive were the only ones I spoke to regularly." *Clive would know what I should do with my life if he were still here,* she thought.

When they finally pulled up in front of their grandfather's house, the large front lawn was completely overgrown. The paint on the black and white house was peeling, and a few shutters were falling off from around the windows. Most of the windows around the house were either cracked or broken. For a minute, Zac and Ben sat in the car, staring at the property in front of them.

"Great," Zac said. She pushed her door open, swung her legs and her crutches out, and hauled herself out of the car. She shoved the door closed behind her with one crutch as Ben got out and retrieved her ruck and her suitcases. Then she eyed the house in front of her. Gray concrete steps- steep, cracked, uneven- went up to the front door. *Can I do this?* Zac wondered.

"Come around back," Ben said from behind her. "Grandpa had a ramp built so that he could wheel Grandma into the house easier."

"When did Grandma use a wheelchair?" Zac asked as they made their way around to the back of the house.

"Only in the last couple of years," Ben replied. "Probably around the time you deployed to Iraq the second time." He fished the keys to house out of his pocket.

Inside the house, a thick layer of dust covered everything, including the furniture. "Oh, man," Zac sighed.

"Nothing a vacuum won't fix," Ben said. He nodded towards the small bedroom on the first floor. "It might be easiest for you to sleep in there until you can get up the stairs."

Using her crutches, Zac swung over to the small bedroom and looked inside. It was the bedroom her grandparents had always used. *I guess this'll do for now,* she thought.

The next morning, Zac awoke to the sound of a lawn mower outside. Looking at her clock, she saw that it was after 0900. *I've been sleeping a lot since that grenade went off,* she thought. She sat up. *I can't wait until I'm better.* She looked outside and saw Ben mowing the lawn in the front of the house. The smell of fresh cut grass reached her nose. Glancing out a different window in the living room, Zac could see that Ben had mowed the lawn in back as well. Feeling guilty, Zac grabbed her crutches and hobbled into the kitchen.

By the time Ben came inside, Zac had nearly finished cooking breakfast. Ben watched his sister cook as he washed his hands. "I'm impressed that you can do all that even with the crutches," he said.

"Yeah, well, I don't have much of a choice. You hungry?"

"I ate when I got up," Ben said. Nonetheless, he poured himself a cup of coffee from the pot his sister had made, and helped himself to a small plate of eggs and bacon when Zac finished cooking.

"Thanks for putting all that food in the fridge," Zac said. "Let me know how much it cost, and I'll write you a check. Thanks for mowing the lawn, too."

"The vacuuming is next," Ben said.

Zac looked away, the guilt rising inside of her again.

"It's fine, Zac," Ben reassured her. "This is why I'm here. What are you going to do when I'm gone? How are you going to get to your doctors' appointments? There's no way you should be driving with your leg like that."

"The Army has a shuttle that's going to take me to the

hospital and back. It's in conjunction with the Wounded Warriors office in Tulsa."

"What about stuff like grocery shopping? Do you need me to set up an account online so that you can get groceries delivered?"

"That's not a bad idea," Zac said.

A few days later, when Ben left, Zac had a cleaner house, new windows, a kitchen full of food, and a couple of closets full of tools, toilet paper, and other necessary supplies. *I also have house that's completely empty otherwise,* Zac thought. *What the hell am I going to do now?*

CHAPTER 2

Two months later, Zac watched as a local carpenter affixed round metal bars on either side of the staircase going to the second floor of the house. The loud hammering seemed to echo through Zac's head, but she tried her best to ignore it. *I've been having trouble getting up these stairs even since they took the cast off my leg,* she thought. *Those burns were really bad, but they weren't as bad as the damage to my leg.*

I could deal with all of that if it weren't for the nightmares, Zac thought. *I haven't had a good night's sleep in forever, and I can't always get up in the morning. Sometimes my physical therapy has been my only reason to get out of bed at all. Same with the work I've been doing on the house.*

As she watched, the carpenter, an older guy named O'Brien, finished his hammering. "Why don't you give it a try now?" he asked.

Obligingly, Zac put her hands on the bars and hoisted herself up. The metal felt cool against her skin. In a second she was shimmying up the stairs, using only her upper body strength. She made it all the way up in one try, hoping the carpenter did not notice that she had gotten out of breath doing it. "That was easy," she said. "Wish I'd done this earlier."

"Glad to be of service," O'Brien replied. "Always happy to help a returning soldier."

"Thank you," Zac said sincerely.

"From your accent, I'm guessing you're from nearby," O'Brien said.

"I'm from Bearden, Arkansas," Zac admitted. *Guess my accent is still audible, despite my efforts to the contrary.*

"This area was hit hard by the war."

"Has it been?" Zac asked. "This is actually my first stint back since going to West Point."

O'Brien nodded. "Lotsa young people went off to fight, never made it back."

"I think that's true all over the country," Zac said. "We were attacked. A lot of people rushed to enlist to fight back."

"It still wasn't enough, though," O'Brien said as he started returning his tools to his bag. "Congress almost passed a draft a couple of years back."

"I remember that," Zac said. "People were really worried about it." *Including me- mostly because I thought Ben would get drafted.* Uncomfortably, she rubbed her hand back and forth across the top of the railing at the end of the staircase and felt how rough it had become.

After O'Brien had left, Ben called. His regular phone calls were something Zac had begun to look forward to. "How are you doing?" he asked.

"Not too bad," Zac replied, and Ben could tell she was being honest for once. *My cast is off, which is nice, but my leg has really been killing me.* "I'm still getting groceries delivered from that online account you set up, though- I think the delivery guy likes me."

"What makes you say that?" Ben asked, amused.

"He's always nice to me," Zac said. "Though maybe he just feels sorry for me, with my broken leg and all."

"Gotta be careful, then," Ben teased. "Now that your cast is off, maybe he'll start delivering moldy food."

They both laughed, and Zac said, "listen, Ben, I really appreciate everything you've done for me. I know I've certainly snapped at you plenty, but..." She swallowed. "I really don't mean to act like that." As she spoke, Zac noticed the dust around the staircase, newly created from O'Brien's work. *I'll have to clean that up,* she thought.

"No, I understand," Ben said. "I'm sure it's hard being back."

"It's not what I would have expected at all," Zac admitted. "I spent my whole life training to fight. I didn't expect it to be this difficult once the fighting was over."

Zac almost smiled as she hung up the phone a few minutes later. *I still remember when Ma was pregnant with Ben. I was already in high school, and there was that one time she dropped me and Clive off at school on her way to do some shopping- it was one of the only times she did that.*

*   *   *

As Zac and Clive got out of the car and moved towards their school, Zac heard her mother calling her. When she looked back, her mother had gotten out of the car and was holding her math textbook. "Oh, yeah," Zac said, running back for the book. "Thanks." When she got back to the door of the school building that housed both the high school and the junior high, Clive was still waiting for her.

Just inside the entrance, Mrs. Jackson, Zac's history teacher, watched them as they came into the school. "Looks like you two are going to have a new sibling soon," she said.

Zac and Clive nodded. "Looks like it," Zac said, and she and Clive moved down the hallway towards their lockers. "I'm glad people see that Ma's pregnant," Zac said to Clive when her teacher was out of earshot. "Otherwise people would think the kid was mine, or Melanie's."

"Don't worry, Zac, no one's gonna think that kid is yours," a voice said from behind them, and Zac and Clive turned to see James Huntington, a sophomore at the high school. "No one around here wants to touch you enough to give you a kid."

Zac dropped her book bag and grabbed James by his hair. Then she slammed his face into the closest wall. James' nose produced a satisfying crunch. The rest of the student body suddenly surrounded them, chanting, "fight! Fight! Fight!"

Just as quickly, several teachers pushed through the crowd and separated them. Among the teachers was Mrs. Jackson, who looked back and forth between Zac and James before speaking to Zac. "What's gotten into you?" she asked. "This isn't the kind of behavior I expect of you."

"He deserved it," Zac replied. "He was being an ass."

"It's still no excuse for fighting," Mrs. Jackson said.

At home that night, Clive thought otherwise. "You really beat him good," he said, laughing.

*   *   *

It was the middle of the night in Afghanistan, and Zac was on patrol, comfortable in her cammies and reassured by the machine gun at her side. The night was dark, but Zac had no trouble finding her way around the perimeter of the base. Then, up ahead, she saw flashing lights and frowned in confusion. *Flashing lights?* she thought. *Are they from our trucks? Or the enemy's?*

"Ma'am!" she heard someone saying loudly. "Ma'am!"

Zac turned, hoping to see Matt Edwards coming over with some intelligence. Instead, she saw a blue-uniformed police officer coming towards her, and the cop car behind him was one source of the flashing blue and red lights. Slowly, Zac blinked. *Where am I?* she wondered. She looked around and saw houses and traffic lights, sidewalks and paved roads. Police cars and an ambulance were up ahead. *This isn't Afghanistan,* she realized. Her eyes focused on the cop in front of her, the one who had been trying to get her attention.

"Are you okay?" the cop asked.

"I'm fine," Zac replied automatically.

"Then what are you doing walking out here at two in the morning?"

Zac looked around, then looked at her watch. The cop was right- it was the middle of the night. The cop eyed her, his eyebrows coming together in a frown. Then he started walking towards her, and Zac reached for her weapon. It was gone. *Shit!* Zac thought.

The cop noticed Zac's movement, and his frown deepened. He put his hand on his own gun. "Are you carrying any sort of weapon?" he asked.

"No," Zac replied.

"You looked like you were reaching for one." Behind this policeman, Zac could another one coming towards her, watching suspiciously.

"I'm used to carrying one," Zac admitted. She was fully awake now, cognizant of the fact that she had just walked into something that she was not supposed to be near. "I just got back from fighting in Iraq. I guess I'm not used to being home yet."

The cop relaxed slightly, and his look conveyed something that resembled sympathy. "Still," he asked, "what are you doing out at this time of night?"

"I'm not sure," Zac admitted. Her mouth was dry and her heart had started pounding. "I don't know how I got here."

"Do you live nearby?"

Zac looked around again. It was only when she saw the small green street signs at the intersection nearby, with their street names in white lettering, that she realized that she was about a mile from her house. Then she nodded. "Yeah."

"Do you remember going to sleep last night?" the officer asked.

As she thought about it, Zac realized that she did remember falling asleep. "You think I've been sleepwalking?" she asked.

The officer nodded. "Where did you think you were when

18

I first called you?"

"Afghanistan." Zac could feel sweat trickling down her forehead, but she realized that the officer's intuition provided the most logical explanation for how she had gotten a mile away from her house on foot, all the while thinking she was still deployed. "I'm sorry to bother you," she said. "I guess I'll head back home."

"No, wait," the second officer said, speaking from behind his partner for the first time. "We're not going to just let you walk home by yourself."

"What are you going to do, arrest me?"

"No, we're just going to give you a ride home," the first officer said.

"What about whatever's happening here?" Zac said, jerking her thumb over her shoulder to indicate the ambulance and police cars behind her.

"The situation is under control," the second officer replied. "We were just leaving anyway."

Zac eyed the cops, and the police car behind them, with trepidation. *How safe is this?* she wondered.

"Ma'am, you're in Tulsa, not Baghdad," the second policeman said, correctly gauging her expression.

I never said I was in Baghdad, Zac thought. *Is that the only place in Iraq the American public has ever heard of?* She took a deep breath. "Fine," she said. The cops turned back towards their car, and Zac climbed into the back seat. She was relieved when they took the quick route to her house.

"What branch of the service were you in?" one officer asked as he drove.

"Army," Zac replied.

"What rank?"

"Colonel."

"Wow, that high up there," the other officer said. "Do you think you'll deploy again?"

"Probably not," Zac said. They had arrived at her house. "Thanks for the ride."

The officers nodded. "Please be careful," said the one

who had been driving.

Inside, Zac made sure her doors were locked, and watched the cop car drive away from her house, watching long enough to make it sure it was completely gone. *They know where I live now,* Zac thought. *That's not good.*

She took a deep breath and sat in one of the chairs in her living room. When she looked down, she realized she was wearing her combat boots and cammies, but that she was holding her cane rather than her gun. *I really must have been dreaming about going on patrol, even if I don't remember a damn thing about it,* she thought. *It's incredible that I managed to get dressed and wander out in my sleep, though.*

Zac stared across her dark living room and into the fireplace in the opposite wall. *I'm not tired anymore,* she realized. *I can't go back to bed.*

She was still sitting in that same chair, in the same position, when the sun finally peeked above the horizon a few hours later. By then, her mind was working again. *I need to call the doctor,* she thought. *I don't even know what to do about this- sleep medication? He'll probably also make sure I go in for that talk therapy appointment he had me set up months ago,* she realized. *I was planning on blowing it off, but I almost got killed tonight. Something's gotta give. I didn't survive three tours in Iraq and Afghanistan to be killed by a civilian in Tulsa.*

It was pouring when Zac drove into Tulsa for her next physical therapy appointment two days later. *At least this outpatient clinic is conveniently located,* she thought, even as her whole body ached with frustration. *It's been raining for days now,* she thought. *I hate this weather. I hate my life.* Angrily, she stepped on the gas pedal and swerved around the car in front of her.

When her physical therapy was over, Zac drove over to the liquor store near the clinic and parked in its parking lot. She shut her car off and sat there silently for a few minutes. *I really shouldn't be doing this,* she thought. *But so many of us started drinking during that last tour in Iraq, just to get through it, and I haven't been able to stop.* She took a deep breath and stared at the store in front of her. Then she got out of the car and went to the store, using her umbrella skillfully enough that she managed not to get soaking wet.

Inside, the clerk barely looked at her as he rang up her purchases, and Zac was glad. She really did not want to interact with anyone right now, and she certainly did not want anyone commenting on her purchases. A minute later, she was back out in the rain, her frustration with the weather somewhat lessened by the bag she held. *The liquor really does make me feel better,* she thought. *I'm definitely going to take advantage of it later today.*

At 0300 the next morning, Zac awoke, sweating. Then she reached for her M-16. When her hand touched something square instead, Zac jerked into a sitting position, and then yelped as shooting pains tore through her leg. *Where am I?* she wondered. Then she recognized her bedroom in Tulsa.

I wasn't even having a nightmare, and still I'm awake in the middle of the night, thinking I'm back in the desert, she thought. She looked around and realized that the lights in her bedroom were still on. *Shit, did I fall asleep without turning off the lights?* she wondered.

Swinging her legs over the side of her bed, Zac realized that she was still wearing the clothes she had worn the day before rather than her pajamas. *Damn, I must have simply fallen asleep,* she realized. *I didn't even change my clothes or anything.*

Groaning, Zac stood up and went into the hallway. From there, she could see that there were lights on downstairs as well. *Fuck,* she thought, and went downstairs. In the kitchen, a sink full of dirty dishes awaited her as well. *I'll leave that for the morning,* she thought as she shut off the lights and headed back upstairs.

In her bedroom, Zac finally changed into her pajamas and brushed her teeth. Then she went into the hallway and turned off the last of the lights. With the house finally dark, Zac stared outside. Rain lashed at the window, and Zac could see a wall of rain pouring down into her yard. *I can't believe it's still raining,* she thought. *Will it ever stop?*

Suddenly, tears came down her face in the same shape as the drops outside. Feeling a sudden combination of anger and sadness, Zac swung her fist at the wall in front of her. The newly repainted plaster crumbled, and Zac found herself staring at a hole in the wall. A second later, the pain in her hand registered, and Zac winced.

Then the tears fell harder, and Zac leaned on the table in the hall, crying. *I've put so much work into fixing up the house, and here I am destroying it,* she thought. *It's a lot like my life- I've spent so much energy working my way up through the ranks in the Army, and it's all for nothing. I'm nothing but a crippled nobody.*

It was awhile before Zac's sobs subsided, and even when they were over she didn't feel any better, only more tired. But at least her bed finally looked inviting, and Zac wandered back into her bedroom to see if she could sleep, at least until the sun came up.

*   *   *

Seventeen-year-old Zac Madison clutched the strap of her heavy book bag and peered around the corner into her high school guidance counselor's office. Her body remained in the hallway, and only her head was visible in the office. Clive stood on tiptoes behind her, also trying to see into the office without being seen. Inside the office, a man in uniform stood talking to Mrs. Davies, the guidance counselor. In a second, however, he looked towards the doorway and saw Zac and Clive. Clive ducked away, backing further down the hallway, but Zac remained in the doorway, looking back at him.

"Hello!" said the man in uniform. "Come in!"

Zac obligingly slid into the office and sat down at the little table in the center of the room. Clive followed in on tiptoes and sat next to her, looking up at the man in uniform with a certain amount of wonder. Zac shared his feelings but kept her expression neutral.

"I am Cadet Drew Jamieson. I am a cow at West Point. What are your names?"

"I'm Zac Madison, and this is my brother, Clive."

Cadet Jamieson sat across the table from them and smiled. "Are you Melanie's brother and sister?"

"Yeah," Zac said, surprised. "How did you know?"

"I grew up here, and she was in my class through high school. What year are you guys in?"

"I'm a senior, Clive's a sophomore," Zac said.

"Zac is one of our more high-achieving students," Mrs. Davies said. "She would fit in nicely at West Point."

Yeah, right, Zac thought. *She's only saying that to be nice.* "I didn't know West Point recruited here," she said to Cadet Jamieson, trying to hold herself steady on her unevenly balanced chair. *He's going to think I'm an idiot if I can't sit straight.*

"I went to school here myself, and I wanted to make sure West Point was firmly represented," Jamieson replied. "The Academy specifically gave me leave for this weekend so that I could come down here for this visit."

"Are you really a cow?" Clive asked, wrinkling his nose in confusion.

Jamieson laughed. "It means I'm a third year student at West Point."

They can't just call themselves juniors? Zac wondered as her friend Harvey Rendell came into the office and sat next to her. *Harvey's one of the only people I've told that I may apply to the service academies,* Zac thought. She looked at him gratefully and he smiled back. Two other students- also seniors- came into the room, and the small table was soon full. Everyone around the table introduced themselves, and Cadet Jamieson launched into a sales pitch of West Point.

"What kind of scores do I need to get in?" Zac asked during a pause in the conversation.

"The Academy only accepts the best candidates," Jamieson replied, and rattled off the standardized test scores and GPAs of the most recent class of cadets.

"Zac's got those scores, easy," Clive said, pointing his thumb at his sister.

"Shut up," Zac hissed.

Jamieson smiled at her. "Do you play sports, Zac?" he asked. "They're required at West Point."

Zac nodded. "I run indoor and outdoor track."

"She's good, too," Harvey said. "She made the National Championships last year for the mile." Zac elbowed him to shut him up.

"But you don't run cross-country?" Jamieson asked.

"Nah, I gotta help my parents harvest the crops on the farm in the fall," Zac replied, ducking in embarrassment. "But I would if I could."

Jamieson smiled at her and handed her an application to West Point. "Perhaps you should consider cross-country at West Point, then," he said. He handed applications to Harvey, Clive, and the other two seniors in the room, who promptly bolted as soon as they had the paper in their hands. Jamieson watched them go. "I may have scared them off," he said.

Slowly, Zac, Clive and Harvey stood up and left the room. From the hallway, they watched Jamieson leave a few minutes later. "Please consider applying," he said when he saw them. "The Academy has really changed my life."

"We will," Zac said.

Jamieson turned and left, marching down the hallway towards the door of the school. His boots clicked on the floor with a sense of purpose.

"You should definitely apply," Harvey said to Zac. "You'll get in."

"I'm going to," Zac said. "You should too."

"I will," Harvey said. "But my grades and SAT scores aren't anywhere near yours. I think I'll probably end up at the University of Arkansas." He sighed.

"That's a fine school," Zac said. "I'd probably go there if

I didn't need to get away from home so badly."

*   *   *

At the outpatient clinic in Tulsa, Zac groaned as she hauled herself through the exercises and stretching the physical therapist ordered. Shooting pains raced down her leg every time she moved, and every time she stretched, her muscles felt like they were being pulled a mile. All around her, both in the main exercise room and the smaller rooms off the main room, was exercise equipment she had never seen before and couldn't even name- equipment she never would have needed if she had been healthy. *There are a few pieces of equipment here- that chin-up bar, that set of parallel bars that a gymnast would use- that I was able to use quite well before that grenade went off,* Zac thought.

To make matters worse, all around her were men without arms, women without legs, veterans who were relearning how to walk without being able to see in front of them or hear the orders they were being given. *And those are the ones who are healthy enough for P.T.,* Zac thought.

When the appointment was over, Zac winced slightly as she rubbed her leg- it still hurt in places, and her limp was still more noticeable than she wanted. *The therapy isn't going as fast as I'd like,* she thought.

A call to Dr. Taylor the morning after her sleepwalking had gone as she had expected- she had a new prescription for sleep medication and extra encouragement to attend her appointment with a social worker. With her physical therapy now over, Zac drove to the Vet Center a few miles away for the therapy appointment. *It's a pain that all these appointments aren't in one place,* she thought. *At least I have a car and can drive now. If I'd had arrange for the Wounded Warrior Program to shuttle me to all of these places like when my cast was on, it would take all day, and I'd never get anything else done.*

Inside the Vet Center, she looked around the waiting

25

room, first at the other soldiers and families who were also waiting, then at the dilapidated ceiling tiles that were threatening to come down. *I hope this social worker thing isn't a waste of time,* she thought. *Talking about my feelings for an hour? I'd rather spend an hour killing the enemy. But after the other night, I really can't skip it.*

Zac looked around the waiting room again, and noticed how crowded it was. *I heard that they've been transferring a lot of soldiers here because this Vet Center offers decent care and there are other good hospitals in the area,* she thought. *It wasn't until I got home after being wounded that I even heard about what's been happening in the VA and military hospitals- the long waiting lists to see doctors, the hospital closures.*

When the social worker was ready to see her, a nurse called her name and Zac got up to follow her. "Hold up a second," she said as the nurse disappeared down a hallway. Her limp made her move more slowly than usual.

"Sorry," the nurse said apologetically, but she did wait. A minute later, she led Zac to one of the small offices in back, where a tall, dark-haired man was waiting for her.

"Zahara?" he asked.

Zac was so unaccustomed to being called by her full name that it took her a second to respond. "Yes," she said finally. "But most people call me Zac."

"Of course," the social worker said. "I'm Ron. Come in." As Zac followed him into the small office, she noticed the sign outside the door: "Ronald Adler, LMSW." "Have a seat," Ron said, so Zac chose one of the chairs across from Ron's desk. Ron himself pulled a chair next to the desk and sat facing her. "So," he said, looking interested. "The last Zac I knew was a man. Is it usually a woman's name too?"

"Not usually," Zac admitted. "But my mother spent her entire pregnancy with me thinking I would be a boy. She was set on the name Zachariah, so when I turned out to be a girl, she made one concession to reality by putting the name Zahara on my birth certificate. But she'd spent her entire pregnancy calling me Zac, so she just continued doing that."

Ron regarded her with amusement. "When did you get back from Iraq?" he asked, and Zac could hear his New York City accent.

"About three months ago."

Ron nodded. "The war looks like it's ending," he said.

"It might," Zac answered. "You ever serve?"

"Nope," Ron said. "Been a civilian my whole life."

"Great," Zac said sarcastically, her voice rising. "There's no way you understand what I went through." She stood up and made for the door.

"Wait, wait, wait," Ron said hurriedly as he stood up. "Most of the therapists are civilians. At least give it a try."

Zac glared at him.

"You seem very angry."

"Of course I am," Zac said. "Did you know I'll probably be given a disability retirement?"

"Your wounds are pretty bad."

"Don't you think I know that?" Zac snapped. "I can't even fucking walk straight!"

Ron put a hand on Zac's shoulder and led her back to her chair. Then he sat down as well. "I'm sure it must be difficult for you."

"You don't know the half of it. Did you know I used to run competitively?"

"Actually, I did. You were nationally ranked while you were at West Point, in addition to being fifth in your class academically."

Zac arched her eyebrows.

"I looked you up in addition to reviewing your file," Ron said. "A lot of people are very impressed by what you've done in your life."

"That's bullshit. I'm a total loser."

"That's not true at all."

Zac shrugged and looked away. The yellow walls with sunlight dancing on them were a more appealing sight than this social worker staring at her. The silence lengthened.

"Listen, Zac," Ron finally said. "I think you might also

benefit from group therapy in addition to these individual sessions."

Zac shrugged again. "What would a group of civilians know about what it's like to be in combat?"

"No, this would be a group of other vets or active duty personnel. I know of several social workers and psychiatrists who are looking for additional people to round out their groups. I can submit your name if you'd like."

Zac frowned, nonplussed. "I guess it's worth a shot," she said finally.

The rest of the hour passed slowly, and Zac felt empty when she left. *That wasn't as bad as I thought it would be,* she thought. *But it was a waste of time. I'll keep the physical therapy appointments,* she decided, without any question in her mind. *It's the only way I'm going to get better. I just can't see the utility in this social worker nonsense, though.*

That night, Zac was glad to go to bed. The physical therapy always tired her out, and, much as she hated to admit it, she was upset at the lack of progress in her talk therapy. *I finally got in there because I almost got myself killed,* she thought, *and it didn't help one bit. I'm still stuck where I've always been. Ron doesn't give a damn about me.*

It was less than two hours later when she was awoken by the sound of a bomb. Still in the desert, Zac yelped as the tent she was sleeping in collapsed around her. As she struggled to get out from under it, Zac looked for her gun. As she searched, the tent became wrapped around her, tighter and tighter. In a second, she was struggling to breathe...

Zac jerked awake and leapt out of bed, looking for her gun. Her heart was racing. It took her a full minute to realize that she was at home in Tulsa. Taking a deep breath, Zac turned on the lamp next to her bed. In its light, the square shape of the bedroom revealed itself. Zac took a deep breath as her eyes glided over heavy dark wood dresser and the lighter colored desk that stood next to it. Then she looked at the small table next to her bed. *I don't even need to open that drawer to know that I have my gun in there,* she thought. *If these nightmares continue, I may have to make use of it.*

As her heart finally slowed down, though, Zac shook her head at herself. *Maybe I should put that gun somewhere else,* she thought. *Then I won't be so tempted to use it on myself.*

Leaving the light on, Zac opened her bedroom door and headed downstairs, taking advantage of her new bars to get down the stairs easily. She finally stopped in the kitchen and stared out into the darkness of the spring night. Then she opened the window in front of her, and was rewarded with a chilly breeze. *See?* she thought. *Much different from the weather in Iraq.*

The next day, Zac drove into Tulsa to do some shopping. *Grandpa left me his two broken-down trucks along with the house,* Zac thought as she drove. *They weren't worth much, but selling them both gave me enough money for this used Toyota, and that's good enough for me.*

She merged onto the highway and sped up. *I can't imagine why Grandpa was so generous with me,* she thought. *I never did much to warrant it. But he did always think Melanie, at least, was a lost cause. Besides, Grandma was gone, and Clive had already been killed by the time Grandpa passed away, so...*

Zac eyed the car in front of her, momentarily forgetting what was thinking. *Why is that driver going so slowly?* Annoyed, Zac changed lanes and sped up. *Finally,* she thought as she pressed the accelerator to the floor and eyed the open blacktop in front of her. A minute later, she heard a siren behind her, but it was not until the police car was behind her, lights flashing, that Zac realized that the cops were after her.

"Shit!" she said aloud. *What could they possibly want?* It was only when she glanced down at her speedometer that she realized that she was going more than ninety miles an hour.

"Where'd you learn to drive like that?" the policeman

asked after Zac had pulled over to the side of the road. The cop car sat behind her, and its flashing lights sent alternating red and blue flashes through Zac's car.

"Iraq and Afghanistan," Zac said through her open window, hoping to sound apologetic, even if she really wasn't. *The civilians around here really can't drive.*

The cop next to her window eyed her and swallowed. Zac could see his Adam's apple move up and down in his throat. "What branch of the armed forces did you serve with?"

"The Army."

"How long you been back?"

"A couple of months. Why?" *What is this, an interrogation?*

The cop sighed. "We've been having a lot of issues with returning soldiers and the way they drive."

"Can't say I'm surprised," Zac said, suddenly becoming angry. "You have no idea what it's like to drive in those convoys, driving around bombs and being shot at- if your Humvee didn't break down in the first place."

"I've heard stories," the cop said. He looked away from her and to the highway behind them, where cars continued speeding by. "Here's what I'm going to do," he said finally, as he looked back at Zac. "I had you going nearly twenty-five miles an hour over the speed limit, but I'm only going to give you a ticket for going ten over. It's a much smaller ticket. Please try to drive more safely in the future- if I pull you over again, I won't be so nice."

Zac did her best to control her anger. *Just stay quiet,* she thought. *If you blow up at him, you'll only make it worse.* A few minutes later, the policeman drove off, and Zac waited until she could no longer see his car before she merged back onto the highway.

Inside the city limits, she pulled up at a Target that had just opened the week before. Red, white and blue triangular flags hung all around the story and the parking lot. In front of the store was a huge red and white banner that read, "Grand Opening!" *I saw an ad for this place in the paper,* Zac thought. *It better be good.*

Inside, however, the store seemed huge, much larger than it had looked from the outside. Zac grabbed a cart and pushed it towards one of the aisles. *I need towels,* she thought. *Where would those be?* Several aisles over, she finally found the first of three aisles dedicated to towels. Towels in all colors and sizes lined the shelves, and Zac quickly found herself getting overwhelmed. *Who needs towels in this many colors?* she wondered. *It never even occurred to me to figure out what size I needed either. Damn it!*

As she stood in the middle of the aisle, Zac suddenly felt as though the store was spinning around her. Her heart raced, and she gasped for breath. *I need to get out of here,* she realized. Leaving her cart in the middle of the store, Zac raced outside and made a dash for her car.

Once inside the car, Zac put her head on the steering wheel. Tears ran down her face. All around her, other shoppers- mostly women with kids, though there were plenty of adults that were there alone- seemed oblivious to her pain. Teenagers with iPhones stared into them as they wandered across the parking lot. Further away, a group of kids laughed as they grabbed their shopping carts.

Zac stared around her, feeling like she was a million miles away from the people that surrounded her. *You'd never know that the country was still at war,* she realized. *These people have no idea what I've been through.*

$$* \qquad * \qquad *$$

Towards the end of her first deployment in Iraq, Zac was en route to the mess hall for dinner when Private David Maynard rushed towards her. "Ma'am, come quick," he said. "It's Specialist Randolph, ma'am. He's out on the roof- with his small weapon."

"Damn," Zac said. She raced up to the roof, and got there faster than Maynard.

A number of her grunts had gathered, looking uneasily towards Glenn Randolph, who stood at the edge of the roof, clutching his small sidearm tightly, his finger on the trigger. The soldiers parted to let her through. For a moment, Zac stood behind Randolph, trying to figure out what to say.

Randolph glanced over his shoulder. "Go away, ma'am," he said. "I don't want you to see me do this."

"I don't want to see you do that either," Zac said. "Put the gun down and we can talk about it."

"What's to talk about?" Randolph asked in a shuddering voice. "This is my third deployment to this shithole. I ain't never going home."

"Sure you are," Zac said reassuringly. "I'll make sure of it."

"Why?" Randolph asked. "What is there to go home to?"

"What about your wife, your kids?" Zac asked, thinking of the pictures of Randolph's family that he always carried with him.

But Randolph shook his head. "My wife is as sick of these deployments as I am," he said. "She just sent me divorce papers- in an email!"

The grunts around them winced, and Zac cringed as well. "That's awful," she agreed. "But it isn't worth your life."

"Nothing is worth anything anymore," Randolph said. "We patrol these streets every day in front of a population that hates us and does nothing but blow us up."

"I know what it's like," Zac said. "I'm out there with you every day. The loss of each of the men that have been killed under my command has been terrible for me too."

Finally, Randolph took a deep breath as he turned around and looked at Zac squarely in the face. "I know that, ma'am," he said. "Seeing such a high ranking officer doing the same work we're doing has been made it more worth doing."

"It's still worth our effort," Zac reassured him. "And I want to continue working with you- but first I think you need to work things out with your wife."

"Can you get me a few days leave to do that?"

"I can," Zac said. "I want this to work out as much as you do."

Finally, Randolph lowered his gun. Zac held out her hand. Randolph held the gun out to her, even as he turned his head away and stared in the opposite direction. Without hesitating, Zac strode forward and took the gun from him. Then she backed off a few steps and tossed her head towards Specialist Fred Richter and Corporal Dean Webster, whom she knew were friends with Randolph. They understood her, and both jumped forward.

"Come on, man," Webster said, put his hand on Randolph's shoulder. "We'll get this sorted out."

Randolph followed Webster and Richter back inside without even glancing back at Zac. Once he was gone, the other grunts slowly followed him in, and Zac was left alone on the rooftop. Slowly, she took a few deep breaths. *Thank God,* she thought. *But I'd better put in the paperwork for his leave.*

CHAPTER 3

With her physical therapy finally helping, Zac's discharge date from the Army approached. *At least I'll get to continue PT until I'm actually finished with it,* Zac thought. *It's just that now, the VA will be handling it. I don't know what's going happen with that talk therapy shit, but I'm not going back to see Ron again.*

The next morning, her official discharge papers in her hand, Zac waited in line for four hours at the VA to fill out the paperwork for her veterans' benefits. When she got to the window, however, the clerk closed the window and put up a sign that said "closed."

"What the hell?" Zac demanded. "Are you just going to walk away?"

"It's lunchtime," the clerk said with a shrug. "Sorry."

Zac banged on the window. "I've been on line for four hours," she yelled. "I was told to get here at 0900, and I still haven't gotten any help."

"Sorry." The woman shrugged again as she continued to walk away.

"What am I supposed to do now?" Zac demanded.

The clerk did not respond. Soon, she disappeared out of the office and into a back hallway where Zac could not see her anymore.

"Fuck!" Zac yelped. The line of people behind her looked just as frustrated. "Is it always like this?" Zac asked.

"Every day," someone said.

Zac turned back to the office in front of her and exhaled in frustration, struggling not to give vent to the curses that were running through her head. *Maybe if I don't turn in my discharge papers, the Army will take me back,* she thought. She almost smiled at the thought. *I wish that would happen.*

As she was deciding what to do next, a younger woman who had been on the phone in the office finished her call and came to the window. "Can I help the next person?" she asked.

"Yes, please," Zac said. "The other woman just got up and left. I've been in line forever."

"Yup, that's the standard around here," the new clerk replied. Her nametag read Tonya. "It is lunchtime, after all."

"So I hear," Zac replied. As she glanced at the office behind Tonya, she could see that Tonya was indeed one of the few people that was still there. "You're not taking a lunch break?"

"Not now," Tonya replied. "Not with this line."

"Someone who's willing to do their job at the VA," Zac said. "That's new." Tonya looked amused, but she did not say anything. Zac handed over her paperwork, which Tonya processed quickly and efficiently. In less than twenty minutes, Zac was ready to go. "Thanks for getting this done," she said.

"My pleasure," Tonya replied, looking past Zac to the next person in line.

As she left the building, Zac glanced behind her to the line she had been standing on, which had grown even longer as she had been waiting on it. Then she shook her head, relieved to be heading outside into the sunshine.

Two days later, Zac was at home, finally getting some work done on the second story of the house. *Grandpa was sick for awhile before he died,* she thought. *And Ben's work on the place my first weekend here was only superficial. The place was really a mess. The first floor and the outside look okay now, but the second floor still needs a lot of work.* She continued dragging the paint roller across the wall in front of her. The paint fumes clogged her nose, but the newly white walls looked much better for her effort. The sound of the telephone interrupted her work. "Hello?" she said into the receiver.

"Good morning, is this Zac Madison?" came the voice on the other end.

"It is," Zac said, glancing out the living room windows to her backyard, where she had been thinking of planting some flowers.

"My name is Jane Sayed, and I am an administrative assistant at the VA."

Uh oh, Zac thought, but she stayed silent, waiting for the punch line.

"We've decided to transfer you to a different therapist when you begin your talk therapy here at the VA," Jane said.

I guess I wasn't the only one who thought my last appointment with Ron wasn't helpful, Zac thought. "Okay," she said. "Who's the new guy?"

"A woman, actually," Jane replied. "Her name is Alexandra Bittman. Your appointment with her next week is in the same time slot as before."

"Alright." *I can't complain.* "Another social worker?"

"No, Dr. Bittman is a psychologist."

"Okay." *I'm moving up the food chain.* "I'm surprised I have an appointment so soon, though. When I filed my paperwork, I was told it would be at least four months, and that was just for the appointment with Ron."

"There have been several cancellations recently," Jane said.

"Works for me," Zac replied. "Is the appointment at the VA itself?"

"Not, it's at one of the Community Based Outpatient Clinics we have near the VA."

"Where is that?"

"I can email you the address and driving directions," Jane

said.

"That would be great," Zac said. "How come it's not at the VA itself?"

"We don't have the resources. If you stayed with the VA for your therapy appointments, you'd only see a social worker once a month, but these clinics are staffed with psychologists and social workers who can see their patients once a week."

"It's unbelievable that the VA can't handle the volume of veterans that need help," Zac said.

Jane sighed. "We've only recently set up services to help female vets in particular, and this appointment is through the CBOC that caters to that. Otherwise, you'd have to go to the CBOC in Vinita."

"Where the hell is that?"

"About an hour away."

Zac clenched her teeth to keep from cursing. There was a brief silence on the other end, and Zac could hear Jane typing at her computer. *She's probably emailing me that information,* she thought. "What about group therapy?" she asked. "Ron said he thought that would help me."

Jane sighed again. "Our groups are completely full, and we have a waiting list a mile long."

"If I put my name on that list, when could you expect to fit me into a group?"

"Some vets put their names on this list over a year ago and are still waiting."

"Fuck!" Zac yelped. She slammed the paint roller she was holding down onto the small table in front of her. White paint splattered across the table and onto the floor.

"I'm sorry," Jane said.

"What the hell am I supposed to do?" Zac demanded.

"Some vets have been getting help from the vets organizations in the area, like the Wounded Warrior group. Maybe it's worth calling them."

"That's a disgrace!" Zac shouted. She slammed the phone back into the receiver.

That afternoon, Zac checked her email to find a message from Jane with all of the information about her appointment with Dr. Bittman. She was about to sign out of her email account when she noticed that Jane had used the VA motto as her email signature. "To care for him who shall have borne the battle, and for his widow and his orphan," it read.

Zac burst into laughter as she signed out of her email account. *If this had been a combat injury, I'd be dead by now,* she thought.

For a minute, Zac stared at her computer, mentally replaying the conversation she had had with Jane that morning and wondering if any of the local veterans organizations could really help her find group therapy at all. *The Wounded Warriors chapter out here has already helped me so much, getting me to my doctors' appointments when I had my cast on and everything. I'd hate to bother them again.*

Still, Zac could not help herself from running a search on veterans' organizations nearby. One of the first websites that came up was for a very specific veterans' group- the Iraq and Afghanistan Veterans of America. *I didn't even know there was such a thing,* Zac thought as she clicked on their website and watched their distinctive acronym dance across her screen. *Guess it's worth a phone call.* When she heard the phone ringing on the other end, though, Zac suddenly felt uncertainty in the pit of her stomach. *What do I even say?* she wondered.

In a second, the phone was being answered, and a man identifying himself as Chris was asking what she needed help with.

"Good morning, Chris," Zac began politely, even as she struggled to control the rage building within her. "I'm an Army officer who's returned from Iraq and Afghanistan after being injured, and the VA has been telling me they don't have the resources to help me out. Is that something your organization would step in for?"

"Absolutely, ma'am," Chris replied smoothly. "Where are

you located, and what services are you looking for?"

"I'm out in Tulsa, Oklahoma," Zac said, before explaining her situation.

"We've had a lot of vets from your area contact us," Chris said.

"The VA here sucks," Zac complained.

"It's not just the one there, unfortunately. The upside is that we have a number of contacts in your area- let me make a few phone calls and I'll call you back. And ma'am-"

"Yeah?"

"If you ever need to talk, even before I get back to you, feel free to give us a call. We always have someone available."

"Thank you," Zac said sincerely.

Later that same day, Chris called Zac back with the names of several therapists who worked with groups. "That was fast," Zac said.

"That's how we roll," Chris said. "I did two tours in Iraq myself, so this one's personal."

Zac almost smiled at that.

"That first woman on the list said she only needed one extra vet to complete the group," Chris added, "so if you call her, you could probably start real soon."

Zac thought about it. "Yeah, that's a good idea," she said finally. *Might as well see what that's like. I won't go back if it sucks.*

When her physical therapy appointment was over the next day, Zac stopped at a hardware store near the outpatient clinic for some carpentry and painting supplies. *My cane and limp definitely make it hard to get around,* she thought. *I really hope my limp clears up soon and that I won't need the cane anymore.*

As she hobbled through the store, Zac was impressed by the rows and rows of merchandise- gleaming hand tools and electrical tools that looked functional and in good shape. *A lot of these tools would have come in handy when our convoys broke down in Iraq,* she thought. *How is it that some of the stores in middle America are better stocked than the United States Army?*

When she finally located the aisles she needed, Zac was also struck by the amount of customers in the store. *It's the middle of the day on a Thursday,* she thought. *Don't these people have jobs?* She thought again of the Target from which she had recently fled. *A lot of people were shopping there too.*

As she added what she needed to her cart, Zac felt the stares of the other customers and was glad when she finally found everything she needed. At the counter, the clerk rang up her items and put them in a brown paper bag. "You find the wrong end of a tractor?" he asked.

"Come again?" Zac said, completely bewildered by the question.

The clerk nodded at her cane. "I never once met a woman who could operate farm machinery," he said. A few other store employees around them snickered as they continued helping other customers and talking amongst themselves.

Zac, wanting to avoid a scene, kept quiet as she paid for her purchases, even as her anger boiled within her. *Farm machinery accident my ass,* she thought.

"So what happened?" the clerk finally asked.

"I was injured in Iraq, leading my unit in combat," Zac replied. "My injuries are from a grenade and a machine gun, not a tractor."

Suddenly, all the conversations around her stopped. The store fell silent, and Zac could feel the eyes of everyone around her boring into her, feel the waves of discomfort that hit her. The clerk, seeing everyone watching, finally looked embarrassed. "I'm sorry," he said. "A lot of veterans that were lucky enough to come home have been having trouble being back."

"Must be because of your attitude," Zac replied, feeling a little better for being able to stick it to him.

"I'm sorry," the clerk said again, his face red.

This time, Zac simply grabbed the bag with her purchases in it and headed for the door, wishing again that she could move more smoothly, but feeling some satisfaction from hearing the door slam behind her.

*   *   *

One night in March of Zac's senior year in high school, she and Clive returned home from school to find their mother in the kitchen, cooking dinner. A large glass of wine sat on the counter next to the pot she was stirring. A double-sized bottle of the same stuff sat on the counter nearby. It was late in the day, and it was dark out. *That's the only downside of running track,* Zac thought. *It's late, and I'm tired.* Behind her, Clive, who had just gotten through a grueling few hours of basketball practice, looked equally exhausted.

Three-year-old Ben, sitting in his high chair at the kitchen table, grinned at them as they entered. Zac smiled back at her little brother, and Ben pointed at the stack of mail that sat on the table in front of him. "Dat's for you," he said.

"All of it?" Zac asked, bewildered, as she started thumbing through the pile.

"Yeah, you're real popular," their mother said sarcastically. "The only thing that wasn't for you today was our bills. Maybe I should give those to you too."

You do that normally anyway, Zac thought as she glanced over at Clive in time to see him roll his eyes at their mother. She smiled. *At least someone here agrees with me,* she thought as she continued glancing through the mail. When she was satisfied that all of it was, in fact, addressed to her, she picked up the whole pile and headed towards the bedroom she had shared with her sister Melanie until Melanie had gotten married and moved out the year before.

Clive was on Zac's heels as they headed out of the kitchen. "Do you want the first shower?" he asked.

"No, you take it," Zac replied. A large envelope from West Point was among the items she held in her hands, and she could not wait to open it.

"Awesome," Clive said, and disappeared into his own bedroom, which he had shared with their older brother Abe until Abe had married and moved out a few years ago. Now Clive shared the room with Ben.

As Zac sat on her bed a second later, dumping all of her mail next to her, she heard Clive heading for the bathroom. Then she heard the shower running. Picking through the mail again, Zac reached for the envelope from West Point and ripped it open. Inside was a large, glossy folder stuffed with papers, which could only mean one thing. Zac's heart skipped a beat as she opened the folder and grabbed the cover letter in it. "Congratulations!" it began.

"Whoop!" Zac shrieked. She waited just long enough for Clive to get out of the bathroom before dancing towards him, holding the letter.

"What is that?" Clive asked, looking at his sister with amusement.

"My acceptance letter to West Point."

"Yes!" Clive yelped. He threw up his hand, and he and Zac high-fived. Rubbing his hand dry on his towel, Clive took the letter from Zac and read it. "That's awesome," he said.

Their parents' reaction to the news was more subdued. "I'm amazed you got in there," their mother said as they ate dinner. "I never thought you were good enough."

"It's kind of far away, too," their father added. "If you want to go there, you're going to have to get there on your own."

Zac looked at him, biting her lips. *I hadn't thought about how I would get there,* she thought.

"I'm serious," her father said, and Zac could tell that he was. "It's too expensive to fly, and we can't spare the time away from the crops to spend several days driving you there."

What the hell am I going to do? Zac wondered. The family was quiet around the table, and Zac and Clive shared a look. Zac could already see Clive's mind working, so she did not say anything. *I hope he has some ideas,* she thought. *Because I don't.*

When dinner was over, Clive snuck into Zac's room rather than going into his own room to do his homework. "What am I going to do, Clive?" Zac asked. "I have to go there. I gotta get outta here!"

"I know that," Clive said. "But we've been earning money from selling our blueberries every summer for awhile now. Ma and Pa don't know anything about that money- they don't know we have those bank accounts. We should have enough money for a plane ticket to West Point."

"What about getting to the airport?" Zac asked. "I'd be happy to drive the truck there if you're willing to drive it back, but I doubt Ma and Pa will let us borrow it."

"Definitely not," Clive agreed. "Besides, I don't think that truck could make it to the airport and back without falling apart."

Zac threw up her hands. "So what am I going to do?" she asked.

"Why don't you talk to Harvey while we're at school tomorrow?" Clive suggested. "His family's always been better to us than our parents have been. Maybe he'd be willing to give you a ride."

At lunchtime the next day, Zac waited in line for the school's free lunch for what seemed like forever. When she finally had her food, she sought out Harvey and plunked her books and her lunch next to him.

"What's up?" Harvey asked, picking up on Zac's sense of purpose.

"I got into West Point," Zac replied.

"That's awesome!" Harvey said, whacking her on the back.

Zac shook her head. "My parents aren't helping me out at all," she said. "They won't drive me there or even take me to the airport."

"Book a plane ticket," Harvey said. "Someone in my family will drive you to the airport. I'll do it if no one else does."

"Really?" Zac asked disbelievingly.

"Oh, yeah," Harvey replied. "You have to do this, Zac. You

have to go there."

Zac eyed him. "What about you?" she asked. "I know you applied there too. Did you ever hear back?"

"I got my rejection letter awhile ago," Harvey said, looking down at his food.

"Why didn't you tell me that?"

"It wasn't important."

"It's important to me."

Harvey just shrugged.

"But you got into U. Arkansas, right?"

Harvey nodded. "I've gotten into a couple of their campuses. I'll probably end up in Little Rock."

"It's a good school," Zac said. "You'll do well there."

*   *   *

When it came time for Zac's first group therapy appointment, she drove into Tulsa. *The VA is letting us use their space to meet, even though it's a private group,* she thought. *I guess that's positive, even if IAVA had to raise money to pay the VA to use this space.* Zac shook her head. *Maybe the VA should use that money to hire more therapists and doctors.*

Once inside, she approached the room with interest, if nothing more. There were three other female veterans, and four males. *An evenly split group,* Zac thought. *That's unusual. They must have done it on purpose.* One of the females was missing a leg and walked on crutches. Zac eyed her in particular. *She looks really young, too. I wonder what happened to her.*

They went around the room and introduced themselves, saying their names and platoons. Then there was a silence. Everyone in the group looked at each other. "How many times was everyone deployed?" Annemarie Jensen, the therapist, asked.

Most of the patients there replied twice or three times, but the young woman with the missing leg, whose name was Jenny

Nichols, said she had only been deployed once, and was injured a month into the deployment. *That's rough,* Zac thought.

"In these first few sessions, we're going to be focusing on reintegrating back into civilian life," Annemarie said. She got up and pulled notebooks from a box on a table behind her and distributed them. Then she pulled boxes of pens out and handed those around to the group. "I want to start you on your first writing assignment for next time," she said. "You can write as many entries as you want- free write as much as you'd like- but one specific thing I'd like to see you write about is spending your birthday in country," she said.

After the therapy session was over, Zac went to talk to Jenny specifically. *I'd really like to know what happened to her,* Zac thought, and yet she felt bad about asking. *What's your problem?* she wondered. She could not answer her own question, and was relieved when the other two female veterans in the group, Gail Murphy and Jessica McKinnley, joined them.

After a few minutes, Jenny glanced at the door. "I told my husband I'd meet him when this appointment was over," she said apologetically.

"It's not a problem," Zac said. *She's married already?* she thought. *She's definitely further along in her life than I am.* "Having family around must ease the transition home somewhat."

Jenny nodded, and seemed relieved to be understood. "My husband served in Afghanistan too," she said. "So he understands where I'm coming from." She looked at Zac in particular. "Did anyone else in your family serve?"

"Uh, my brother was a Marine," Zac stumbled. "But he didn't make it through his second deployment."

"I'm sorry," Jenny replied.

"Thanks," Zac said, struggling to force the word out through the swelling in her throat that always occurred when Clive's death was mentioned.

After another moment of silence, Jenny headed for the door. Zac watched her go before looking back at Gail and Jessica.

"It's been tough being back," Gail admitted. "Only other

veterans truly seem to understand it, and I've been finding that other female vets in particular have been the easiest for me to connect with."

"Really?" Zac asked. "I haven't even managed to connect with many vets at all."

"Are you planning on coming back to this group?" Gail asked. Zac nodded. "I think it'll help," Gail continued. "I've also been attending other veterans' events. That's where I've met other female vets- would you be interested in coming?"

"Absolutely," Zac replied.

The next week, Zac sat in the waiting room at the local Community Based Outpatient Clinic, waiting for her appointment with Dr. Bittman. *This appointment better be good,* she thought. *If it goes the same way as my appointment with Ron, I'm outta here and I'm not coming back.*

A few minutes later, she was hobbling back to Dr. Bittman's office. Inside the small office, Zac was left with a young woman- *she could be my age or even younger,* Zac realized. Her office was also decorated differently than Ron's had been. Ron's diplomas had been the foremost decoration. Here, wallpaper with flowers danced across the office.

"I'm Alex," the woman said, extending her hand to Zac and smiling.

"I'm Zac," Zac said as she eyed Alex.

"What are you thinking?" Alex asked as they sat down- Alex at her desk, Zac in one of the chairs facing it.

"I'm surprised that they reassigned me to a new counselor."

"Ron actually thought I would be a better match for you as a clinician."

"You know Ron?" Zac asked.

"He splits his time between this clinic and the one where you saw him," Alex said.

"Oh," Zac said.

"You don't seem disappointed by the change in providers,"

Alex said, trying to tell what Zac was thinking.

"I guess I wasn't impressed by him either," Zac replied. "I wasn't planning on going back because I didn't think he could help me."

"Unfortunately, Ron is one of our more, um, inconsistent therapists," Alex admitted. "He's been spectacular with some of his patients- veterans that were not making progress with other counselors have improved dramatically with him. But he's had... problems with other patients."

"Like me," Zac said. *Great*, she thought. *Even the therapists think I'm a loser.* She looked around the small office, wishing there was more space separating her from Alex.

"I wouldn't take it personally," Alex said. "Ron is usually better with the male veterans, maybe less with the women."

"Sounds like his mother dropped him as a child."

Alex laughed. "Luckily, his faults have given me a few opportunities."

"How so?"

"I've been concentrating my psychology practice on veterans re-entering civilian life, and female veterans in particular. I've been finding that they have unique issues- even dealing with my colleagues, it seems."

"It isn't just your colleagues," Zac replied, and related her experience in the hardware store.

Alex sighed. "This is the first large-scale war the U.S. has had in decades, so a lot more veterans are returning home than in recent memory," she said. "For the first time in history, a decent percentage of those veterans are women, but public perception hasn't caught up to that yet."

I don't know, Zac thought doubtfully. *We've been at war for ten years. How long does it take?* She looked past Alex and through the small window behind her. Outside, clouds caused dappled sunlight to fall across the parking lot.

"What are you thinking?" Alex asked.

"In the Army, I never wanted to remind people that I was a female," she said. "I always made sure I kept up with the males in terms of the fitness requirements, and in terms of the academic requirements at West Point. I wanted to make sure I wasn't treated differently."

"So many of the cadets there thought that as a woman, you couldn't succeed?"

"Plenty did," Zac admitted. "But plenty were supportive." She shrugged. "These things go both ways sometimes, too. You can't be a whiner and expect to get ahead."

"Do you think a lot of your female classmates and colleagues were whiners?" Alex asked.

"Most were not. But plenty didn't make it, too. West Point is hard. Being in the Army is hard too, and you have to be tough to get through it. But if you do well, there's respect for that too."

Alex nodded as she glanced at Zac's file, which was laid out on her desk. "So I noticed that you've been having nightmares and flashbacks about the war?"

"Yeah." Zac intertwined her fingers uncomfortably, wishing she did not have to stay in this tiny office.

"When these things happen, what are they about?"

"The flashbacks are always the same- the grenade goes off and I get thrown a few feet from the blast. Then the enemy is standing right nearby, firing at us with machine guns."

"And the nightmares?

"Similar, except I can't get away. I get smothered by a tent, or the enemy aims at me directly."

"So there's always a fear of getting killed?" Alex said.

"It's stronger than fear- in the nightmares, I'm usually dying before I wake up." Zac bit her lip. "And when I do wake up, I feel like I should have been the one driving that first vehicle- I was the one leading that operation, after all." For a minute, Zac examined the rosebuds on the wallpaper, noticing how they seemed about to open.

"That guilt you feel is often symptomatic of survivor guilt, and nightmares and flashbacks are typical symptoms of Post Traumatic Stress Disorder," Alex said.

Zac looked back at her and shook her head. PTSD was something that happened to other people.

"This isn't about being strong enough to not get these symptoms," Alex said. "In fact, 'being strong' and bottling it all up as has lost me a few patients."

"What happened to them?"

"I've had several veterans who have refused to talk about happened, who couldn't handle the stress of keeping it all inside and committed suicide."

The statement struck Zac to the bone. "It took me four months to even get that initial appointment with Ron," she said. "And then it was moved up a month because of 'cancellations.' Did patients 'cancel' by committing suicide?"

Alex looked uncomfortable. "That could be one reason," she said.

"You have to be kidding me!" Zac snapped, the color in her face rising and her heart racing.

"It could have been anything else, too," Alex said, regretting her first answer. "The people with those appointments could have moved out of state, or gotten treatment elsewhere."

"Do you believe that?" Zac asked, her eyes spitting fire and ice. Alex took a deep breath and exhaled, and Zac interpreted her silence as a negative response. "Is there anything we can do to change this?"

"Lobby Congress," Alex said. "Some of my colleagues and I have tried to get better funding and better administration for the VA, and we've gotten nothing but silence."

"So what makes you think they'd listen to me?"

"You're an injured veteran whose care is affected."

Zac gritted her teeth and looked away. The floral wallpaper was less attractive now. Then she crossed her arms across her chest and leaned back in her chair, grimacing. "When I was in the hospital in Germany, my CO mentioned a couple of inquiries that might happen, including one into Victor Rice's conduct." *I've been repressing that conversation. I still can't believe Victor may have done anything wrong.* "If anything comes of that, I'll have to go to Washington to testify. Maybe that trip will do double duty."

"It's definitely a place to start," Alex agreed. "But, getting back to your treatment, a lot of the veterans I've treated have been helped by this type of talk therapy, or a combination of therapy and medication."

Zac shook her head. "There's no way I'm taking medication," she said.

"Then let's see how the therapy goes by itself," Alex replied. "What do you want out of these sessions?"

"I want my symptoms to go away. I'm also hoping the physical therapy helps me get past my injuries."

"Are you looking to get back to active service?"

"That would be ideal, yes."

Alex looked away for a second. When she looked up again, she said, "you know, I looked through your medical records and spoke with your doctors before this session. Have they spoken to you about the possibility of re-enlisting?"

"They think it's a long shot," Zac admitted gloomily.

"If it's something you want to work towards, I'm not going to stop you, but I think you should consider other options as well."

"Like what?" Zac asked. "I've been active military my entire adult life. I don't know what else to do at this point."

"It's certainly something we can discuss and develop."

CHAPTER 4

The next week, Zac actually found herself looking forward to group therapy, and the chance to share her story of spending her birthday in country. To her surprise, the other members of the group seemed reluctant to share, and they all seemed glad when she volunteered.

"My younger brothers always made a big deal about my birthday when I was deployed," she said. "My youngest brother more so than my middle one. During my first deployment, my middle brother called me to wish me happy birthday, but my youngest brother actually sent me a cupcake and some candles." She smiled. "Of course, by the time the cupcake reached me, it was stale, but I still lit the candles and blew them out."

The rest of the group was smiling now. "What about the other times you were deployed?" asked Jimmy Brooks, a Marine veteran.

"The same thing happened during my second deployment, and by my third deployment, I was already commanding a platoon, so my men got together and made sure I got a cupcake that was still fresh." Zac was laughing by the time she finished speaking.

"What kind of cupcake was it?" Jenny asked.

"It was a small one with chocolate frosting and few sprinkles- my favorite kind."

"You mean you don't like the huge ones they sell nowadays, the ones the size of your head?" Gail teased.

The group laughed. "Those huge ones are actually pretty gross," said Daniel Smith, an Army private who had barely said anything so far.

"They'd be alright if I felt like spending a week eating them," Zac said.

"It sounds like the men and women under your command really respected you," Jenny said.

Zac had to think about that. "I guess," she said.

"Come on, Zac, it's definitely true," Jimmy said. "Even in the Marines, we knew your reputation. You weren't the type of commander to hang back and give orders- you were right out there going on missions with the grunts."

"Commanders fighting like that is based on history," Zac replied. "I don't understand why it's not a more pervasive practice nowadays."

"What kind of historical precedence do you mean?" Annemarie asked.

"Well, Ranald Mackenzie comes to mind," Zac said. "He fought in the Civil War and then made a name for himself in the Indian Wars. He was always out in front with his men, even as a Colonel- it's what won their respect."

"That's not something to minimize," Annemarie said. "Your leadership style sounds like it was different from the norm, and that it made a real impression on the people that served with you."

At Zac's next individual therapy session, Alex began by saying, "tell me about your upbringing- I hear a slight Appalachian accent. Are you from around here?"

"I grew up outside of Little Rock," Zac said, rolling her eyes.

"Are you embarrassed by that?"

"I did try to lose the accent as soon as I got to West Point. I guess I haven't fully succeeded."

"Why would you do something like that?"

"I thought it made me sound stupid."

"Why would you think that?" Alex asked. "Were you ever treated like you were stupid?"

Zac nodded. "Certainly my parents thought I was. I had an older brother who was very smart, and they treated the rest of us like we were dirt."

"Why do you think they did that?"

"Well, my older sister was genuinely dumb as dirt, and I think my parents were frustrated with her, so they treated the rest of us the same way." Zac stared at the carpeting of the office, noticing what a dull beige it was.

For nearly an hour, Alex bombarded Zac with questions about her childhood, which Zac used as few words as possible to answer. "Ma and Pa started having kids before they were twenty," she said. "We never had enough money, and Ma and Pa drank all the damn time."

"And no one ever reported this to the state or anything?" Alex asked.

"Oh, they did," Zac said. "I never found out who called it in, but one day, these people showed up on a Saturday to take a look at our house and our farm, to take a look at us. It turned out they were from the state. It was early afternoon, but Ma and Pa were already drinking." Even now, Zac remembered the clink of her parents' alcohol bottles against their glasses.

"Oh, man," Alex said. "How old were you when this happened?"

"I was twelve when they showed up that first time."

"What came of it?"

"A bunch of hearings that turned out to be custody hearings. I was thirteen by the time my parents lost custody of me, Melanie and Clive. We went to our grandparents' house here in Tulsa, where I'm living now."

"What about Abe and Ben?"

"Ben hadn't been born yet. Abe had turned eighteen by then, so he was an adult and the state couldn't touch him. He ended up staying on our parents' farm and working on it to keep the property together while my parents went into rehab." Zac tugged unhappily on a string of her jacket.

"How did he run the farm? By himself?"

"No, he'd just graduated from high school, and since college isn't exactly a thing where I'm from, he had a bunch of friends that were looking for something to do, so they all came over and helped run the farm. One of those friends was this girl June, who's now Abe's wife."

Alex was genuinely interested in hearing more, but the hour was up, and Zac was glad. "I'll see you next week," Alex said.

*   *   *

Thirteen-year-old Zac Madison sat in the back seat of a social worker's sedan as it drove down the highway between Arkansas and Oklahoma. Clive sat in the middle seat between her and sixteen-year-old Melanie, and for a minute, Zac took her eyes of the highway to look at her siblings. Melanie sat glowering, staring out the window. Her arms were crossed, and her headphones were on her ears. The music she was listening to was loud enough for Zac to hear it across the car. Zac looked at Clive to find him staring back at her, his blue eyes wide and sad.

"Why do we have to go live with Grandma and Grandpa?" Clive asked.

"Because Ma and Pa can't take care of us right now," Zac said.

"Why not?"

"I don't know," Zac said. "I guess there are a lot of us, and it's hard. Farming is hard work." *The fact that they've always hated me doesn't help much either.*

"I've always tried to be a good kid," Clive said.

"You are a good kid," Zac told him. "You're not the problem."

"Then why can't we stay with Ma and Pa?"

"They just need a vacation for a little while." *I'm out of ideas here, kid.*

"When are we going back home?" Clive asked.

"I don't know," Zac said honestly. *I'm not sure I want to.*

"We shouldn't have to go live with Grandma and Grandpa at all," Melanie said sullenly, and Zac was amazed she could hear their conversation over her music.

"It wasn't much fun with Ma and Pa either," Zac said. *Their fights have gotten scarier and scarier. I'm tired of hiding in the house and praying they don't find me.*

"I don't care what you think, or what anybody thinks!" Melanie snarled, her voice becoming louder. "All of my friends were at home. I could have stayed with one of them."

From the front seat, the social worker turned down the car radio. "Staying with your friends is not a stable enough situation, honey," she said.

"It would have been better than going to Tulsa," Melanie replied.

"Why do you feel that way?"

"Tulsa is in the middle of nowhere. None of my friends are there. I'm losing my whole life. I have nothing."

"Your grandparents live there," the social worker reminded her. "And you'll be going to school there. Maybe you'll make new friends."

"No way." Melanie shook her head. "Everybody that lives there are losers."

"I like Grandma and Grandpa," Clive said.

Zac nodded in agreement. *They've always been better to us than Ma and Pa.*

"Zac and Clive will be in Tulsa with you," the social worker reminded Melanie. "You think they're losers too?"

"Yes," Melanie snarled. "I hate them and everybody else." She turned up her music again and stared back out the window.

Zac rolled her eyes at her older sister, but Clive's tears had started running down his face. "I'm sorry, buddy," she told him, reaching into her backpack for some tissues.

That night, long after the social worker had left to go back to Arkansas, Zac and Clive sat on their beds in the room they were now sharing on the second floor of their grandparents' house. Melanie had a room to herself down the hall. It was already dark outside, and Zac wasn't looking forward to sleeping in a new place, even if it was a place that was somewhat familiar.

"Are you scared, Zac?" Clive asked.

Zac nodded.

"Me too," Clive admitted.

"So how's school going?" Zac's grandfather, Jeffrey, asked one night as her grandmother, Elaine, served dinner.

Zac and Clive looked at each other. "It's okay," Zac said finally.

"It's not easy being the new kids, is it?" Jeffrey asked.

Clive shook his head. "The teachers are okay, though," he said.

"Good," Jeffrey said.

"What about you, Mel?" Elaine asked. "Are you enjoying your new classes?"

Melanie just shrugged, as sullen as ever. "It's the same as it was at home," she said shortly, and began eating.

It was later that night that the shouting began. Zac and Clive, who had been upstairs doing their homework, snuck downstairs to listen to the argument and hid just outside the living room.

"Zac and Clive are upstairs doing their homework," Elaine was saying to Melanie. "All I was asking was whether you have work of your own?"

"Well, Zac and Clive are just wonderful little robots, aren't they?" Melanie yelled back.

"I didn't say that at all," Elaine replied.

"We know you're unhappy, Mel," Jeffrey said. "But I agree with Elaine- your schoolwork may be the path to get you out of this situation. College can set you on a completely different path."

"Nobody goes to college," Melanie said. "Especially not me!"

"If you work hard enough, you certainly can," Jeffrey said.

"Don't you know that I'm too stupid for that?" Melanie said, raising her voice again. "Everybody else knows it."

"Don't say that," Elaine said.

"It's true," Melanie said. "I'm failing all my classes. Everybody at school hates me. The boys won't even look at me. I don't see why I should have to put up with this shit! I'm sixteen! I'm an adult!"

Outside the living room, Zac rolled her eyes. *Sure you are,* she thought sarcastically. Next to her, Clive was groaning also.

Inside the living room, Jeffrey glared at his granddaughter. "You know, your mother had the same attitude," he said. "She was your age when she ran away from home, and look where it's gotten her."

"I'd still rather be at home than in this hellhole!" Melanie shrieked. She stomped out of the room and stormed upstairs, barely noticing Zac and Clive as she shoved past them.

In a second, Zac could hear the door to Melanie's room being slammed. *That door is gonna come off its hinges if she keeps doing that,* Zac thought.

*   *   *

"So, a lot of the female veterans I've worked with have faced either sexual harassment or worse throughout their career," Alex said at Zac's next appointment. "Has that affected you at all?"

"I've been pretty lucky," Zac said. "I mean, I've heard it

occasionally, from time to time, but…" She shrugged.

"You've never had it be a major issue?" Alex pressed. "Not once?"

Zac looked down. Her face got warm and red. When she looked back at Alex, she found that the therapist was waiting for an answer. "I know you've staked your career on this," she said finally. "I wish I could help you."

"I think you can," Alex replied. "I think there's something you're not telling me."

Zac stared out the window, clenching her teeth. The silence lengthened. Then Zac sighed. "It was only bad once," she said.

"What happened?"

Zac frowned. *I've spent sixteen years trying to forget this incident,* she thought, feeling her stomach sink. But Alex was looking at her, waiting for an answer, so she started talking. "My plebe year at West Point, we'd just started classes. We'd already made it through Beast Barracks, so I figured that a lot of us would make it through the next four years."

"Beast Barracks- that's the initiation period for first year students before classes start?" Alex asked. Zac nodded. "So what happened after your classes started?"

"It was the middle of the night, and my roommate- Jen was her name- and I were asleep in our bunks. All of a sudden, our door was thrown open, and a bunch of our classmates burst in."

"All men?"

"Yeah. They were a bunch of plebes too, and apparently they'd been interested in me and Jen since we'd arrived."

Alex eyed her patient. "What happened next?"

"We woke up in a second, thinking it was a combat drill. It wasn't. Three of them pinned Jen down on her bed. She screamed, and one of them put a hand over her mouth. The other three came after me." Zac took a deep breath. She swallowed.

"What did you do?" Alex asked.

Zac shifted in her seat. "West Point's dress uniforms include a bayonet. I grabbed mine and started swinging at their faces. The first one I hit got a gash on one side of his face. He screamed and pulled away. I hit another one a second later-twice, once on each side of his face. The third one who had come after me tried to grab the bayonet from me, but I pulled it back once his fingers were around it. He almost lost his fingers."

Zac stopped speaking and stood up. She paced the office, which was so small that she could take no more than three strides before having to turn around.

Alex allowed a minute of silence before asking, "what about the cadets that had gone after Jen?"

"They jumped off her immediately. I mean, the guys I'd attacked were literally screaming in pain. In a second, I went after the last three, but they were already running out the door."

"Did any of your other classmates hear what was going on?"

"Yeah. A bunch of them had come running to see what the screaming was about, so when the three guys ran into the hallway, they ran into a bunch of cadets who stopped them. A few of the older cadets also came to settle things. Of course, by then, there was blood all over the floor of my room, and Jen was cowering in the corner, but the older cadets really calmed things down."

"What did they do?"

"They got the plebes I'd injured to the hospital, and the unharmed ones to our officers for punishment."

"Did they get punished?" Alex asked.

"Yes, they all did," Zac said, her satisfaction obvious as she stopped pacing around the office for a second. "Apparently, there were two ringleaders, and one was coming after me in particular- that was the guy whose fingers I almost chopped off. The other one wanted Jen. They both got expelled from the Academy. The rest of the guys got various forms of punishments."

"How did you feel about that?"

"I would have liked to have seen them all expelled, but at

least the whole school knew what they'd done, and nobody really bothered me again after that. Besides, the two guys whose faces I scratched up still had their scars when we graduated. Our classmates called them Scarface and Frankenstein." She broke into a grin.

"What about Jen?" Alex asked. "How did she handle all of that?"

"Not well," Zac admitted, her smile disappearing. She felt like kicking the chair in front of her, but instead, she sat down again. "She had nightmares about it for weeks before she finally dropped out of the Academy."

"What do you think accounted for how differently she reacted?"

Zac frowned as she thought about it. "Well, those guys were on top of her in an instant. Besides, we came from different backgrounds," she said. "My family was dirt poor and wasn't anything I could go back to. Jen came from old money. She was from Georgia- her family had been in the country forever and had owned a plantation and thousands of slaves before the Civil War."

"Wow," Alex said.

Zac nodded. "I thought that was fascinating," she said.

"What happened to her after she left West Point? Did you guys keep in touch at all?"

"For a little while. She took some time off, and then went in a different direction entirely- she ended up at one of the all women's colleges up north- Mount Holyoke, I think. But I haven't heard from her in years."

It was morning, and bright sunlight streamed through the windows, but Zac didn't feel like getting out of bed. *I don't have anywhere to be or anything to do,* she thought. It was one of the few days during the week when she had neither physical therapy nor an appointment with Alex. All of a sudden, the sheer directionless of her life, coupled with her lingering physical immobility, hit her with full force, and Zac could feel a wave of sadness rolling over her. She looked at her clock. *If I were healthy, I'd get up and go for a run,* she thought. Then she realized, *if I were healthy, I'd probably still be deployed.*

What else can I do? she wondered. *Maybe I could look into gyms nearby. Maybe they have a pool I could use, or some machines that won't hurt my leg.* But instead, she felt herself drifting off to sleep again.

When she awoke for a second time, it was nearly 12:00. "Shit!" Zac yelped, and tossed off her covers. *A whole morning wasted- how did I do that? I could at least have been getting some work done on the house.*

As she picked up her paintbrush and hammer a little while later, her sadness hadn't abated much, but Zac was determined anyway. *Tomorrow morning I'm setting a fucking alarm- I don't care if I have to drag my sorry ass out of bed, I'm not sleeping until 12:00 again.*

In therapy a few days later, Zac complained to Alex about her continuing nightmares, sleeplessness and oversleeping. "It sounds like you could be depressed," Alex replied.

"But what about all this therapy stuff?" Zac asked. "Isn't it supposed to be helping?"

"It will," Alex said. "But it takes time. You have to be patient."

Zac glared at her. "I need this to move along faster," she said. "All of it. I need the nightmares to go away, I need to be a normal person again and have a regular job."

Alex did not back down. "When has anything that's been worth achieving happened quickly?" she asked. "When you got into West Point, was that based on a single test? Or was it based on the grades you got over the course of several years before that?"

"Both," Zac said. "My SAT scores were really high."

"Did you prepare for the SATs?" Alex asked.

"Barely," Zac said. "I had to steal some books from my

school's library to prepare because my parents couldn't afford a prep course." Even now, Zac remembered those books, their glossy covers folded and torn by so much use, their paper written all over and threadbare.

"But you studied the books, though, didn't you?" Alex asked. "That's preparation."

"I guess."

Alex's eyes narrowed. "You didn't really steal those books, did you?"

"I did, actually," Zac admitted. "I got sick of never being able to use them because other kids had checked them out. One day, they were on the shelves as the library was closing, and I grabbed them and ran."

"I'm having trouble believing that," Alex said.

Zac shrugged. "I returned them after the exam was over."

"That might be more in keeping with what I've seen of your character."

"Whatever," Zac said. "It wasn't the first time I'd stolen something from the school. Our parents didn't always have enough money for food or even toilet paper, so Clive and I often took rolls of toilet paper from the school bathrooms."

"Really?"

"Uh-huh. There was one time the janitor left his cart in the hallway outside one of the bathrooms and we filled our backpacks with rolls of toilet paper. We must have taken close to twenty rolls between the two of us." For a minute, Zac remembered the smell of the janitor's bleach, emanating from the squeaky floors he had just cleaned.

"That's a tough way to live."

"I don't know how much we thought of it in those terms when we were young," Zac said. "We thought more in terms of how to get around our problems. It was only when we got older that the full force of it hit us- quite literally sometimes."

"So your parents were abusive?"

"They could be, especially when they were drunk."

"And both you and Clive chose the military as a way to get out of it," Alex noted.

"We were a lot alike in many ways," Zac said. "It's why we got along so well."

"It sounds like you never had a stable family situation."

Zac shrugged. "My friend Harvey's family was always good to me and Clive, and my first CO out of West Point treated me like family."

"Who was this?"

"Victor Rice."

Alex's eyes narrowed. "This is the general they think might have committed treason?" she asked. "You mentioned that before, and it's certainly been on the news plenty."

Zac nodded, her teeth clenched. *I still don't know what to think about that.*

"He's been opposed to these wars- especially the one in Iraq- for some time now," Alex said, again wondering what Zac was thinking.

"We were always running out of supplies, and we were fighting for years without a specific mission, so he wasn't completely wrong." Zac shook her head. "I really hope there isn't a trial or anything. I'd hate to have to testify." *I really dread it, actually.*

*　　　　*　　　　*

Early on a Sunday in late June, only a couple of weeks after her high school graduation, Zac stood at the window, watching for Harvey's car. Her four suitcases stood next to her. Clive stood in a corner of the room, also looking out the window. The house was quiet until Zac heard a set of small footsteps patter into the room. She turned to see little Ben waltz through the doorway. He grinned at her and threw his arms open wide. Zac's heart melted as she went to hug her little brother goodbye.

"Mommy and Daddy are still asleep," Ben said, "but I wanted to say goodbye."

Zac smiled. "I'm glad you did," she said.

Ben looked at Clive. "Are you going away too?" he asked.

"I'm just taking her to the airport," Clive said. "I'll be back soon."

Ben looked at Zac. "When will *you* be back?" he asked, pointing at her as he asked.

"I don't know," Zac admitted.

"It's gonna be quiet around here without you," Ben warned.

I doubt that, Zac thought, remembering the row their parents had raised just last night. *Given the amount they drank, I'm not surprised they're not up yet. It's one reason I'm taking such an early flight.*

At that moment, a car horn honked outside. Clive jumped. "That's Harvey!" he exclaimed. He grabbed two of Zac's suitcases and headed for the door.

Zac gave Ben one last hug. Then she grabbed her two remaining suitcases and followed Clive out the door and to the waiting car. Harvey had already gotten out of the front seat and was helping Clive lift the suitcases into the trunk. His mother Maria sat in the driver's seat. Harvey helped Zac with the last two suitcases. Then he went around and got back in the front seat as Clive got into the back seat. Zac turned around and looked back at her house once more. Ben still stood at the front door in his pajamas. Zac waved at him. Ben grinned and waved back enthusiastically. Then Zac climbed into the back seat of Harvey's car and closed the door. She could see Ben closing the door to their house.

"Ready?" Harvey asked.

"Ready," Zac said.

*　　　　　*　　　　　*

Zac had been attending group therapy for over a month before she finally worked up the courage to ask Jenny what had happened to her leg, and even then, she waited until after the therapy session was over.

"I was commissioned a second lieutenant when I graduated from Norwich University about a year ago," Jenny began. "About a month after graduation, I deployed to Baghdad. We were patrolling the streets when a bomb went off under me. The medic was right nearby, and still he couldn't save my leg."

"It's incredible you survived," Jimmy said from behind Jenny.

I didn't realize he was listening, Zac thought.

Jenny shrugged. "At the time, I didn't want to die, but now I really feel the loss of my leg- a part of me is really missing." She swallowed and shook her head. "But you want to know the worst of it?" Zac found herself leaning forward to hear what Jenny was about to say. "It must have been a premeditated attack- there was actually some guy on a rooftop nearby filming the whole thing!"

Zac recoiled slightly, and Jimmy grimaced.

"One of my troops shot at him as the medic tended to me, but the guy just disappeared," Jenny continued. "I don't even think he was hit or anything."

"You're really brave," Zac said. "I got hit by a grenade and shot in the leg, and I was very worried about losing my leg."

"It's been hard," Jenny admitted. "But I just didn't want to die over there."

Two weeks later, Zac sat at her kitchen table and studied the day's newspaper, whose large headline read: "Iraq and Afghanistan Wars Officially Over!" All at once, Zac found herself thinking many different things, her emotions in turmoil.

The wars were over. More than ten years and thousands of lives later, the enemy had finally surrendered. *Well,* Zac thought, *the United States hasn't lost face. We're still the most powerful nation in the world. Thousands of American soldiers lost their lives, including Clive, and I lost my career, but the United States didn't lose face.*

Zac folded down the paper and looked at the bottom half of the front page. Just as quickly, she wished she had not. The headline at the bottom read, "General Victor Rice Captured Alive Behind Enemy Lines." Zac's heart rate shot up, and her stomach sank. *Oh no*, she thought. *Oh no*. A smaller headline read, "Rice proclaims innocence, claims prisoner-of-war status." *There's no way that's true*, Zac thought, feeling unshed tears against her eyes. *I really thought Victor's situation would be resolved internally. I don't like the way this is going at all.*

All at once, the grenade exploded again in Zac's mind, and the bang made her jump. "Oh, please," she whispered. "Not again." But she could do nothing to shut out the cries of the other soldiers, the firing of the guns, the bang of the grenade. The pain.

Zac took a deep breath, struggling to return to the present. *When will it all go away?* She swallowed. *You should tell Alex that this keeps happening,* she said to herself, even as another part of her replied, *she hasn't asked about it recently.*

Zac got up and went to the window. *Were these wars really worth it?* she wondered. *I don't know that we can ever fully stop terrorism.* She sighed, listening to the silence of the house around her. *I really got accustomed to the constant sound and movement of the Army,* she realized. *Besides, thinking of the war and its aftermath makes me think of all the friends and family I lost, all of the lives wasted.*

Finally, however, Zac's eyes focused on the scenery in front of her. The house had a large front lawn- nearly an acre- that now looked neat and proper, in direct contrast to when she had first seen the place. *When I haven't been repairing the house, I've been trimming the vines, mowing the grass, and planting flowers,* she thought. The chores had become heavier as her leg healed, and now, looking outside, Zac was pleased at how much better the place looked. *I still haven't touched most of the few acres behind the house,* she thought, *but I'll get there eventually.*

Then the sun came out from behind the clouds, and Zac, remembering that summer was here and that the weather was warm, went outside.

Later that day, Zac received a letter in the mail, an official one from the United States Army. She ripped it open immediately, but soon she was sorry for her haste. The letter was from Washington, and it detailed the inquiry into General Rice's conduct during the war. A huge trial was planned for the end of the summer. *The headline about this only appeared in today's paper*, Zac thought as she read and reread the order to testify. *Maybe the military is ahead of the press on this one after all.*

She frowned and took a deep breath. *What to say while testifying?* she wondered. *I knew Victor and his family well, but if he betrayed his country, he doesn't deserve any leniency.* Zac stared out the window in front of her. *On the other hand, I really don't know the facts behind what he's accused of. It also wouldn't surprise me if the Army is going after Victor because he's been such a visible opponent of these wars. It couldn't look good to have one our own generals talking about how our contractors' corruption meant a lack of supplies and vehicles that were always broken.* Zac sighed, and pushed the letter away.

Just as much, however, questions about her long-term future still hung in Zac's mind. *What am I going to do for the rest of my life?* she wondered. *I asked Jim Conrad the same question in the hospital when I first woke up. I don't have any more answers now than I did then.*

At least I'm healthier now, she thought. She reflected on Jim's suggestions, one of which was writing about herself and her experience in the war. *Not exciting at all,* she thought. *I don't have much to say, nor do I think my experience is much to write about, except that I'm lucky enough to have survived.*

Then she thought of Jim's next suggestion- teaching at any of the service academies. Zac swallowed at the thought. *I still don't think I have much to say to the cadets,* she thought. Even so, memories of West Point suddenly swelled in her mind, and she breathed in the scent on the campus' fresh cut grass on a morning run, the sound of taps as the flag was lowered each evening, the feel of the cadets all marching in a single line.

Those were the best years of my life, Zac thought. *I would give anything to get it back.* Once again, involuntarily, tears rose in her eyes, and, even worse, they overflowed and rolled down her cheeks.

Grabbing a napkin from the napkin holder on the kitchen table, Zac shook her head at herself. This would not do, getting all weepy at a moment's notice. *You're only getting weepy at your memories of school,* she told herself. *It's really the only time in my life I feel that way about. Maybe Jim was right. Maybe going back there would do me some good.*

It was 0230 the next morning when Zac blinked awake. *Dammit,* she thought. *I don't even have to look at the clock to know what time it is. Whenever I've been drinking, I always wake up at 0230. It's why I'm exhausted all the time- I don't sleep well at all.*

At 0300, Zac was still wide awake, so she hauled herself out of bed and went to the window. Outside, the two tall trees in her back yard were illuminated by the full moon, and in a split second, Zac thought of the Twin Towers in New York City, whose collapse at the hands of terrorists had plunged the nation into war. *So much has changed since then,* Zac thought. *Before that, I was a First Lieutenant who was hoping to make General before I retired. Now I'm just a crippled civilian.*

Zac clenched her teeth as tears rose up in her eyes. *I really wanted to make General,* she thought. *I really thought it was possible when I got promoted to Colonel during my third deployment. I was so close.* She thought of the gun in the drawer of her bedside table. In her mind's eye, her hand ran over the ridges of its handle, the curved trigger...

You really shouldn't kill yourself, the rational part of her mind said. *Why not?* she immediately countered. *It's not like I have a future worth living for.* Taking a deep breath, Zac looked around her bedroom. Even in the darkness, she could see notebooks piled on her desk, with rows of pens next to them. *Annemarie gave us those,* she thought. *We're supposed to be writing in them.* In the darkness, Zac had a sudden urge to pour out what she was thinking. She turned on the light and sat at her desk.

"I was stationed in Hawaii when the towers fell," she wrote. "I had spent four years in a school just north of those towers, but now I felt far away. Palm trees and paradise were all around me as I watched the smoke and debris from the TV on the base. More than three thousand people slain, and still I could see palm fronds swaying in the wind.

"I had trained for war, but our attackers were killing innocent civilians. It was not something I could understand or support. Less than a year later, I was glad when the United States declared war- we couldn't let such a heinous act go unpunished.

"But what we found when we shipped out was not the enemy we'd envisioned. The perpetrators of the terrorist acts we sought to avenge had disappeared into the mountains, and the desert populations we camped among were often families with kids. But the enemy often came from everywhere, even from among the children..."

For the first time since she had started writing, Zac looked up from her journal and stared at the blank wall in front of her. She had more she wanted to say, but she was not sure what words to use. Finally, she simply pressed the pen against the paper and let her hand move. "We may have declared victory in this war," she wrote. "But at what cost? It's ten years later, and so much has been lost. Are we any better off than when we started?"

CHAPTER 5

Two days after her arrival in New York, eighteen-year-old Zac Madison stood in line at West Point as the cadet in front of her yelled, "you will report to the Cadet in the Red Sash! You will salute like this-" he raised his fingers to the brim of his hat- "and you will say, 'Sir, New Cadet X reports to the Cadet in the Red Sash as ordered.' Can you idiots do that?"

"Yes, sir!" Zac shouted at the same time as the new cadets around her. Then she moved in a straight line with two new cadets in front of her and three behind her. They lined up in front of a tall cadet in a perfect uniform who had a red sash around his torso. *He's really tall,* Zac thought. *I'm five-six, and he still towers over me. He's got to be at least six-four. He's handsome, too.*

As she waited, a breeze floated over her, and it felt good against her sweaty face. Zac took a deep breath, trying to calm her flip-flopping stomach as the Cadet in the Red Sash yelled repeatedly at the two new cadets in front of her. "Drop your bag!" he howled at the first new cadet in line. "I said drop it, not put it down softly! Now pick up your bag! Drop your bag! Pick it up! Drop it!"

That poor kid, Zac thought. *He can't do anything right.*

The second new cadet in line did not even make it as far as the first one had. "Get your feet off my line!" the Cadet in the

Red Sash yelled. "I said step up to my line! Not *on* my line! Not *over* my line! Step up *to* my line!"

Oh my God, Zac thought, feeling her legs start to shake. When she was first in line, the Cadet in the Red Sash took one look at her and yelled, "drop your bag!"

Zac dropped her bag, saluted, and yelled, "Sir, New Cadet Madison reports to the Cadet in the Red Sash as ordered!"

The Cadet in the Red Sash stared at her, frowning, his thick black eyebrows coming together in a single line. As Zac waited for him to scream at her, she eyed his nametag. *Sheffield,* it read. Then, to Zac's amazement, he said, "that actually wasn't bad, New Cadet Madison, but your salute needs work. May I touch you?"

"Yes, sir," Zac said, her heart racing again. *Touch me? In front of all these people?*

But the Cadet in the Red Sash simply reached over and adjusted her hand, pressing her fingers together, and pressing her hand closer to her cap. "Now, try again," he ordered.

Zac dropped her arm to her side, then brought it back up again into a salute before shouting out the same words again.

"Very good," the Cadet in the Red Sash said. He inspected Zac's tags, and a tumble of words fell out of him, directing her to her to report to the First Sergeant of Third Squad, her new company. "Do you understand that, New Cadet Madison?"

"Yes, sir!"

"Good, post!"

Zac turned and marched through the doorway on her left. *Cadet Sheffield,* she thought as she headed upstairs. *I'll have to keep an eye out for him in the future.*

*   *   *

It was almost a week after the end of the wars before Zac could talk to Alex about it. "How do you feel about them ending?" Alex asked characteristically.

"I'm glad they're over."

"Do you wish these wars hadn't happened?"

"That's always a tough question," Zac said. "As soldiers, we train for war. But that doesn't mean I'm happy to have lost my brother or my career. I mean, I still have no idea what to do with my life now."

"Let's talk about that," Alex said. "You're not married, right?"

"Correct."

"Do you have any romantic prospects?"

"Definitely not." *I'm a loser, Alex. Don't you get that? Who would be interested in me?* Zac crossed her arms and glared at Alex.

Alex remained calm. "Why do you think that is?"

"Anyone that I was ever interested in was killed in the war."

Alex winced. "That's harsh," she said. "Every last one of them?"

"That I know of." Once more, Zac pictured the handgun in her bedroom. *Why should I still be alive when so many good people were killed?* It took some effort to bring her mind back to the small, square office in which she now sat.

"Were there men at West Point that you would have been interested in, even way back then?" Alex asked.

Zac shrugged. "If it had been allowed, I might have been. But fraternization between the cadets was discouraged, especially between the older cadets and the plebes."

"So there were some older ones you were interested in?"

Zac nodded. "A couple."

"Like who?"

"What's it matter now?" Zac asked, shifting in her chair to ease the pain she still felt in her leg. "It was fifteen years ago!"

"I'm just asking, to get a better sense of who you are and where you might go from here."

"Fine," Zac replied. "One was Eric Johnson."

"The Olympic gymnast?" Alex asked. "I remember him! It was a big deal when he competed in the Olympics that year-the fact that he was at West Point was a major part of his story line."

Zac nodded, impressed that Alex would know who he was. Even so, she found herself tugging at a loose piece of thread on her chair.

"So what happened between you two?" Alex asked.

"Well, we kept in touch after West Point- sporadically, anyway," Zac replied. "As it turns out, he was interested in me, but we were never stationed in the same place at the same time."

"Did you ever ask to be?"

"I didn't know to try."

"Did he ever marry?"

"No. He was always involved with lots of women, but he didn't marry any of them."

"And when the wars started?" Alex asked.

"We actually met up again when we were getting deployed the first time, if you can believe it," Zac said. "We kept in touch more seriously after that. Towards the end of the war, when it looked like we would both survive, he finally said he was interested in getting married- in an email." Zac rolled her eyes.

"And?" Alex prompted.

"*And* my CO gave me that email along with the news that Eric had just been killed."

"I'm sorry," Alex said.

"Me too," Zac replied, swallowing to get rid of the lump in her throat. She looked around, wishing she could get out of the office. *How does Alex stand working in such a tiny space?* she wondered.

"Was there anyone else that you were interested in, even from your time at West Point?" Alex asked.

Zac heaved a breath. *I really don't want to talk about this,* she thought. "My plebe year, it was Max Sheffield. He was a firstie."

"Did you ever tell him you were interested?"

"No way! I told you-"

"Yeah, I heard. Fraternization was discouraged. But you

73

guys only overlapped for a year- what about after he graduated?"

Zac shrugged. "He got stationed in California somewhere. We lost touch."

"And you never followed up at all, with other cadets that knew him or anything?"

"A couple of his classmates visited one time as I was starting my firstie year, and I asked after him, but they said he was already married, so I dropped it."

"And you haven't tried to get in contact with him recently, like since you've gotten back to Oklahoma?"

Zac shook her head. "How would I even do that?"

"Doesn't West Point keep tabs on its graduates, especially with two wars ending? You could also try social media. Are you on Facebook at all?"

"I used to be," Zac said. "But most of my friends were people I knew from West Point or from serving with them. As more and more of them got killed in the war, I didn't want to keep looking at it, so I closed the account."

"Maybe it's worth reopening it, and using it to see if you can reconnect with people."

It took Zac nearly a week of agonizing before she finally took Alex's advice and decided to reopen her Facebook account. Even then, she felt slightly intimidated by the task as she sat down at her computer. *It's been a few years since I've done this,* she thought. *What if it's different? What if I can't figure it out?*

But, once at the website, she was surprised by how easy it was to restart her account. To her shock, most of the information that had been stored in her profile when she had closed it was still there. *Guess they don't actually delete anything,* she thought cynically. Her heart sank as she saw how many of her friends' profiles had been deleted. *Those are all people I knew who were killed in combat,* she thought. Without those people who were no longer alive, her list of friends was down by over ninety percent, and Zac could barely stop herself from crying. *That list includes Clive,* she thought. *Why am I alive and all these people aren't? I really didn't deserve to survive that grenade, or those shots. The enemy was firing at me, and they wanted me dead.*

She bit her lip, willing her tears not to overflow. *I'll bet Ben has a profile now too, though, even though he didn't when I closed my account,* she thought. She searched Facebook's listings, and found her brother quickly. *That's a little scary,* she thought as she sent Ben a friend request.

Then she scrolled through the photos she had in her account, and smiled at the ones she had of herself in her fatigues and her dress uniform. *I'll leave the ones I have of me and Clive,* she thought. *I also have a few more recent ones I want to add.* Over an hour later, she had finished uploading the last of the photographs. With that done, Zac had one more task- searching out Max Sheffield. *It's the only reason I'm doing all of this anyway,* she thought as she typed his name into the search field.

To her surprise, several people's profiles, all with the same name, came up, and Zac had to scroll through them and look at their pictures to find the one she wanted. *No, that guy's blond,* she thought. *No, that one's old.* Finally, she clicked on the next to last profile, and her heart jumped. *That's him,* she thought. *No doubt about it.*

With her heart rattling in her chest, Zac sent Max a friend request. *He probably won't remember me,* she thought. *It's been fifteen years.* Nonetheless, her feelings of fear remained unabated. Her heart continued pounding, and her stomach was beginning to hurt. *That's enough for now,* she thought, and signed out of her profile. *I need a drink. Or a few.*

When Ben called the next day, he had already accepted Zac's friend request. "When did you rejoin Facebook?" he asked.

"Yesterday," Zac said, groaning.

"Why?"

"My therapist suggested it. She thought it might help me reconnect with people."

"Oh, speaking of that- I met someone the other day who knows you. I've been meaning to call you about it."

"Really?" Zac asked.

"Yeah, he said he was an old friend of yours and Melanie's, but I didn't really know who he was, so I thought I'd call you about it." Zac could hear him digging around for something on his end. Then he said, "here it is. His name's Drew Jamieson."

For a minute, Zac stood silently, feeling like she had been nailed to the floor.

"You still there?" Ben asked.

"Yeah... God, I haven't heard from Drew in for*ever*."

"He said he went to West Point with you."

"Yeah... yeah... Of course I know who he is, it's just been awhile. He's from Bearden- he went to our high school and came to recruit for West Point when I was a senior."

"He said he was in Melanie's class in school growing up."

"Yeah, they were the same age. How'd..." Zac swallowed. "How'd you even meet him?"

"He lives in Little Rock now. He's Vice President of this big tech firm here in the city, and he came to campus on a recruiting visit. He gave a speech and mentioned being from Bearden, so of course I went to talk to him. As soon as he heard my last name, he asked if I was related to you."

Zac shook her head in disbelief. "Un-fucking-believable."

"Tell me about it," Ben said. "But he gave me his business card and asked if you'd be interested in getting in touch."

"Definitely."

"I'll send you a message on Facebook with his contact info."

*   *   *

Thirteen-year-old Zac Madison sat in the hallway of her

school in Tulsa, Oklahoma, right outside the guidance counselor's office. Clive sat next to her, holding a book in his lap, kicking his feet back and forth. Inside the office, the guidance counselor was meeting with their grandparents and some of their teachers, and Zac strained to hear what they were saying. "Melanie's behavior is a continuing problem," one teacher was saying. "She cuts class, she's failed most of her exams, and we've caught her smoking outside the school."

"She takes after her mother," Zac heard her grandfather mumble, and she almost smiled.

"It sounds like she's acting out," someone else inside the office said. "It's a difficult time for all three kids, and they're at a difficult age."

"Still, Zac and Clive are adjusting as well as can be expected," someone else said. "They're doing well in their classes and don't have the discipline problems that Melanie has. So it's not just a genetic personality issue."

"Part of the equation is that Zac and Clive are smarter and more focused," another teacher said. "They study harder, but they also seem to grasp the material more easily than Melanie does."

In the hallway, Zac and Clive looked at each other and grinned. *That's the first time I've ever heard anyone call me smart,* Zac thought. *Ma and Pa always told me how stupid I was.*

"Would Melanie benefit from counseling?" Zac heard her grandmother ask. "Are there counselors on staff that could help her?"

"We have one social worker," came the response. "But whether we could get Melanie to go to that any more than we've been able to get her to go class remains an open question."

In the hallway, Clive nudged his sister. Zac looked over at him. "We may be getting good grades, but it's still really hard to get the other kids to like me," he said.

"I know," Zac replied. "Everyone's already got their own friends. No one wants to deal with us."

A couple of weeks later, it was a quiet night in their grandparents' house when Zac tiptoed down the hall to see if Melanie was in her room. To her surprise, Melanie was sitting on her bed with her schoolbooks open. "Yes, I'm actually studying," she said when she saw Zac sticking her nose into the room. "They'll only let me go home if I pass my classes."

"Do you need help with anything?" Zac asked.

Melanie hurled a pen at her. "I don't need help from my little sister!" she said. "Besides, they got me a better tutor than you could ever be."

"Oh yeah?" Zac asked. "Who?"

"Larry Jansen. He's the cutest senior at the school. It's worth going to the tutoring sessions just to stare at him."

Zac made a face. Melanie made a motion to throw another pen at her, and Zac ducked.

"Just wait 'til you're into boys!" Melanie said.

"Why would he want to tutor you?" Zac taunted.

"The school is paying him," Melanie said with a shrug. "But if I pass my classes, I'll probably have to sleep with him anyway."

"You really are turning into Ma," Zac said. Then she ducked again to avoid the book that Melanie hurled at her. "Did they ever force you to go to those counseling sessions they were discussing?" she asked a minute later, keeping her body in the hallway but sticking her face into Melanie's room.

"Yeah," Melanie said. "Worst waste of an hour, *ever.*"

"So why bother?"

"It's a condition of getting out of here before I'm forty. Tulsa sucks. I want to go home."

Yeah, because Bearden is so much better, Zac thought sarcastically as she went back to her own room.

When Zac's parents finally regained custody of their three

younger children, Jeffrey and Elaine drove their grandchildren back to Bearden, following the social worker on the highways until they reached the smaller streets of Arkansas. *I can't believe it's been a full year since we did this ride the last time,* Zac thought. Once more, she was sitting next to the window, with Clive in the middle and Melanie on his other side.

Melanie looked over at her younger siblings as the car neared their farmhouse. "Finally," she said.

I'm not sure, Zac thought. *It'll depend on how Ma and Pa are doing.*

To her surprise, her parents were waiting for them outside the house when the car pulled up. Abe was waiting with them. *They do look better, I'll give them that,* Zac thought as she got out of the car. In front of her, Melanie had gotten out of the car first and was already hugging their parents. Then her parents looked at her and Clive, and Zac was not sure what to do. The fact that her grandparents were also hanging back increased her uneasiness.

"Zac, look at you," Linda said finally. "And Clive! My God, you both have gotten so tall."

"Come here, you two," Jack said, holding out his arms. "It's good to have you back."

Yeah, right, Zac thought, but Clive was already hurrying over to their parents to give them a hug, so she followed.

After a few minutes of hugs, Zac went back to her grandparents' car to get her book bag and the several suitcases that were hers. Clive followed her and unloaded his own bags as the social worker kept an eye on them. Melanie had already brought her stuff back into the bedroom she and Zac had always shared, but Zac moved more slowly, looking around the house as she did.

"It looks better in here," Clive said, voicing his sister's thoughts as well.

Zac nodded. "Yeah, it's not such a mess."

"That's because we've spent the last year cleaning it up," Abe said from behind them, making both Zac and Clive jump.

"Thanks for doing that," Zac said.

TAMAR ANOLIC

Abe nodded. "It's not like I had anywhere else to go, though," he said.

A girl his age stood next to him, and Zac recognized her. *She was in a few of Abe's classes in school,* she thought. "Did you stay here too, June?" she asked.

"Yeah, I wanted to help Abe out," she said. "A few of us have been living and working here since you guys left."

CHAPTER 6

Sixteen-year-old Zac Madison hesitated on the staircase of her house, listening to her parents' angry voices in the kitchen. "He's just a baby," Linda was saying. "After four other children you should know that they don't always sleep through the night."

"He's over a year old now- he should be sleeping through the night," Jack snarled back. "I'm exhausted all the time. I can't stand it."

They're talking about Ben, Zac thought. *He's been waking up at night a lot.*

"What are you going to do about it?" Linda replied. "If the state comes back, they'll take the kids away again, including Ben, and we won't get them back this time."

"That sounds like a good solution," Jack said.

Only to you, Zac thought. Plucking up her courage, she continued walking down the stairs and into the kitchen.

"Get out of here," Jack snarled when he saw her. "Your mother and I are talking."

"I need my history textbook," Zac said. "I left it in here."

"I don't care," Jack replied, and when Zac made a move to get the book, Jack threw an empty bourbon bottle at her. Zac ducked, and the bottle clanged against the wall behind her.

"Jack," Linda admonished him. "Her book is right here on the table. Would you just let her get it and leave?"

"I don't see her doing that," Jack replied, glaring at his daughter.

Linda glanced uncomfortably back and forth between her husband and her daughter. "Why don't you hurry up and get your book?" she said to Zac.

Zac ducked into the room, grabbed her textbook, and dashed back out again, keeping an eye on her father until she got to the stairs. Then she raced back to her bedroom, taking the stairs two at a time, even as she cradled her heavy textbook. Relieved to be back in her own room, Zac closed the door tightly and put a chair up against it.

Melanie made a face at her sister. "I wouldn't have even gone down for the book," she said.

"I need to finish my homework," Zac replied.

Melanie's face remained scrunched up. "I can't wait until I get out of here," she said. "I'm moving out the minute I graduate from high school."

"You spent our entire year in Tulsa counting down the minutes until we got back here," Zac reminded her.

Melanie shrugged.

"You're already eighteen- almost nineteen," Zac added. "That makes you an adult. Why don't you just move out?"

"I don't have anywhere to go yet."

"And you think that'll change as soon as graduation rolls around?"

"It might."

"Better start planning instead of dreaming. Otherwise you'll be coming right back here."

*　　　*　　　*

Zac spent several days staring at the contact information that Ben sent her before she finally picked up the phone to call

Drew Jamieson. *I really am nervous about this,* she thought. *It's been so long. What if he got injured too?* Nevertheless, as soon as Drew's familiar voice answered the phone, Zac found herself smiling. "Drew, it's Zac Madison," she said.

"Zac Madison," Drew replied, and he sounded like he was smiling too. "I wondered if I'd get to talk to you again."

"Yup," Zac said. "I heard you ran into my little brother."

"Yes, I did," Drew said. "I was as surprised as anything. He said you were back living at your grandparents' place in Tulsa?"

"I am," Zac said. "He's been out here a bunch to help me out."

"You make it back to Arkansas much?"

"Not if I can help it."

"Sounds like things haven't changed that much since we went to West Point."

Drew still sounded like he was smiling, but now Zac could hear a question in his voice, and she was not sure how to answer it. "It's certainly been a long time since the Academy," she began. "There's plenty that has changed."

"That much I know," Drew said. "War and deployment change a person."

"Definitely."

There was a slight pause. "So, Zac, I have plans to be in Oklahoma for work next week- Oklahoma City, at least. I know it's a bit of a drive from where you are, but would you be interested in meeting me there?"

"I'd be happy to. It's not that much of a drive."

After getting Drew's schedule and spending a couple of hours thinking about it, Zac decided to spend an overnight in Oklahoma City, heading down there after her group therapy appointment on a Friday and staying through late Saturday, when Drew had to head back to Little Rock. On the drive down, Zac found herself struggling to breathe normally. *What's your problem?* she asked herself. *I'm just nervous,* she replied. *Generalized unspecified anxiety.* Then she almost smiled. *Guess I'm learning more of that psychobabble from all the therapy I'm in.*

Later, after she had checked into her hotel, she made her way to the restaurant she would be meeting Drew at for a late dinner. *I hope his meetings went well,* she thought. *And that they don't run late. I'm hungry.*

She was not waiting much longer when a light blue sedan parked across the street, and Drew got out. It took Zac a second to recognize him. *He looks different,* she thought. *I wouldn't have thought he was going to age that way.*

But Drew grinned when he saw her, and Zac smiled back. "Zac!" Drew said, and held out his arms.

Zac hugged him back. "It's great to see you," she said. "I was surprised when Ben said you'd met up."

"I was surprised too," Drew said as they went into the restaurant. "I'd forgotten you had a brother that was so much younger. At first I thought he might have been Abe's son."

"He was born right around the time you went to West Point. It must have been just outside of your consciousness."

Drew looked at Zac for a long moment and smiled as they were seated and given their menus.

"What?" Zac asked.

"It's been a long time," Drew said. "But I'd still recognize you anywhere."

Zac smiled at that. "West Point really does feel like a long time ago- and that recruiting visit you made to our high school, forget it. That feels like an entire lifetime ago."

Drew laughed. "I can't believe you remember that," he said.

"It was the first time I thought the service academies were a real possibility," Zac admitted.

"I'm glad I had such an influence. Clive ended up at the Naval Academy, right?"

Zac nodded. "I can't believe *you* remember *that.*"

Drew shrugged, and the smile disappeared from his eyes as he put his menu down. "I certainly remember hearing that he didn't make it through his second tour of duty. I'm real sorry about that."

"Thanks," Zac said, hoping her tears did not show in the

dim light of the restaurant. "It doesn't get any easier."

The waitress came and took their order. Drew waited until she was out of earshot to shake his head and sigh. "We lost so many good people in this war, especially from our area, that I still haven't decided whether it was worth it."

"We were attacked," Zac replied. "It seemed like a good war at the time."

"I agree with that," Drew admitted. "The attacks came right before my service time after West Point was up. I was about to five and dive, but when we were attacked, I enlisted for a tour in Afghanistan. It really felt like the right thing to do, especially after all my training."

"What changed?" Zac asked as their drinks came.

"A lot," Drew said. "My deployment split my family apart."

Zac frowned. "Your family was so supportive of you while we were at West Point. That time they met us at the airport my plebe year, it made my coming back to Bearden seem like the right thing to do."

"I didn't mean that part of my family," Drew said. "I got married about a year out of the Academy. By the time we were attacked, I had two children under the age of five and was looking at a number of lucrative jobs in the private sector." He took a swallow of the beer he had ordered.

"You gave up those jobs to reenlist, didn't you?" Zac said.

Drew nodded. "My wife never forgave me for it. She'd moved across the country to marry me- away from her own job and family, and suddenly it was like she was a single mother while I was half a world away fighting. The extra money from the private sector also would have gone a long way."

"You must have gotten combat pay."

"It was still a single salary for a whole family."

Victor Rice managed to support his whole family- all eight kids of it- on a soldier's pay, Zac thought. "So what happened?" she asked. "You obviously survived the deployment."

"And I came back to a bunch of divorce papers. My wife

couldn't handle the pressure of me being gone."

"I'm sorry."

"Me too."

They were quiet as their soup came and they ate it.

"So what do you think you might want to do tomorrow morning?" Drew asked when their soup dishes had been cleared. "We have most of the day before we head home."

Zac nodded. "This is my first time in Oklahoma City, so there were plenty of things that made my list," she said. "But I have to admit that going to the memorial for the Oklahoma City bombing is actually at the top." She paused for a second to gauge Drew's reaction. "As much of a nerd as that might make me look like."

Drew laughed. "No, I actually thought that might interest you," he said. "It's at the top of my list as well. I mean, we did just spend ten years fighting terrorism." He shook his head. "And you're worried about looking like a nerd after graduating fifth in your class at West Point? I'd say it's a little late for that, Colonel Madison."

The next morning, Zac and Drew quietly passed through the memorial's Gates of Time, which marked the time that the bomb had gone off. As they walked, sunlight streamed across the reflecting pool of the memorial, but it was the Field of Empty Chairs that haunted Zac the most. "Each of those, and more, could be for the men and women I lost in the wars," she said.

"I know," Drew said, putting an arm around her shoulders. "It's so difficult to lose people in the field."

Zac shook her head. "I was just a kid when this happened," she said of the Oklahoma City bombing. "But I remember it. I remember when they put of the sketch of the guy they thought did it, and how much I thought it actually looked like the guy when they caught him."

Drew nodded. "I was already applying to the services

academies when it happened. It was the first time I'd thought much about terrorism, let alone domestic terrorism. Until then, I'd always assumed that I'd go abroad to fight unjust wars."

They continued walking for awhile in silence before Zac asked, "what about the war we did fight in? Were you only deployed the once?"

Drew nodded. "After that I left the service. I thought maybe if I was home I could save my marriage and my family, but…" He shook his head. "My ex got primary custody of the kids and I took the private sector job I thought I was going to take before I deployed."

Zac sighed. "These wars destroyed so many lives. I've stopped counting and still there are more."

"I know," Drew said. "What about that General you served under, who was found behind enemy lines? That's not over yet, is it?"

"God, Drew, it's just beginning. It kills me to even think about it."

"What happened?"

"He's being charged with treason."

"Did you see any of what they're charging him with?"

"I have no idea!" Zac exclaimed. "I barely know what the charges are based on."

"Then how do you even know they'll ask you anything? You could be worrying over nothing."

Zac shook her head. "When I woke up in the hospital after I'd been injured, my CO came to visit me. He made it clear that if the matter went to trial, I'd be called to testify, and I've already received the order in the mail."

Drew groaned, his sympathy obvious. "Well, you know what they say about the Army," he said. "That your last interaction with it is one of rejection."

"Great."

They continued walking, nearing the end of the memorial now. "If you don't actually know anything of the facts on which they're trying him," Drew said, "then there's not much you can say."

"I wish it were that easy," Zac said. "But this guy treated me better than my own parents did. If I said anything against him, it would be a betrayal."

"And what I'm saying is, if you don't know what these charges are based on, you don't have to say anything against him."

Zac shook her head. "Victor had eight kids, and the family barely survived on his salary, even with his combat pay. I think that if the other side can prove that he or his family benefited- monetarily or otherwise- from any kind of treason, then it's a problem."

"It's not your problem," Drew said as they got to the end of the memorial. "It's the other side's burden to prove everything. If they're prosecuting him, they have to prove he did something wrong."

Zac frowned as they left the memorial and got into Drew's car to go to lunch.

"I'm serious, Zac," Drew said as he drove. "Don't give them any more fuel for this fire."

*   *   *

Two weeks into Beast Barracks, Zac stood in West Point's Field House while the captains of the men's and women's cross-country teams looked out over the platoon-sized crowd of new cadets who were trying out for the teams. "Alright new cadets, listen up," shouted Wendy Simpson, the women's cross-country captain. "I'll be splitting you up by events." She sent various new cadets to different parts of the Field House until only the distance runners stood in front of her.

Zac bit her lip and eyed the other distance runners among the new cadets. *I hope I can do this*, she thought. *I only have this one shot of making the team, and I really want it. But I'm already exhausted too- having already done drill practice and a two mile run during the P.T.*

test won't exactly help me here.

"Alright," Wendy said, looking back at the distance runners as the men's captain, Jackson Jones, eyed them as well. "You'll be running a mile around this indoor track here. If you want to make the team, you'll have to run the mile in under 4:40 if you're a male, and under 5:30 if you're a female."

Zac took a deep breath. *My mile time at Nationals was better than that,* she thought. *I got this.* As she looked around at the other new cadets, though, she realized from everyone's expressions that she was one of the few people who felt confident. She looked back at Wendy and Jackson to find that Jackson in particular was eyeing her.

"You think you can do this, smack?" Jackson asked. "You look like a skinny string bean to me."

Wendy rolled her eyes at him, but she also looked slightly amused. Zac took another deep breath and stared past them both. "Good," she said. "In competition, I always thought it was a good strategy to have my opponents underestimate me. It made it that much easier to smoke them because they didn't try as hard."

Wendy grinned at Jackson. "Serves you right," she told him. "And if New Cadet Madison makes the team, you've just hazed her for the last time."

Zac looked at her and could not contain a small smile. Looking back at Jackson, she found that he was smiling too.

"Alright new cadets, on the track," Wendy shouted.

Zac lined up with the rest of the distance runners. She shot forward as soon as the starting gun went off. Even so, the track was only 200 meters long, and Zac soon felt like she had run a million laps and still had more to go. *It doesn't help that my legs are killing me,* she thought. *I had meets in high school where I would run the mile, and then the two mile race, but I was resting in between, not doing all of the shit I've done today.*

With three laps left, Zac felt a second wind coming, and picked up the pace. *Hallelujah!* she thought. *I have a shot at this!*

As she turned around the last curve, Zac shot forward again, heading towards the timekeeper at a dead sprint. As she crossed the finish line, she heard him counting her time: "Five eleven, five twelve, five thirteen."

I made it! Zac felt like shouting. She hopped off the track and slowed down to a jog, then to a walk, trying to catch her breath. Then she looked up just in time to see Wendy stick her tongue out at Jackson.

On one of the last days of Beast Barracks, Cadet McKnight, the leader of Third Squad, pulled Zac aside- but not far aside. The rest of the new cadets in her squad stood right nearby, listening to everything they said. "Madison, can you swim?" Cadet McKnight asked.

"Yes, sir," Zac replied. "My track coach in high school used to take us to the pool so that we could cross-train."

"Very good," McKnight said. "By now, I'm sure you've heard about the Iron Man competition that's happening tomorrow afternoon?"

Zac nodded.

"Each Company needs four people to represent it in this competition. Our entire chain of command met about it an hour ago to come up with a list of names, and yours was on it."

"Mine, sir?" Zac asked, doubt etched on her face. "Are you sure?"

"Yes, I am. Are you interested in competing?"

"Yes, sir!"

"Great," Cadet McKnight said. "You know about all the requirements, right? Swimming to a raft in the middle of the lake and back, fifty pushups, fifty sit ups, and running around the lake- that's close to three miles."

Zac nodded. "I can do that."

Cadet McKnight grinned. "Awesome," he said. "I'll be counting your pushups and sit ups for you. See you tomorrow."

As she lined up for the competition the next afternoon, Zac glanced around at the other new cadets she was competing against. *There are hardly any females,* she thought. *Maybe one per company, at most.* She looked at the lake in front of her. *I can do the swimming piece easily,* she thought. *And the running piece too. It's the sit ups and the pushups that are going to kill me. Or just the pushups, anyway.*

As soon as the starting gun went off, Zac leapt into the water. *Goggles would have helped,* she thought, but, remembering all the times she had swum without them as a kid, she powered through the water to the float and back. As she pulled herself out of the water, gasping, Cadet McKnight raced towards her, holding her regular clothing and sneakers. "You're the fourth female!" he said. "You can do it!"

Not wanting to disappoint him, Zac raced into her clothing and started on the sit-ups. The first half of the set went just fine, but by the thirty-seventh sit-up, Zac could feel her stomach muscles complaining.

"Thirty-eight, thirty-nine, forty," Cadet McKnight counted for her. "Come on, Madison, you're almost there!"

As soon as she had finished her fiftieth sit-up, Zac gasped and lay on the ground for a split second.

"Move it, Madison, time for the push-ups!" McKnight boomed.

Immediately, Zac rolled over and began the push-ups. She made it through seventeen of them before groaning. "I need a break!" she gasped. McKnight looked disappointed, but he gave her a few seconds of rest. After several deep breaths, Zac pumped out fourteen more before her arms gave out again.

"Come on, come on, you're almost there!" McKnight encouraged. "Then you're off to the run, where you can haze everyone around you."

That was all the encouragement Zac needed. She planted her hands in the sand and made it through the last of her push-ups. Then she leapt to her feet and ran for the starting line of the nearly-three mile run.

"Go, Madison, go!" McKnight cheered.

Zac broke into a grin as she set her watch and moved forward. *Only two females are in front of me now, and I'm going to catch them.* Zac's body felt tired, but at least she was running. *I really do love to run,* she thought. *It's such a shame I could never do cross-country in high school. It would have prepared me for this race.*

Nevertheless, Zac could feel her leg muscles warming up, and as her feelings of fatigue left her, Zac picked up the pace. As she did, she passed two other cadets, one male and one female. "Come on, you're doing great," she encouraged them as she passed them. *Only one female left ahead of me,* she thought. *Where is she?*

As Zac continued running, she neared the lake's halfway point. Cadets were lined up along the road, cheering. Then, up ahead of her, Zac finally saw the one other female that was still in front of her. *Get her!* she thought.

Picking up the pace, Zac caught the female in front of her, and then two male cadets. By now, she could see the cadets from Third Squad on the side of the road, and she could hear them yelling her name and cheering. *You're almost there!* she yelled at herself. *Move, Zac, move!*

As the finish line came into view, Zac picked up the pace one last time and sprinted towards it. As she did, she heard Cadet McKnight's unmistakable howl. "Come on, Madison!" he shouted.

Zac crossed the finish line, then doubled over in pain. Her breathing came in ragged gasps, and her leg muscles ached. A stitch in her side made it nearly impossible to breathe. "Ooowww," she yelped.

Suddenly, a strong arm was lifting her upright. "Alright, Madison!" Cadet McKnight said. "You did great!"

They were surrounded by other cadets of Third Company, who lifted Zac's arms onto their shoulders and supported her until she could walk and breathe on her own.

"How did I do?" Zac asked when her heart and breathing rates had slowed down.

"Sixth overall, and the first female," Cadet McKnight said. All around him, the cadets of Third Company whooped in encouragement.

*   *   *

The sound of imams chanting woke Zac up one night in Iraq. She groaned as she checked the clock next to her head. *It isn't even light out yet,* she thought. *Did they start prayers early? Why do they have to be so damn loud about it? No one at home prays like that.*

She sat up and pulled her boots on, making sure to stay as silent as possible so as not to wake the soldiers around her. Then, with her machine gun at her side and a pair of binoculars around her neck, she went to the roof of the FOB to get a view of the surrounding area. She had hardly gotten onto the roof when she saw a grave out back, behind the base. Lifting her binoculars to her eyes, Zac tried to read the gravestone. The name on the stone jumped out at her even in the early morning light. "Matthew James Edwards," it read.

They buried him there? Zac's mind screamed. *No, no, no! His body was supposed to go home!*

She stormed down off the rooftop and sprinted down to the desert outside the base. When she got to the grave, she began digging frantically with her hands. As she removed the dirt, the sounds of the Islamic prayers grew louder and louder around her. Then she looked up to see a number of enemy soldiers coming her way, holding rifles.

"Go away!" Zac screamed at them. As she struggled to get the words out, one of the soldiers raised his rifle...

Zac jerked awake in the early morning light of Tulsa, Oklahoma. Her heart was racing and she struggled to get her bearings. As she looked around, she realized that she was kneeling in her backyard. Something dark covered her hands. Zac shrieked and jumped up. *Blood! I'm bleeding all over the place!* she almost screamed.

Then she realized that her hands were covered in dirt. *Where is it from?* she wondered. She looked down at her feet. She was standing in the middle of her flowerbeds, all of which had been torn up. Rows and rows of flowers now lay on their side or buried in mounds of soil. *Shit*, Zac thought. *I was literally digging up a grave.*

Her breath came in gasps as tears fell down her face. Wiping them off only transferred the dirt from her hands to her face. "Fuck," Zac said. She turned and walked back into her house as the sun slowly peeked over the tops of the trees in her yard. *Time for a shower- and probably some sort of medication. I've been trying to avoid that route, but I don't think I can anymore.*

That afternoon, when it was completely light out, Zac checked her email and was glad she had. She had exchanged her email address with the other veterans in her group therapy, and now she saw a message from Gail to both her and Jenny about a concert in Tulsa. "It's a concert for vets- thank you for your service!- I guess," Gail wrote, and Zac tried not to laugh as she pictured Gail's sarcasm. "But it's being given by a local band who's pretty popular, so I'm interested in going, just to see them perform."

Zac clicked on one of links in Gail's email, which brought her to the band's website. *Oh, yeah, I've heard of them*, she thought. *They're totally a boy band- not my kind of music at all. I remember when girls were falling all over them. I had a few grunts that were into their music too- all females, of course.*

I didn't know they were from around here, though, Zac thought as she continued clicking around the band's website. *It might be worth going just for that. And to see Gail and Jenny, too, of course. I'm really starting to like them.*

As she looked at the concert's website, however, Zac frowned. "This is the band's first concert back in Tulsa," the site read.

Where have they been? Zac wondered, and typed the band's name into a search engine. The news stories that came up answered her question pretty quickly- the three band members, ages 21, 19 and 17, had spent the last two years living with an uncle in Canada while they finished their last tour and started work on a new album.

So much of their marketing is about how proud they are to be from this area, Zac thought. *Why would they move to Canada for a couple of years? That's kind of random.* As she thought about it, though, Zac realized that two years ago was right around the time that Congress had been considering implementing a draft. *I'll bet anything they ran to Canada to escape the draft if it was implemented,* Zac thought, her resentment boiling within her. *That's why they're back now- because the wars just ended!*

Zac stood up and went to the window, her teeth clenched. She stared out to cloudy skies that looked like they were about to drop more rain on the earth below them. *What gave them the right to disappear to Canada and shirk their duty to this country?* she thought. *They were all safe in another country while my brother was being killed, and I was nearly killed.*

Zac took a deep breath. *Should I skip this concert on moral grounds?* she wondered. *I don't know. I like the fact that vets get discounted tickets, and that all the money from the concert is benefitting local vets' organizations. The band won't see a penny from it.* As she stared out the window, the clouds parted and a large ray of sunshine splashed into Zac's eyes. She squinted. *I guess I'll go,* she thought. *It'll be good to get out of the house, and it'll be good to see Gail and Jenny.*

When Zac pulled up to the outdoor field where the concert was being held, she was smiling. She parked her car and got out, feeling the warmth of the sun on her face. *Summer is finally here,* she thought as she spotted Gail and Jenny and went over to them. *It'll be nice when I don't have to use this cane anymore, though.*

"I think that's the most I've ever seen you smile," Gail said to Zac as she joined them.

Zac nodded. "There are a couple of vets that I knew from West Point that I've managed to reconnect with," she said. "I just heard back from one of them."

"That's nice," Jenny said.

"Yeah, that's great," Gail said. "Is one of them the guy you went to Oklahoma City to meet?"

Zac nodded.

"How'd that go?" Jenny asked.

"It was very nice," Zac said.

"You look kind of relieved," Gail said.

"I guess I am," Zac said as she thought about it. "It's been awhile since I've seen him, and I wasn't sure how it would go." *Actually, my heart is coming out of my chest, but it's mostly from finally getting a message back from Max on Facebook. It's incredible that he finally responded. I didn't think he would.*

"Well, I'm glad it's working out," Jenny said.

"Me too," Zac said.

"Anyone want a drink?" Gail asked, opening a cooler at her feet and pulling out a couple of beers and a wine cooler.

"Yes, thanks," Jenny said, taking the wine cooler.

"Cool," Zac said, taking one of the beers. *I hope I can stop after one or two,* she thought. *I haven't been able to recently.*

As they drank, Zac, Gail and Jenny looked at the stage in front of them. Behind the stage, a huge banner read, "Welcome Home Veterans!" On the stage itself, three young men were setting up their instruments- Zac could see amplifiers, a keyboard, and part of a drum set. *That's definitely the band,* she thought as she recognized them from the pictures she had seen online.

"The oldest one is only a year or two younger than I am," Jenny said. She glanced down at her missing leg and crutches and then back at the stage. "It's incredible what a different life they have."

Zac and Gail nodded sympathetically. "You have nothing to apologize for in how you've lived your life," Zac said. *I get what she's saying, though,* she thought. *These guys are quite famous- and pretty wealthy at this point, I'm sure. I earn a decent salary as an officer, especially as a Colonel, but I doubt it's anywhere near what these guys have.*

"Yeah, these guys are young, but they've put out a few

albums already, and all of them have sold millions of copies," Gail said, making Zac wonder if she could read her mind.

The three of them watched as a middle-aged couple and a few younger kids helped set up the stage. *I'll bet that's their family,* Zac thought. *Their parents only look about forty. They must have started having kids pretty young- probably around the same age my parents were when they started having us.*

"Their parents are helping them set up?" Gail asked, a combination of sarcasm and amusement in her voice. "I guess these guys really still are kids." She laughed, and Zac joined her.

"Don't knock it," Jenny said. "I heard their family is pretty close. My own family is like that, and it's what's kept me going since my injury."

"I didn't mean any offense," Gail said. "I would expect your family to help you out."

"I know," Jenny said, and it was clear she was not offended. She nodded back at the stage. "I read that these guys were barely even teenagers when their first album came out. Their parents had to drive them to all of their concerts."

Onstage, Travis Lamont set up his keyboard and helped his younger brother Robby set up his drum set. Their older brother Cole plugged in his amplifier and guitar. "It's good to be home again," Robby said as Travis adjusted his cymbals.

Travis and Cole nodded, and Travis surveyed the crowd in front of them again. More people were finally arriving, and he could see a number of people with visible injuries joining some of the more able-bodied veterans. In particular, he saw a group of three women standing off to the side, talking and laughing as they watched the band set up. One was on crutches and was missing a leg. Another was holding a cane.

Cole followed Travis' eyes. "That girl without the leg looks about our age," he said.

Robby nodded, turning his back to the crowd so that only his brothers saw his grimace. "Can you imagine losing a leg?" he said. "I'm not sure I'd want to live like that."

"Tell me about it," Travis said. "I thought the blond one

in that group looks like she could be related to us."

His brothers glanced back at Zac, whose pale blue eyes were visible even from where they stood. "She only looks like you," Cole teased Travis. "We might all be blond, but you're the only one in the family with blue eyes."

Travis eyed Zac again, noticing her cane. "I wonder what happened to her."

"You can ask her after the concert," Robby said with a grin, and he and Cole laughed.

"No way," Travis said. *We ran away from the war so that we wouldn't have to risk getting killed. These people went towards combat and have obviously suffered for it. What could we possibly talk about?*

"Oh, come on, Travis," Cole said. "You were the one that wanted to hold this concert. Maybe you should go meet some of the people that came to it."

Travis just shrugged.

CHAPTER 7

During the first week of classes of her plebe year at West Point, during study hour after dinner, there was a knock on Zac's door- one knock, which meant official business. "Enter, sir!" Zac said loudly, and she and her roommate, Jen, jumped up to stand at attention.

The door opened, and to Zac's surprise, Drew Jamieson entered. He looked at her and smiled, propping the door open at a ninety-degree angle as he did. Then he eyed Jen. "At ease, Cadet Newman. You may go back to studying."

"Yes, sir," Jen replied. She went back to her chair and her books.

"Cadet Madison, I see you made it to West Point," Jamieson said.

"Yes, sir!" Zac replied.

"I hear you made the cross-country team as well."

"Yes, sir!"

"Well, I'm glad to hear that. How are you settling in?"

"Very well, sir. I'm glad to be here."

Jamieson smiled again. "That's good to hear," he said. "It's good to know that someone from my hometown made it here." Then he extended hand. "Drew," he said.

"Zac," Zac replied, shaking his hand.

"Well, don't let me disturb your studying anymore," Drew said, giving a last nod to both Zac and Jen before disappearing back out into the hall, closing the door behind him.

When he was gone, Zac and Jen looked at each other and dissolved into giggles. "Wow, I can't believe you've already been recognized by an upperclassman," Jen said.

"I've met him already," Zac admitted. "He came to my high school last year on a recruiting visit."

"Even so," Jen replied. "The fact that he came by means he remembered you and looked you up to see if you came here."

"That is pretty incredible," Zac agreed. "But he went to my high school, so I guess he was just looking for hometown pride."

"I still wouldn't minimize it if I were you."

"Oh, I'm not. But we do have enough of a history that I guess it would occur to him to check on me."

For a second, Jen stared at their closed door, thinking. "So Drew's a senior, right?"

"A *firstie*," Zac corrected.

"Oh, right, a firstie," Jen said, rolling her eyes. "Maybe one day I'll get this place's lingo down." She shook her head. "But that makes him in the same year as the Cadet in the Red Sash we saw on R-Day."

Zac nodded. Even now, she remembered that cadet's last name- Sheffield. "I wonder what his first name was, though," she said.

"Cadet," Jen replied. They both laughed.

"So are you enjoying it here?" Zac asked.

Jen nodded. "I am. Are you?"

"Yes," Zac said. "This is quite a welcome relief from home."

"Tell me about it," Jen replied, rolling her eyes. "The rest of my friends from home have been doing nothing but partying and wasting their lives."

"That must be nice," Zac said. "My family never had enough money to party."

"My family and circle of friends had the opposite problem. We always had enough money that it wouldn't matter what we did with our lives."

"Why are you here, then?"

"To do something with my life," Jen said, looking at Zac squarely in the face. "It was all partying and drugs. I was so bored- and I was scared of not having a direction in life."

"Wow," Zac said. "My life lacked direction, but for the

opposite reasons as yours. If I hadn't gotten out of there, I'd be married with at least one kid by now."

Jen shook her head. "That's rough," she said.

"It's why I gotta survive this place," Zac answered. "I can't go back there." She shook her head. "But you don't miss that carefree lifestyle at all?"

"Generally not," Jen said. "But every once in awhile I wish I could go clubbing, like on a Saturday night. It was probably the worst when we were in Beast, marching around with our faces painted at one in the morning. At that point, I was like, what am I doing here?"

They both laughed again. "I think it's worth it, though," Zac said.

At the end of her second week of classes at West Point, Zac left her last class of the day and began marching back to her company barracks. All around her, cadets poured out of their classrooms, plebes and upperclassmen alike. All of a sudden, a voice howled over the din, "Cadet Madison, halt!"

Zac immediately came to a stop. *Shit*, she thought. *What was I doing wrong?* A tall cadet appeared in front of her, and Zac recognized him immediately. *The Cadet in the Red Sash*, she thought. *Cadet Sheffield. This has to be the fourth time he's hazed me this week alone.*

"Cadet Madison, where are you from?" Cadet Sheffield yelled. Behind him, a number of firsties watched with amusement.

"Sir, I am from Bearden, Arkansas," Zac shouted in response.

"Where is that, Cadet Madison?" Cadet Sheffield boomed. "Not all of us are familiar with the boondocks."

"Sir, it's about an hour and a half south of Little Rock."

"An hour and a half by car, smack?"

"No, sir, my family prefers a horse and buggy."

All around, cadets burst into laughter. "Whacked by a

smack!" a firstie yelled. "Nice job, Max!"

Max, Zac thought. *Cadet Sheffield's first name is Max.*

In front of her, Max's face turned bright red. "Careful how you address me, smack," he roared. "Or I'll haze you every day until I graduate!"

Zac cringed inwardly, wondering if she'd gone too far. But then she saw that Max's eyes were twinkling, and she had to suppress a smile.

*　　　　*　　　　*

"So have you made any progress with Max?" Alex asked during Zac's next session with her.

Zac nodded. "He's meeting me when this session is over."

"Good! I'm really glad to hear it! See, I knew it would work out."

How could she possibly have known that? Zac wondered, feeling claustrophobic in the small office. She eyed the doorway. *At least I can get out of here quickly if I need to.*

Then Alex switched gears entirely. "Do you want some fresh blueberries?" she asked, holding out a green container full of the blue fruit. "A friend of mine bought a bunch."

But Zac shook her head. "I don't like blueberries."

Alex stared at her. "I've never met anyone who doesn't like blueberries."

"I can't deal with them."

"Why not?"

Zac's face crinkled in frustration. "When I was growing up on the farm, before I went to West Point, we lived on several acres of land. One summer, Clive and I found blueberry bushes growing at the edge of the property, filled with ripe blueberries."

"How old were you when this happened?"

"Ten. Clive was eight. We made the mistake of telling our

parents about those bushes. Next thing we knew, our parents put us to work, picking the berries and selling them so that they could have more money to buy alcohol."

Alex put her container of fruit away. "Were there a lot of berries on those bushes?" she asked.

Zac nodded. "Clive and I used to get up as soon as it got light and pick as many berries as we could. Then we'd take the bus into Little Rock and sell them to the stores there. At the height of the summer, we sold gallons of them at a time. By the end of that first summer, our parents had us plant more bushes."

"So you guys earned a decent amount of money doing this?"

"Yeah. A lot of times, if Ma and Pa fell behind on the bills, we'd take the money we got from the blueberries and go to the companies' offices in Little Rock and pay off the bills that way. Or we'd use the money to buy groceries that we knew our parents wouldn't- and I don't mean candy and treats," Zac added.

"You guys had to buy stuff like milk and real food?" Alex asked.

"Yeah," Zac said. She pictured her twelve-year-old self, with Clive in tow, walking up and down the aisles of the grocery store. *The store clerks never even asked us why a couple of kids would be buying groceries for their family- they just rang up our purchases and took our money.* "As the bushes we planted that first summer grew and bore fruit, Clive and I often put a few containers aside and kept the money for ourselves- we always split it evenly."

"And your parents never found out about that?"

"No. After I went to West Point, Clive kept doing that, only he kept all the money for himself. He had a decent amount saved up by the time he went to the Naval Academy."

"What happened after he passed away?" Alex asked. "Did your parents get his belongings?"

"No," Zac said. "He drafted a will before his first tour of duty that left everything to me." She shrugged. "I'd rather have my brother than his money."

"I didn't mean otherwise. How did your parents feel about his passing?"

Zac swallowed. Images from Clive's funeral flashed in her mind, and immediately, tears stung her eyes. Alex pushed a box of tissues across her desk. Zac ignored them, even as her tears threatened to overflow. "I'm not sure what they thought," she said finally.

"What do you mean?" Alex pressed.

"At the funeral, they had no expressions on their faces at all. If they had been kids, I would have said they didn't understand what was happening. Even when they got presented with the flag from the top of Clive's coffin, it was like they were somewhere else."

Alex shook her head in sympathy. "That must have been tough," she said.

"It was horrible," Zac admitted.

When the appointment was over, Zac gratefully closed Alex's door behind her and followed the exit signs through the maze of offices until she got to the main waiting room. She was already thinking of the bright sunshine outside, and would have made a dash for the exit, but for a familiar face in the waiting room.

Zac did a double take, and then took another look. She smiled. As she looked at him more closely, the more certain she became. He had not aged much- she'd recognize him anywhere. "Max," she said.

In a second, he was looking at her. Then his face split into the grin that Zac remembered from their days at West Point. "Zac!" Max said as he got up. "It is so good to see you!" He was as tall as she remembered, with the same black hair in a crew cut, the same thick black eyebrows.

He threw open his arms, and Zac hugged him without reservation. She had not missed the hook that had replaced his left hand, though. "What happened to you?" she asked.

"Roadside bomb in Afghanistan. What happened to you?"

"Grenade and machine gun fire in Iraq." *I actually forgot I was holding my cane- unbelievable.*

"Sounds like war."

"It was."

For a second, Zac and Max stood looking at each other, amused looks on their faces, oblivious to the hustle and bustle of patients and nurses around them. Then Max looked at his watch, which he now wore hanging around his neck instead of his missing left wrist. "Do you want grab breakfast?" he asked.

"Sure," Zac replied. "There's a diner near here that I've always wanted to try."

"I think I passed it on my way here," Max replied as they headed outside into the heat. "You know, you still have your Southern accent."

"So I'm told."

"I don't think it's as strong as when I first met you, though."

"Because I've worked on lessening it."

"Oh, come on, Zac," Max said, giving her a playful whack on the shoulder. "Why would you do such a thing? Your accent was awesome!"

"I don't know about that," Zac replied. "Plenty of the cadets at the Academy teased me about it."

"Only because they thought it was awesome too!"

"Yeah, right," Zac said.

"I'm serious," Max said as they got to their cars. "Meet you over there is a few minutes?"

"Sure," Zac said, and a little while later, they walked into the diner together. "So... I was surprised to hear that you were living so close to me. What brings you to this area?" Zac asked as they walked. *I'm not even sure where to start this conversation. It's been so long since I've seen him, and our Facebook conversations have just been about setting up this meeting.*

"A few things," Max replied as they were led to a booth inside the diner. "First, I found a temporary job down here."

"Doing what?" Zac asked. The brown cushion of the diner's booth, with its plastic covering, crackled as they sat opposite each other.

"Manufacturing plastic prosthesis for veterans. I'm hoping to get one soon myself. It's got to be better than this." He waved his metal hook around.

Zac frowned as she looked at where his hand used to be. "I hope I can get used to that," she said.

"You'd better," Max teased.

"Didn't you used to work in a factory before you got to West Point?"

"You have a good memory. Yes. Manufacturing is a big thing up in Rochester. Or was, before all the business went overseas." Max shook his head. "There's no way I'm going back there. Not to live there or anything."

"And yet you still took a manufacturing job."

"At least it's a better gig than the one I had in high school," Max said. "It pays better, and we're actually doing good work. Lotsa good soldiers can walk now and do a buncha stuff they couldn't do before."

"And business should be good, based on what I've seen in physical therapy," Zac said. She concentrated on extracting her fork and knife from the paper napkin in which they were tightly rolled.

Max nodded. "That's good and bad. It's sad that so many vets need these services, but it's good that an American business is meeting that demand."

Zac eyed him. "Even so, how'd you end up in Tulsa?" she asked. "I'm only here 'cause my grandpa left me his property."

"Some coincidence, huh?"

Zac shook her head. "No way," she said. "I was just talking about you to my therapist. I find it hard to believe that you just happen to be down here."

"Who's your therapist?"

"Alex Bittman."

Max did not look surprised. "She treated me too when I first got out of the service about a year and a half ago."

"I wondered if she knew who you were!" Zac said. "She would never say anything, though!" She shook her head.

"Confidentiality be damned, I wish she could have given me your number or something- all of this would have moved a lot faster if she had."

"It's not just about confidentiality, it's about helping us do this stuff on our own," Max said. "She can't impose what she wants for us onto what we do, we have to do it ourselves."

Zac eyed him. "So did you mention me at all when you were in therapy?"

"You mighta come up," Max answered, deliberately looking over at the waitress as she came to their table.

"Are y'all ready to order?" the waitress asked.

"We haven't even looked at the menu," Zac said apologetically. "Sorry."

"Take your time," the waitress replied. She moved on to a nearby table.

"What do I want to eat?" Zac asked, opening her menu for the first time.

"Are you still allergic to blueberries?" Max asked.

Zac blinked at him uncomprehendingly.

"Oh, don't tell me you don't remember," Max said. "Your first week of classes at West Point, you said you were allergic to blueberries."

"I can't believe you remember that," Zac said.

Now it was Max's turn to look incredulous. "You know, there was one time Jason Stratem cooked a whole batch of blueberry pancakes," he said of another cadet, "and I had him disinfect the entire kitchen afterwards so you wouldn't have an allergic reaction."

"I didn't know that!" Zac said. She burst out laughing. "Oh my God!"

"So you mean to tell me you're not actually allergic?"

"I'm not actually allergic, but I couldn't deal with blueberries for awhile. It's a long story. It was just easier to say that I was allergic."

Max shook his head at her, but he was beaming.

Zac laughed again. "I can't believe you did that," she repeated. They both laughed and picked up their menus again.

The waitress came back. "Know what y'all'd like?" she asked.

"I do," Zac said, and ordered French toast with bacon on the side.

Max ordered blueberry pancakes. "Now that I can," he said teasingly as the waitress left.

Zac shook her head and laughed. "Whatever happened to Jason?" she asked. "I remember him. He was a cow my first year at the Academy."

"Killed in Iraq about a year into the war. And that's true of many of our classmates."

Zac sighed. "What a waste," she said.

"I can't disagree," Max said. They were quiet for awhile, and Zac looked first at Max, and then outside, where the heat rose in shimmering waves. "So, what have you been up to since you got home?" Max asked finally.

Reluctantly, Zac pulled her eyes away from the parking lot outside. *I haven't been doing shit with my life,* she thought. "It's mostly just been the therapy," she said. "I was pretty badly wounded, so I really couldn't do much at all for awhile. And I've been fixing up my house. Like I said, my grandpa left me his property, so luckily, I don't have to pay anything to live there. I'd be in trouble otherwise."

Max nodded. "My first few months out were brutal," he said. "Losing a hand was really bad. And I've been out for nearly two years, and I still haven't had more than temporary jobs."

"How long does your current job last?" Zac asked.

"Until the end of the year, and it might get extended."

"That's a decent stretch."

"It's still not like having something permanent, though."

"Like being in the Army."

"Tell me about it. Any thoughts on what you might do eventually?" Max asked.

They both looked up at the waitress as their food came, and Zac took the opportunity to think for a few minutes rather than say anything. But eventually she found Max looking at her for an answer. "I really don't know," she said finally.

"It would be a waste for you not to do anything," Max said. "You were always one of the smartest people around at West Point, and that's saying a lot. Besides, you survived the war, and your reputation has really made its rounds."

"What?" Zac said, bewildered. "No one knows who I am, except the people I served with."

"Not true," Max said, shaking his head as he cut his pancakes with his fork.

Zac watched him uneasily, realizing that he couldn't use a fork and knife at the same time anymore.

"Ever read a newspaper?" Max was saying. "Every paper covering the war had news stories about you- how your unit advanced, especially towards the end of the war."

"You can't be serious."

"I am serious, Zac. You don't give yourself enough credit. It's been pretty easy to follow your career for years now. Especially when you got wounded and moved back here, the papers had large articles about it."

"I didn't notice at all."

"Probably because you were in the hospital. You should look it up when you get home today."

"I might do that." Zac paused to eat a piece of bacon. "So, is that another reason you landed here in Tulsa? Because I'm here?"

"It was one motivating factor," Max admitted, even if he could not look at her while he said it. "I got a decent job here, don't forget, but I thought it would be nice to know one person who understood where I was coming from."

Zac studied him. "I thought you were already married," she said. "What happened to your wife?"

"She was someone I knew from back home in Rochester before I went to West Point. It seemed like a good idea at the time. I was interested in getting married, and there she was."

"But?"

"*But* she cheated on me during one of my first tours of duty. With a Marine, I might add."

"Wow." Zac didn't know what else to say. "I'm sorry to hear that."

Max shrugged. "We divorced pretty quickly after that. I don't have the patience for that kind of nonsense."

"That sucks."

"Yes it does."

A few days later, Max invited Zac to dinner at his apartment, and she was only too glad to accept. Anything that broke the monotony of the endless days at her house. *The house still needs plenty of work,* Zac reminded herself as she drove into Tulsa, also reminding herself to drive at the speed limit. *So does the land around the house. Grandpa used that place as a farm until Grandma passed away and he got too old to work on it. Those back few acres haven't been touched since. Not sure what I'm going to do with all that land. There's no way I'm going back to farming, and anyway, I can't do it all myself.*

In the city, Max grinned at her when he saw her waiting outside his apartment building. "I have to warn you, though, I do have a puppy," he said when they were in the elevator going up to his apartment.

"Oh, yeah?" Zac said, grinning back. "What type?"

"Black lab."

"They're really adorable."

"Yeah, this one in particular is the cutest."

As soon as Max stuck his key in the door to his apartment, they heard the thump of paws hitting the floor. Max broke into a grin. "He must have been on the couch," he said. A second later, they heard the puppy whining at the door.

"Aawww," Zac said.

Max swung open the door and the puppy immediately jumped all over him. "Hey Blackie!" he cried, picking the dog up and moving into the apartment so that Zac could get inside too. "Happy to see me?"

"Woof!" Blackie replied.

"If he'd said anything else, I would have been worried," Zac teased.

Max grinned. "He's great," he said, scratching the dog's ear as he held him. "Really gave me a reason to get out of bed there for awhile."

"Maybe I should get a dog, too, then," Zac said as she pet the puppy.

"You really should consider it," Max said seriously. "If you're having nightmares and trouble getting out of bed and all that, then you're having all the same symptoms I was."

"How did you beat it?"

"The therapy helped," Max admitted. "I've had to go back a few times since my regular sessions ended, though. Moving here and having a change of scenery helped a bunch too, as does having a regular job where they understand what happened to me and where I feel like I'm making a difference for other vets. Having a network of other vets helps too."

"Yes, it certainly seems to," Zac agreed. "Even the vets from my group therapy are a good safety net. I've done stuff with some of them already, and it's been good."

"Plus, I'm here now," Max said, his grin lighting up his face. "That makes all the difference!"

Zac laughed at him. "I've also gotten back in touch with Drew Jamieson," she said.

"Yeah, me too," Max said. "His company designs some of the stuff we make at the factory." His grin disappeared slightly. "He got off easily."

"I don't know if I agree with that," Zac said, frowning.

"He didn't get injured at all, and he only served one tour."

"He was about to leave the service entirely when we were attacked. He chose to deploy because he felt like it was his duty."

"And then he got out pretty quickly."

"His wife left him while he was deployed," Zac said. "And the fact that they had young kids meant that his divorce wasn't as clean as yours was. I don't think he's had it as easy as you think."

Max gazed at her steadily. "He didn't get injured, and he has a high level job that he got pretty quickly when he left the Army," he said. "I still think he got off more easily than we did."

Zac sat down on Max's couch. Blackie jumped up on the couch next to her, and Zac gave the puppy a couple of pets to calm herself down. "He's certainly had an easier transition to civilian life than we're having," she agreed finally. "But why are you so bitter? I thought you guys got along when you were classmates."

"We did," Max said. "It's not about that." He heaved a breath. "But these wars have been long, and the transition home has been harder than I was expecting. Seeing others who have it easier doesn't make it better."

CHAPTER 8

Zac smiled at Drew as she held her front door open for him. "On a selfish level, I'm glad you travel a lot for work," she said. "It's good to see you."

"You still fixing this place up?" Drew asked, looking around as he stepped inside.

"Yeah, I've gotten a ton of stuff done, but there's so much more to do."

"You need a new roof, for one thing."

"And new floors. My grandparents were having trouble maintaining the place towards the end of their lives."

"So is this the house you stayed in for that year that you were living away from Bearden?" Drew asked.

"Yeah," Zac said. "My grandparents got custody of us until my parents dried out." She shook her head. "I can't believe you remember that."

Drew looked at her, and his eyes seemed to bore into her face. "I was in Melanie's class growing up, remember?" he said. "I never knew quite how bad you guys had it at home until the state came and took you away. Then you were gone for a whole year. It was a big deal."

"What was Mel like in school?" Zac asked. *Was she different with the boys than she was with me?* "Our grandparents certainly thought she was a pain in the ass."

Drew laughed. "I can understand that," he said. "She was loud and sarcastic, and everyone knew she got bad grades. It was no secret that she had to repeat a few classes, especially when I went off to West Point and she didn't have enough credits to graduate. Did she ever finish her degree?"

"Eventually," Zac said. "But she never did anything more. When we lived here in Tulsa, my grandparents caught her sneaking out a lot at night. They only managed to get her to start studying by getting some good looking guy to tutor her."

Drew laughed again. "That was about the only way to get through to the Melanie I knew," he said.

"Was she really that easy?" Zac asked. "Did you guys sleep together?"

Drew eyed her as he contemplated the best way of answering that. "Come on, Zac," he said finally. "She had a lot to act out against, as you well know."

*　　　　　*　　　　　*

During the first week of classes of her yearling year at West Point, Zac sat in her assigned seat in her mechanical engineering class, waiting for the professor. Michael Strong, another yearling, marched in and took his seat behind her and next to her friends Heather Graham and Lucy Tennyson. Caroline Mack, another yearling, sat next to Heather and Lucy. Out of the corner of her eye, Zac watched Michael put his books down on his desk. Then he leaned over and said, loud enough for the whole class to hear, "I'm surprised you ladies are still here." He twisted the word "ladies" sarcastically. "West Point is usually too difficult for the females."

Zac turned around to stare at him directly in the face. "The day you do better than me on an engineering exam, Strong, or run a mile faster than me, is the day I will consider leaving West Point. Until then, you'd better get used to seeing me here."

All around them, their classmates snickered, and most were watching with looks of amusement. Michael glared at Zac, well aware of their classmates' reactions. The room was silent as he contemplated his reply. Then their professor, Major James Pierce, entered the classroom. The students rose to acknowledge their professor, and the class began.

It was only later, when Zac, Heather and Lucy were on their way to track practice that Caroline, who was on her way to basketball practice, managed to find them. "Thanks for saving my ass in engineering," Caroline said.

"No problem," Zac said. "Strong is such a dick."

"Only because the one he has isn't large enough to satisfy his ego," Lucy said.

"I'm going to defer to Lucy's superior knowledge on the subject," Zac said, keeping her eyes on Caroline and raising her eyebrows.

Finally, Caroline laughed. "I do appreciate it, though," she said. "He has a much harder time arguing against you being here. You really do beat him in everything- sports and academics."

"That's just luck," Zac said. "Ignore him, and everyone who agrees with him."

*   *   *

Zac frowned as she pushed her shopping cart up the long aisle at the Lowe's in Tulsa, looking at the different types of roofing materials the store carried. *I hope this doesn't turn out the same way as my trip to Target did that time,* she thought. *I really need part of my roof replaced, and some new flooring too. But I've been in therapy for awhile now. If I can't even go shopping, then it isn't helping.* She eyed her cane, which she did not particularly need anymore, but had brought into the store just in case. *The physical therapy has definitely been helping- I've thought that all along.*

She reached out to feel some of the rough, dark material in front of her. *This seems to be good quality stuff,* she thought. *And I think it would look nice on the house.*

"Can I help you?" Zac heard someone ask. She looked up to see a man in a Lowe's shirt standing near her.

"Yeah, that would be great," Zac said. "I'm looking for

both roofing and flooring materials." She glanced at the top of his nametag and saw that he was the store's manager. *The manager is out on the floor, helping customers,* she thought. *I'm impressed.*

"Well, we're in the roofing aisle, so let's start there," the manager said. "Were you thinking of shingles?"

"Yes, I was originally thinking of black or dark gray, but those lighter gray ones over there might look nice too."

As the conversation continued, Zac found herself glancing at the man's nametag again. "Neil Lamont," it read. *Lamont,* Zac thought. *I wonder if he's related to that band whose concert Gail, Jenny and I saw. But what would he be doing working in a store like Lowe's? Aren't those boys making enough money to support the rest of the family?*

Her first question, at least, was answered several minutes later, when she and Neil had moved on to the store's flooring section. Zac was just making a decision on what she wanted when Travis and Robby themselves bounced into the aisle. "Hey, Dad!" Robby said.

"Hi guys," Neil replied. "Is Cole with you?"

"He was, but he detoured into the paint section."

Travis eyed Zac, and she looked back at him with interest. "Hi," she said.

"Hello," he replied quietly.

Robby looked over at her, and it was clear that he recognized her too. "Hi," he said. "I didn't realize you lived around here. Did you just move into the area?" he asked.

Zac nodded. Neil looked back and forth between Zac and his sons. Zac looked back at Travis, who looked at the floor, his face turning red.

"We're going to find Cole," Robby said after a minute. "Come find us when you're done, Dad."

Neil looked back at Zac when they had disappeared. "We're nearly out of that flooring, but we're getting some more in tomorrow," he said, gesturing at the wood that he and Zac had been discussing before his sons had appeared. "We can deliver it if you'd like."

"That'd be great."

"Do you also need a hand with installing it?"

"No, I've got a local carpenter who's been helping me with the heavy work. But thanks for the offer."

"So how do you guys know that woman I was helping when you came into the store?" Neil asked Travis and Robby at the dinner table that night. His wife, Diana, sat next to him. As he spoke, Neil eyed Travis, Robby, and then Cole. After two years of having his oldest sons living with his brother in Canada, he was still getting used to having them home again.

Travis looked at Robby, then at their father. "She was at our vets concert," he said finally.

"Which one was this?" Cole asked, looking interested. "The one with the missing leg?"

"No, the one with the cane and the limp," Robby said.

"The one you thought looked like us?" Cole teased Travis. Travis rolled his eyes.

"Well, she has an Appalachian accent," Neil said. "She's obviously from around here somewhere."

"Is she a soldier?" asked Janet, who was 14. Audra, who was 11, looked first at her sister, and then at her brothers for an answer.

"I don't know," Travis said. "We didn't actually meet her, she was just at the concert with a couple of other vets."

"It looked like she was injured in combat," Neil said.

"It also sounds like she made an impression on you guys," Diana added, trying to get a sense of what her sons were thinking.

But Travis, Robby and Cole just looked at each other and shrugged. *I'd say yes to that question,* Travis thought. *But if Robby and Cole aren't saying anything, neither am I.* He looked back at his parents to find his father eying him.

"Well, she ordered a bunch of flooring that I'm getting in tomorrow that I'm supposed to deliver to her house," Neil said. "If you want to drive over there with the employee that's delivering it, I won't stop you."

"Do you think that's appropriate?" Diana asked.

"I don't see why not," Neil answered.

"We went on deliveries before we went to Canada," Robby said.

"But your father was usually the one doing the delivering," Diana replied.

"What's your problem?" Neil asked his wife.

"I think maybe you should leave this delivery to your employees," Diana said.

All the more reason for me to go, Travis thought. *I think Mom's out of line. I don't know what her problem is.* He glanced at Robby and Cole and found that they were also watching their parents and frowning.

The next afternoon, Travis got into his car to help with the delivery. Diana was just getting home from work as he started his car. Travis rolled down his window to tell his mother where he was going. Even from the driveway, he heard his brother Marshall, who was nine, start pounding away on the old drum set that Robby used to play. At the same time, in a different part of the house, Cole strummed his guitar, and Robby pounded out a beat on the newer drum set he now used. Occasionally, he could hear Cole or Robby playing a few notes on the keyboard he himself usually played while he sang. *No wonder I needed a break,* he thought.

"I thought you and your brothers were working on a new album," Diana said when Travis told her he was heading out for a little while.

"We've started on it," Travis replied.

"Wouldn't it be easier to continue the work if you were in the same room as your brothers?"

Travis clenched his teeth and stared out the front windshield. *We really need our own house,* he thought. *Before, we were too young to live on our own, but Cole and I are old enough now, and we certainly have the money.*

At the same time, Travis admonished himself for thinking of moving out. *You, Cole and Robby wouldn't have a music career at all if Mom and Dad hadn't started you on that path,* he thought. *They were the ones who taught us to sing in harmony as kids and put instruments in our hands soon after.* Even so, Travis chafed under his mother's withering gaze.

"I just want to make sure you're moving along," Diana said. "You haven't put out an album since around the time you went to Canada."

"We were touring for a long time, first in the U.S., and then abroad," Travis reminded her. "Besides, Uncle Chuck continued to home-school us. It's just been in the last year or so that our tour wrapped up, and we were continuing our education. We haven't exactly been sitting on our butts."

"It might not look that way to your fans," Diana said. "They're at an age where they move on pretty quickly. Maybe it makes sense to get more material out there."

"It has to be good material, though. It's not worth it otherwise."

"Still, I thought you would have had more written by now."

Sometimes, Travis wished that one of the trees around them would fall on his mother. "We're moving along nicely," he said. "I just need a break. And if I don't leave now, I'll be of no use to Dad whatsoever."

"Fine," Diana replied, and Travis pulled out of the driveway.

Half an hour later, Zac saw the Lowe's truck pull up in front of her house, and went to open the front door. She was amazed to see Travis get out of his car behind the truck and help with the unloading. "Hi," she said as she held the door open for them.

"Hello," Travis replied as he helped maneuver the flooring into her living room.

Zac watched the unloading for awhile. "I'm surprised you'd be helping with a delivery," she finally said to Travis as he put more of the flooring down.

"Figured I'd help my dad," he said with a shrug.

"My name's Zac, by the way. Zac Madison."

"I'm Travis Lamont. It's nice to meet you."

When the last of the flooring was being left in Zac's living room, Travis looked around a little more. To his surprise, he caught sight of his band's latest CD sitting on Zac's stereo.

Zac followed his gaze as the Lowe's employees left, and was a little embarrassed when she saw what he was looking at. "After I saw you in concert, I figured I'd get your latest," she said. "Your first album made quite a sensation, if I remember correctly."

Travis nodded. "Our first that this record label produced, anyway. We'd done stuff on our own before that."

"I remember hearing all that when you guys got famous," Zac said. "Are you quite as popular now?"

"Maybe not quite," Travis replied. "But almost as much, and it's with a different crowd of people whose music interests aren't so mercurial."

"Which is probably better for you guys in the long run, if you have a steadier fan base," Zac answered.

Travis nodded. "It's weird, though. Almost none of the people who made us famous in the first place listen to our music anymore."

"No more teenyboppers for you, huh?" Zac said, looking amused.

"I guess not," Travis answered. He looked around again. It was the first time he had seen the inside of the house, and the place looked nice. He took a closer look at the diplomas on the wall nearby. *West Point*, he thought, and tried to sound out Zac's full name. "Zahara Lynne Madison," the diplomas read.

"Well, don't let me keep you," Zac said. "I'm sure you're busy. Thanks for the help, though."

"It's no problem at all."

"She did?" Robby asked when Travis told him and Cole that Zac had bought their latest album.

"Yup," Travis said as the three brothers sat around their bedroom in their parents' house.

"What's her place like? Is it nice?" Cole asked. Travis nodded. "What's her name, anyway?"

"Zac Madison."

"Isn't Zac a man's name?" Robby asked. "Like Zachary?"

Travis shook his head as he thought of the diplomas he'd seen. "No, this Zac is short for Zahara."

"How do you get Zac from Zahara?" Cole asked.

"I have no idea," Travis admitted. "But her full name was on her college diploma- she went to West Point."

"Wow," Cole said. "So she's Army. How old do you think she is?"

"Maybe early thirties?"

"I'm surprised she would be interested in our music," Robby said. "She seemed kind of... I don't know, distant?" His brothers nodded in agreement.

I'm sure she's frustrated by her injuries, Travis thought. *I also don't know what she's doing these days, if she's still on active duty or anything. Maybe she's at loose ends. If so, it's no surprise that she'd be irritated by us. We did run from the war.*

Then Neil and Diana appeared in the doorway, and for a second Travis thought his mother was going to yell at him again. But she stayed quiet as Neil looked around the room, taking in how much smaller it looked with his three grown sons in it. "I've been fixing up the attic," he said. "It's been split into two bedrooms and a bathroom. Maybe you guys want to move up there rather than share this room?"

Robby, Cole and Travis looked at each other. "It's not a bad idea," Robby said.

"I have to admit your younger siblings were using this room while you were away," Neil said. "It made more sense for the four of them to be split between this room and the third bedroom, rather than the four of them in one room."

"We've been talking about buying our own place, too,"

Cole said.

Diana and Neil exchanged a look, and Travis sensed that they had discussed that possibility as well. "We thought we'd look for something in the city or the suburbs," Travis said. "Something that would be close to the recording studio we use in the city, or be large enough to build an on-site studio."

"It's certainly something to discuss," Neil said.

Later that night, Travis hung out in the hallway outside his parents' bedroom, listening to their conversation as his younger siblings played outside. "I'm not looking forward to having them move out," Diana was saying. "Are you sure it's a good idea for them to go so quickly? They just got back from Canada."

"Cole and Travis are adults, and Robby isn't that far behind," Neil replied. "We can't expect them to continue sharing a single bedroom here. They've been getting in each other's hair ever since they got back."

"They seem more like adolescents than adults that way," Diana said.

"The transition back home hasn't been easy for them," Neil said. "It's not just about the lack of space."

"That's more what the problem is," said a low voice behind Travis.

Travis jumped. He turned to see Cole standing behind him. "I didn't see you there," he whispered.

Cole tossed his head in the direction of the staircase nearby, and Travis followed him into the attic on the pretense of surveying the work their father had done there. For the first time, both of them were tall enough to have to duck under the staircase's low ceiling. "I don't think Mom wants to see how much the war changed everything," Cole said.

"Dad just wants the family back together again too," Travis said. "It's both of them."

"It won't ever be same way it was before the war."

"I know. Even the music we've been writing recently has been darker, edgier."

"That was true even when we were in Canada," Cole said. "It was hard watching the country get torn apart, and feel like we couldn't do anything about it."

"We could have done something about it," Travis said. "We could have come home and fought."

"You're only saying that because you've been around Zac."

"That's not true."

"I never heard you say anything like that while we were in Canada."

Travis sighed. "I don't know. Everything's been different since we got home. I don't know what I want anymore." A wave of sadness washed over him.

Cole eyed his brother uncomfortably. "We have so much talent, the three of us. It would have been such a waste for any of us to have gotten killed in the war."

"Plenty of talented people got killed in the war," Travis replied.

Cole's intense gaze did not let up. "You feel guilty about not fighting, don't you?" he asked.

Travis looked away. "I'm not sure what I feel," he said. "Maybe there's some guilt. But I couldn't face the possibility of getting killed. That's why I stayed in Canada."

"Then we're both guilty of that," Cole said.

*   *   *

It was November of Zac's firstie year at West Point, and Zac shivered as she marched to Thayer Hall with Heather and Lucy. It was not just the cold that made her quake- the momentousness of the choice in front of her also set her teeth on edge. *You've known since Beast Barracks that you would have to choose your first duty station before you even graduated,* Zac reminded herself.

"We've all made it this far," Heather said, putting her arms around her best friends.

"Against all expectations!" Lucy added.

Zac nodded, her mouth dry. "Only a few more months to go," she said.

"Have you decided what you want, Zac?" Heather asked.

"Not quite," Zac admitted.

"Better hurry up," Lucy said. "You still yo-yoing between Military Police and Military Intelligence?"

"Yeah," Zac said as they arrived at Thayer Hall. "MI appeals to me analytically, but I think I'd go out of my mind spending twenty-four hours a day in front of a computer, analyzing pictures and data."

"MP would let you get out on patrol, and gather intelligence that way," Heather said.

Zac nodded. "I know," she said. "It's a real combination of tactics, strategy, and intelligence. I like that."

The atmosphere in Thayer Hall was electric, and Zac could feel herself getting caught up in the excitement. Within a few minutes, her heart was pounding and her palms were sweating. *We choose by class ranking,* she thought. *I'm fifth in the class, so I should be able to get the duty station I want.*

When the selections started, Zac chewed her lip. The first four cadets, all men, chose their stations, and none of them wanted Military Police. When Zac's name boomed out, she stood, and in a loud, clear voice, said, "Military Police, Schofield Barracks."

The class cheered as the spot for Fort Shafter, Hawaii, was checked off. When Zac sat down, she smiled. Next to her, Lucy and Heather grinned back at her. "Congratulations," Lucy said. "I think that's the right choice for you."

"I hope so," Zac replied.

"A post in Hawaii?" Heather said. "It's an incredible spot. The Army's lucky I'm not the one going there- I'd spend all my time on the beach with a piña colada."

Just then, Brian Stewart, the class' valedictorian, clapped Zac on the back. "Nice choice," he said.

"Thanks," Zac said.

"I was struggling between that and artillery myself." He eyed Zac and laughed. "You look so relieved."

"I am," Zac replied. "I really wanted MP."

Brian nodded. "I'm not surprised," he said. "It's a good combination of the cerebral and the physical. I think it'll suit you well."

"My thoughts exactly," Zac said, and they both laughed. When Brian left, Zac looked back at Heather and Lucy. "That was the longest conversation I've ever had with him."

"Don't be too surprised," Lucy said. "He thinks highly of you. We all do."

When Zac landed in Hawaii for the first time, a military escort in the form of Specialist Paul Gray met her at the airport and took her to her new living quarters. As they drove, Zac looked out the window to see sunshine and palm trees swaying in the wind. Almost an hour later, she put her suitcases down in her new home and examined the space. Her quarters were tiny, and very plain. There was barely enough space for a single bed, a small refrigerator, a desk, and a nightstand.

Just before her graduation from West Point, Zac had purchased her first car, a small Honda that she had had shipped to Schofield Barracks. The car had not arrived yet, though, so the next day, Zac took a bus to the Battalion Headquarters, an imposing building that she almost felt intimidated by. *Take a deep breath,* Zac reminded herself as she tried to calm her nerves. *You didn't get here by accident.*

Specialist Gray had already let the Battalion know Zac was coming, and when the bus arrived, an enlisted soldier appeared to escort her into the building. *This has been very smooth so far,* Zac thought as she was taken down a long hallway to meet the Battalion commander, a Colonel Victor Rice. The colonel's office was empty when they arrived, however, and Zac frowned.

"Don't worry, honey, he should be here any minute," Rice's secretary said. "He's expecting you."

"Thanks," Zac said. *Honey?* she thought. *I hope the Colonel doesn't treat me that way.*

A minute later, the secretary cocked her head towards the hallway. "That's him now," she said.

Zac wondered how she could tell, but then she heard the Colonel coming before she could see him- marching down the hallway with two other officers in tow. *Where did he learn to march like that?* Zac wondered. *He's stomping rather than marching.* She went to the door of the office to watch his arrival.

The Colonel did not see her yet. Instead, he was clearly looking for someone else, and his face looked like an angry storm cloud. Zac felt her knees knock together in fear and hoped it did not show. *Relax, relax,* she told herself. *You made it through four years at West Point. You can take this too.*

In a second, Colonel Rice had located his quarry, an overweight E-5 who had just come unsuspectingly out of the bathroom. "Sergeant Danbury, you little maggot!" Rice shouted, and his voice reverberated down the hallway.

Even from where she stood, Zac could see Sergeant Danbury quivering with fear. *West Point all over again,* she thought. *Danbury could just as easily be a plebe, and Rice a firstie.*

"I have your discharge papers, you little toad!" Rice yelled, waving the set of papers he was carrying.

"But sir-" Danbury protested.

"Don't 'but sir' me!" Rice shouted. "You're lucky you're only being discharged. If that court-marshal had stuck, you'd be in Leavenworth for all time!"

Zac looked over at Specialist Gray. "What did Danbury do?" she asked.

"He was suspected of misrouting some supplies and selling others and keeping the money," Gray said. "Too bad we couldn't prove anything."

Zac looked back down the hall, where Rice was shoving Danbury's discharge papers in his face. "Goodbye, Mr. Danbury," he snarled. "I never want to see your overweight, pockmarked face again!"

His face quivering, Danbury took the papers and practically ran towards the door. Colonel Rice watched him go. Then he turned in the other direction and started walking towards his office, where Zac was waiting. Zac ducked back into the office, not wanting to be seen watching the confrontation, and yet feeling like a kid who was about to be reprimanded. By the time Colonel Rice arrived in his office, Zac was standing at attention.

Colonel Rice entered his office and stopped. He looked at his secretary. Then he looked at Specialist Gray. Finally, he looked at Zac, who was still standing at attention. "Are you Lt. Madison?" he asked.

"Yes, sir," Zac replied.

"Welcome to the Battalion," Rice said, gesturing for her to follow him into the inner office. "Your reputation precedes you."

Really? Zac wondered. *What reputation? I've only just graduated from the Academy.*

"Don't look so surprised, Lieutenant," Rice said, sitting in the chair at the desk and offering Zac a seat opposite him. Specialist Gray sat next to her. "Fifth in your class at West Point, and a nationally ranked runner? We don't get those types every day."

"Thank you sir," Zac said. "I'm glad to be here."

"And I'm always glad to have another Academy grad in the mix," Rice said. Zac looked at him questioningly. "Oh, yes," Rice said. He held up his hand with the West Point ring on it. "Class of '79."

"Yes, sir!" Zac said with a smile.

"And don't worry about the fireworks you saw in the hall. I don't have any tolerance for incompetence, but if you continue on the track you're on, we should get along just fine."

*   *   *

Zac sat at her computer in Tulsa, searching the internet for more information on Travis' band. *They really are huge,* she thought. *I can't believe they released their first album when Travis was only thirteen.* She looked closer at the screen in front of her. *His brother Robby was only eleven. Geez. When Clive and I were thirteen and eleven, we were being shipped off to live with our grandparents.*

As Zac continued reading, she realized that Travis' parents had started teaching him and his brothers to sing so that they could sing in their church choir, and then had given them instruments when their voices had sounded good. *What a different upbringing from what I had.*

Taking a deep breath, Zac turned to her next task- looking herself up, something she had been interested in doing ever since her first meeting with Max. *He thought a lot of people were following my career with interest. That can't possibly be right,* Zac thought, but she typed her own name into a search engine anyway.

To her shock, quite a few results came up. Most were news articles, and Zac started with those. One even went way back to her graduation from West Point, noting how highly honored she had been, and how unusual that was for a woman. *Maybe Alex is on to something after all,* Zac thought. *I was always just so focused on achieving things, I never really thought about it being different in any way.*

She kept reading, and was surprised to see how the newspapers had covered the war while she had been in the Middle East fighting. There were reports on the fighting, and where American troops had gained against the rebels. "Several units in particular, led by Army Colonels Zahara Madison and Jackson Jones, have made significant progress against the terrorists. Army officials credit these colonels' leadership skills and knowledge of military tactics and the terrain for their advance," one article stated.

Unreal, Zac thought. *I wonder who they were talking to. It's incredible that someone would give my name, in particular, and Jack's. Weren't they worried that would make us targets?*

Plenty of articles also detailed her injuries and arrival back in the United States, and Zac was amazed. *I had no idea I was such big news*, she thought. But one of the most interesting things Zac found was a series of posts on a military-related discussion board. "Is Colonel Madison writing her memoirs?" the discussion began, posted by an anonymous poster. "That would be a worthy read from one of the highest-ranking officers to see direct combat in these wars."

"I would definitely read that book," another commenter responded. "If the military lets her talk honestly about her experiences."

Many other posts expressed interest as well, and Zac was ensconced in reading the responses when she was startled by a knock at her door. Surprised, she went to the door to find Max there, and then first remembered that she had invited him over for dinner. "Hi," she said, opening the door to let him in.

"Hello," he responded, holding up a couple of steaks and the case of beer he had brought.

"Nice," Zac said. "I'll start the grill."

In the kitchen, Zac put the beer in the fridge. Max caught sight of Zac's computer and looked closer to see what she had been doing. "See, I told you there's a lot of interest out there," he said.

"Oh, yeah," Zac replied, closing her browser and shutting off the computer. "When I was in the hospital after being injured, my CO suggested I write a book about myself. I couldn't imagine having a sense of what to write about, or that there would be any interest."

"Who was your CO?" Max asked.

"Jim Conrad."

"He's a smart guy. If he encouraged you to do it, it's something to consider."

Zac headed outside to start the grill. Max followed, looking around the large backyard as he did so. "Nice place," he said finally.

"It looks nice now," Zac said. *Now that I've replanted all my flowers after digging them up that night.* "But it was barely livable when I first got here."

Max went inside for a beer, and came back out carrying one for himself and one for Zac. He was also holding Travis' CD, which he had seen in Zac's living room. "So this is your neighboring boy band?" he asked.

Zac laughed as she took one of the beers. "Yeah, that's their latest. They're also working on a new one."

"I could live without it," Max said, even as he continued examining the cover artwork.

Zac shrugged. "I can't say I ever listened to them before this, but some of the songs are pretty good."

"Still no bluegrass for you, huh?"

"I didn't listen to that even back at West Point."

"I remember. We had two cadets from Kentucky who played nothing but bluegrass, and you would put your hands over your ears."

Zac laughed at the memory. "Only because my parents were so into that kind of music that they would play it nonstop. I couldn't stand it anymore." She shook her head. "I think it's mostly classical music for me now. When I listen to music, which hasn't been recently."

"It can be tough when you first get back," Max agreed. "All I wanted was silence."

"I'd take silence over grenades and gunfire, but it would be nice to listen to music again someday."

"Like the stuff Damien Lewis always used to sing?" Max asked.

Zac looked at him, and they both cracked up at the memory of a cadet in Max's year who had been a trained singer- and who had been punished numerous times for singing at otherwise serious moments.

"I can't blame Damien, though," Zac said. "He's how I got into pieces like Carmina Burana."

"He got so many demerits for that one that he marched twelve hours as punishment," Max said, and Zac laughed again at the memory.

"Whatever happened to Damien?" she asked.

"Injured in the war, like the rest of us," Max said.

"What happened?"

"Shot in the head, first six months of the war. Real bad, too. I heard the doctors got him to sing again, though- he was singing before he could talk. The doctors thought it had something to do with his vocal training- he could access that part of his brain better or something."

"What a shame," Zac said. "I remember hearing that he'd gotten accepted to Julliard and some other conservatory too, but that he chose West Point instead."

Max nodded. "That's true."

Zac went inside to get the steaks, and Max followed her, carrying Travis' CD with him and returning it to the living room. When he got back into the kitchen, his eye fell on the letter from the Army, which was sitting on a counter in the kitchen. "You got one of these too?" he asked.

Zac looked up. "What is that?" she asked.

"The order to testify at Victor Rice's trial."

"You got one? How did you know him?"

"He was finishing a Master's at Columbia my plebe year at West Point, and he spent a semester teaching my engineering class."

"I didn't know that," Zac said. "When do you testify?"

"August 27."

"I testify the 28th."

"Oh, good, maybe we can fly out to Washington together."

"Do you have any idea what you're going to say?" Zac asked nervously. *I still have no idea.*

"Not much I can say beyond what I knew of him," Max answered. "I don't know anything about the conduct these allegations are based on."

"Me neither," Zac said.

"Sounds like both our testimonies will be limited, then."

"That's what Drew said too. Even so, it's hard to see a fellow officer brought up on such serious charges. The fact that I knew him and his family personally isn't helping."

"I know," Max answered, looking outside to see if the coals

on the grill were ready.

Seeing that they were close to being done, Zac followed Max outside, holding the steaks on a plate. "The most you can say is what you know," Max added. "Not much more you can do."

Zac frowned. "We'll see," she said.

CHAPTER 9

By the end of September of her plebe year at West Point, Zac was feeling the loss of no longer having Jen as a roommate, and she gravitated towards her classmates and members of the track team as friends. After practice one day, she, Heather and Lucy realized that they had a whole twenty minutes to shower before dinnertime. "What a luxury," Zac joked. "I may even get to use soap this time."

Heather and Lucy snickered. "Well, you can go ahead and shower," Lucy said, a conspiratorial look on her face, "but I'm going to sneak into the gym to see if Eric Johnson is still practicing."

Cadet Johnson- I know him, Zac thought. *He's one of the cadets that came into my room to help me and Jen after we were attacked.*

Heather was nodding. "I'm coming with you," she said. "He may be short, but he's hot- and his muscles have always been visible through his uniform."

Lucy and Heather moved towards the gym, and after a second's hesitation, Zac followed them. "What sport does Eric play?" she asked.

"Gymnastics, dummy," Heather hissed. "Don't tell me you didn't know that."

Zac shook her head.

Lucy shot her an incredulous look as they went into the gym. "What rock have you been living under?" she asked. "I'd heard of him even before I came here. Word has it he's training for the Olympics next year."

When they got to the gym, Zac spotted Eric immediately in the quickly emptying room. At five-foot-seven, he was clearly shorter than most of the male cadets around him, but more muscular. As Zac, Heather and Lucy watched, Eric grabbed his gym bag and headed for the door- the door they had just come through and were still standing near.

"Oh my God, he's coming this way," Lucy said.

Zac rolled her eyes. "What are you, twelve years old?" she asked, but both Lucy and Heather were practically drooling.

As he approached the doorway, Eric noticed them watching him and gave them a nod. Then his eyes focused on Zac, and it was clear he remembered her from a few weeks before. "Cadet Madison, how are you doing?" he asked.

"I am fine, sir," she said. "Thank you for asking."

Eric kept moving towards the door, checking his watch as he walked. "Don't be late for dinner, Cadets," he said.

"Yes, sir," Zac, Lucy and Heather said at the same time.

As soon as the door closed behind Eric, Heather and Lucy looked at Zac, looked at each other, and dissolved into giggles. Zac groaned. "You guys are unbelievable," she said as she headed for the door.

* * *

The next time Drew was traveling for work and was in Oklahoma City, he made a point of taking an extra day and coming into Tulsa. Zac took it as an opportunity to invite both him and Max to her house for dinner, and cook a large meal for all of them. When dinner was on the table, Zac raised her wine glass. "Thanks for being here," she said. "You both have made my life so much better."

"We feel the same way about you," Drew said.

"Keep chugging, Madison," Max added with a grin. "You're a pleasure to have around."

After dinner, Zac turned on the television to watch the women's gymnastics national championships. Drew followed her into the living room and caught sight of Travis' CD on her stereo as he walked. He picked it up and went back into the kitchen before holding it up for Max to see. "Are these the guys whose mother is such a big anti-war activist?" he asked.

"Yeah," Max said.

"What?" Zac asked, getting up from the couch and going back into the kitchen. "I didn't know that."

Drew and Max both looked disgusted. "My office designs a lot of the stuff that Max's factory produces," Drew said. "This woman and her group have protested outside the factory, and they've even sent people to protest outside my office."

"They're protesting vets getting new limbs?" Zac asked, aghast.

"I don't think they know that's what we do at the factory," Max said. "Plenty of the stuff Drew deals with has applications for the defense industry as a whole."

Drew nodded as he went back into the living room and put the CD back on the stereo. "Most of our stuff goes to the defense industry," he said. "But some of it goes to the stuff that Max does, and there was a large news item about a delivery of our products to his factory. We publicized it because it's something that will help injured veterans, create jobs, all that good stuff, and these protesters show up."

"Unbelievable," Zac said as she followed Drew back into the living room.

"As a result, I will not be buying and of that band's music," Drew said as he sat on Zac's couch.

"I only bought it because they're local, and I went to one of their concerts," Zac said as she sat in a chair next to the couch.

Drew eyed the television with interest. "I didn't know you

were into gymnastics," he said.

"Only enough to watch when it's on."

Max took a break from stacking the dinner dishes in Zac's dishwasher to see what program she had turned on. "Ugh, gymnastics," he said, and went back into the kitchen.

"I thought you were into sports," Zac said to his retreating form.

"Football, baseball, basketball, definitely," Max replied from the kitchen. "Maybe even soccer occasionally, but gymnastics? No way."

"I've always liked watching it," Zac said with a shrug. She looked at Drew and grinned. "It reminds me of what I'm still incapable of doing."

When Max was finished with the dishes, he joined Zac and Drew in the living room, taking a seat opposite Zac. Drew watched one gymnast on the balance beam for the remainder of her routine as Max eyed both him and Zac. "Wow," Drew said when the athlete had dismounted. Then he looked at Max, a wicked smile on his face. "That, at least, was impressive."

"Whatever," Max replied, nonplussed.

Zac laughed. "I've always like watching nationals, and Olympic trials. And then the Olympics themselves, of course. They're always incredible." She looked from the TV to Max and Drew. "Do you guys remember Eric Johnson?" she asked.

"I do," Max replied.

"Barely," Drew said. "I knew who he was- mostly because of his gymnastics and the Olympics- but I didn't deal with him much."

"I thought it was incredible that he went to the Olympics, and that West Point let him take a year off to do it," Zac said.

"Well, he won a bronze medal and two silvers, so it was obviously worth the school's while to let him go," Drew said.

"I always liked watching him compete," Zac said.

"You and the rest of the females at the academy," Max teased.

"Yes, I always did have a whole group of friends with me at his meets," Zac remembered with a smile.

"Not to mention the whole group of them who would crowd around the gym while he was working out," Max said.

"I only did that once," Zac said. She laughed. "I guess I wasn't that bad."

"The rest of your friends were, though," Max said. "Lucy, Heather, Wendy- they all followed Eric around."

"I may have known that," Zac said, still looking amused.

"You all should have become gymnasts, just to watch Eric practice," Max said, still teasing. He picked up a pen from the table in front of the couch and threw it at her.

"No way," Zac said, smiling as she threw the pen back at him.

"No way is right," Drew said seriously, holding up a hand in between them so as not to get hit by the flying pen. "West Point would have lost out on a nationally-ranked runner." He looked at Zac. "I hope your leg heals up completely. You were an incredible competitor."

Zac shrugged. "Running away from my pa when he was drunk was good practice for that," she said.

Max frowned. *I always wondered why she was only close to her younger brothers,* he thought. *Maybe I just found out why.*

When her next group therapy appointment was over, Zac made her way down to where the medical doctors had their offices. She was not waiting long when Max got out of his doctor's appointment, groaning slightly. "Everything okay?" Zac asked as they headed outside. *He really doesn't look happy. I don't like that at all.*

"My wrist has been bothering me again where my hand was amputated," Max admitted as he rubbed his arm. "The doctors think it's some kind of nerve issue."

"That's not good," Zac said, making a face as they headed towards a nearby restaurant to have lunch.

Max shook his head. He was about to say something when he and Zac heard someone calling her.

Zac turned to see Travis coming towards her. Looking behind him, she could see Robby and Cole standing near their truck about a half a block behind Travis. *How is it that we keep running into each other?* she wondered. "What brings you here?"

"Oh, my brothers and I were just getting in some studio time," Travis said, gesturing behind him to where Robby and Cole were.

"I didn't know you guys did your recording right here in the middle of the city," Zac said. "I didn't even know there was a studio here."

Travis nodded. "It's on the second and third floors of the building up there. The first floor is a regular store, so it's kind of hidden. We like that."

"Have you met my friend Max?" Zac asked, suddenly remembering that Max was still standing behind her. "We went to West Point together. Max, that's Travis."

"Nice to meet you," Max said.

"Likewise," Travis said, his eyes going to Max's missing hand and the hook that replaced it. "So you're a veteran also?"

Max nodded.

"How many tours did you serve?"

"Two. I was injured during the second one."

There was an awkward pause. "I should probably go," Travis said finally. "My brothers are waiting for me."

"Okay," Zac said. "See you later."

"So that's the lead boy-bander," Max said as soon as Travis was out of earshot.

"That's him," Zac replied as they finished their walk to the restaurant.

"What a wimp."

"He did run as soon as there was mention of a draft," Zac admitted.

"My point exactly," Max said. "The draft was never even instituted, and he still stayed in Canada until the war was over."

"I'm sure his parents played a role in that. I mean, he and his brothers all went."

"He's old enough to have come back and fought,

regardless of what his parents thought. We signed up when we were eighteen."

"I know that."

"Why do you even deal with him, Zac?" Max asked as they examined their menus.

"He's been doing some work with vets since he got back from Canada," Zac said. "I don't mind the effort."

Max rolled his eyes. "He's just trying to sell more music."

"Maybe," Zac said. "But if his work sheds light on what we went through over there, or on what we're going through here, it can't be bad."

*   *   *

In late October of her first semester at West Point, when the campus' leaves were all singing shades of red, orange and yellow, Zac opened a letter that she had received from home. *This is one of the first letters I've gotten from home, and it's from Clive, not even Ma and Pa,* she thought. She smiled almost immediately, though, when she saw the top of the letter, which had the word "Ben" written in blue crayon and in big block letters. *He's learning to write,* she thought. *He's so cute.*

Clive's news, however, made Zac frown. "Now that you and Melanie have moved out, Ma and Pa have taken on a boarder, who lives in your room and pays rent."

If this were any other family, I would laugh, Zac thought, but she could tell that Clive was serious- he wrote that the man that was staying in the house with them commuted into Little Rock for a part-time job three days a week and helped out with chores around the farm on his days off. *Where does that leave me?* Zac wondered. *I don't know that I ever planned on returning home, but it would have been nice to have the option, especially for Christmas.*

At track practice that afternoon, Zac found herself warming up with Drew Jamieson, who was on the field for soccer practice. Across the field, Zac noticed the Cadet in the Red Sash- *Max Sheffield,* she reminded herself. *I can't keep calling him the Cadet in the Red Sash- not after he helped me and Jen out when we were attacked. Now I know that he plays soccer with Drew, though, which I didn't before.*

"Why the long face?" Drew asked her. "I thought you finally got mail from home. Isn't it nice to know your parents actually love you?"

Zac rolled her eyes. "I'm not sure they do," she said.

"What's that mean?"

"The letter was from Clive, not my parents. He said our parents have already rented out my empty room at home because they need the money."

Drew shook his head. "That's tough," he said.

"You don't seem surprised, though," Zac said.

"We come from rough stock, Zac," Drew answered. "The main reason I was down at our high school recruiting is because I wanted people from our area to know what opportunities are available to them."

"And yet I'm the only one from that group that ended up here."

"West Point is a tough school to get into, and many people that get in and decide to come don't last the four years."

"I'm planning on toughing it out because I don't want to go home," Zac said as they jogged around one of the track's curves.

"What about when you have leave?" Drew asked. "What about for Christmas? It would be real sad if you had to stay here for the holidays."

"I don't know," Zac admitted. *I'd like to see Clive for Christmas, at least. Maybe Harvey's family will have me over.*

"Well, think about it," Drew instructed. "I'll certainly be going home for it."

"I'll keep it in mind," Zac said honestly. *Maybe it won't be so bad if I have someone to travel with.*

Two months later, Zac and Drew were on the same flight out of John F. Kennedy Airport in New York City, flying into Little Rock. When they landed, Drew's large family seemed to take up half the airport, and they surrounded him immediately. "Drewdy!" his mother howled as she hugged him.

Zac almost burst out laughing at the nickname. *They must have started calling him that when he was a little twerp,* she thought. *There's no way that nickname fits the big guy he's become.* Still, Zac was just starting to feel sorry for herself, not having any family to meet her, when she heard someone yelling her name. Looking up, she saw Clive racing towards her. "Clive!" she yelled back, and dashed towards him.

Behind him, Harvey and his family were waiting with large grins, and Zac finally got the round of hugs she wanted. Soon, she was saying goodbye to Drew and piling into Harvey's family's van. "Thanks for all the care packages," she said, directing the comment mostly at his mother. "The muffins were great, and so were the chocolates."

"You still look like you've lost weight," Maria said.

"I probably have," Zac said. "It's a lot of physical activity, and we don't always get to eat much."

Maria shook her head. "Well, you'll have plenty to eat at our house," she said.

"I'm looking forward to it already," Zac replied with a grin. *Maybe I won't have to see Ma and Pa after all.*

*   *   *

"Your relationships with Max and Drew seem to be progressing," Alex said the next time Zac met with her.

Zac nodded. She was glad for this time, glad that her nightmares and flashbacks seemed to be less frequent even if they were getting more graphic, but she was tired of coming here, tired of the tiny office.

"You seem to have picked up where you left off," Alex added, trying to draw her patient out. "You guys were on good terms in school, right?"

"Yeah," Zac said slowly. "But we have a shared history. I

mean, I knew them from West Point. It was a different time in my life."

"Before the war and all of the loss."

"Yeah."

"When a lot more seemed possible."

"I guess," Zac said, wondering where her therapist was going with this.

"If you met them now for the first time, do you think the connection would be the same?"

Zac frowned as she thought about it. "It depends. I mean, if they were veterans and officers, we'd still have that much in common."

"And what about that musician who just got back from Canada?"

"He met Max the other day," Zac said.

"How'd that go?" Alex asked.

"It was a little tense. Travis was uncomfortable, and Max didn't like him."

"Why do you think that is?"

Zac sighed, and stared through the tiny window in the office to the shimmering heat outside. "Max feels the same way I do. This is a kid who shirked his responsibility to the country. He and his brothers lived out the war in safety while we were fighting. Max was irrevocably injured. A lot of our most talented classmates were killed or maimed. My own brother was killed."

"Both you and Max grew up in pretty poverty stricken circumstances," Alex said. "Do you think your attitudes towards him are influenced by the fact that he has more monetary resources, as well as supportive parents, which you never had? His parents were instrumental in getting him out of the country during the war, and your parents are the reason you landed in the Army."

"Travis and his brothers have a lot of money because they're talented musicians and they made something of that," Zac said. "I don't think the family was particularly well off before that. I mean, their father still works at the Lowe's that he's been at forever- he's worked his way up to manager, so maybe he makes a decent salary now, but I don't think he always did. It took me some time and research to realize that."

"They still got famous and wealthy at a very young age, and had that wealth and a strong family structure when they fled to Canada."

"I'm well aware," Zac said. "I don't doubt that our family circumstances led us on very different paths."

"You said Travis was uncomfortable around Max- why?"

"His missing hand, definitely. It's also clear that Max took the same path as me- West Point, combat, all that."

"And yet Travis seems interested in dealing with you."

Zac took a deep breath and shifted in her seat. "I read an interview where he said he was the one that wanted to do that veterans' benefit concert that I went to," she said. "But I also heard from Drew and Max that his mother is a pretty vocal anti-war activist."

"What do you make of all that?" Alex asked.

"I don't know," Zac answered. "Maybe their family dynamic is evolving- Travis and his brothers did just get home after a couple of years, and are at an age where they could be rebelling. Besides, they've now had contact with people their mother thinks are the enemy, and they didn't get eaten or anything." She shrugged. "Maybe Travis is starting to realize that his mother's opinions aren't the only ones out there."

Travis Lamont sat at the desk in one of the attic rooms that he, Cole and Robby had taken over in their parents' house, scribbling both lyrics and musical notes. Then he went back to the keyboard next to him and played the chords he had just written to see how they sounded. *That's not too bad*, he thought.

He looked out the window. With his concentration broken, he suddenly became aware of how stiff he was. He looked at the clock on the desk. *Oh crap!* he realized. *I've been at this for nearly four hours!*

He stretched out, trying to shake the stiffness from his muscles. Then he heard the sound of a car crunching on the gravel in the driveway. Going to a different window, he could see Cole and Robby get out of the car and start pulling grocery bags from the back. *Oh yeah,* Travis remembered. *They went to see a house in the city that we were interested in buying. They must have stopped for groceries afterwards.*

He went down to help his brothers unload the car. When the three of them held the last bags in their arms, Cole slammed the car door shut and said to Travis, "you should have come with us to see this house."

"I was writing some more songs," Travis replied as the three of them remained standing in the driveway. "I only stopped because you guys got back."

"More war related songs?" Cole asked.

"Some of it is," Travis said. "But a couple of stanzas are happy."

"It's about time," Cole said.

Travis nodded. *I'm relieved about that too,* he thought.

"Sounds like you got a lot done," Robby said.

"Yeah, I wrote the lyrics for two full songs, and a couple of stanzas for a third that I'm having trouble finishing. I also have a bunch of music written that may or may not go with these lyrics."

Robby and Cole laughed. "We'll take a look," Robby said. "I'm sure it'll turn into something- both the lyrics and the riffs."

"I'm relieved that we have more material," Cole admitted, and his brothers nodded in agreement.

"So how was the house you saw?" Travis asked as they carried the grocery bags they held into the kitchen.

"It was nice," Robby said as Cole started putting some of the perishable groceries into the refrigerator. "It had a basement, two full stories and an attic. Both the basement and the attic could be turned into a studio if we wanted to record there."

Cole stuck his head around the fridge door and nodded.

"I think the basement would be better as a studio," he said. "But the attic would be serviceable."

"How many bedrooms?" Travis asked.

"Four," Robby said. "All on the second floor. One was kind of small, though."

"If we turned the basement into a studio, we could also do what Dad did with the attic here," Cole said, putting a carton of milk into fridge as he spoke. "We could add extra bedrooms and a bathroom."

"It's also pretty close to the studio we've been using in the city," Robby said. "So we have options."

"Sounds good," Travis said. He started unloading more of the groceries from the bags in front of him, and Robby joined him. "I definitely want to take a look at it. We should see a few more places too."

"Yes we should," Cole said, slamming the fridge door shut and watching his brothers unpack the rest of the groceries. "If we do, you'll have to make sure you come with us, and go to the grocery store afterwards." He and Robby exchanged a look and a laugh.

Travis eyed his brothers.

"A bunch of fans recognized us at the store," Robby said, laughing.

"It was like four or five of them," Cole said. "And they were disappointed that you weren't there."

Travis laughed. "I was always the best looking of the group," he said.

Cole pulled a few grapes from the bunch he was holding and threw them at Travis. "You wish," he said.

Travis scooped up the grapes and threw them back at Cole, one at a time. "The girls were always after me," he said. "You were always jealous."

"Whatever," Cole said, throwing the grapes back.

"Hey, watch out!" Robby yelped, ducking as he was hit by a number of battered grapes.

The three brothers looked at each other and collapsed laughing.

Zac was just leaving a session of her group therapy when her cell phone rang. When the caller turned out to be Brigadier General Jim Conrad, Zac took a seat on a long wooden bench in the hallway of the VA to have the conversation.

"We might have you fly to Washington a bit earlier than planned, Zac," Conrad said. "Things here are going quicker than expected."

"That's good," Zac replied. "Is there any indication of how Victor's trial might come out?"

"Not yet. It'll be hard to tell until everyone's done testifying."

"Oh damn. There's really no way for me to get out of testifying, is there?" Zac said, hoping it sounded half-joking.

"No, I don't think so," Conrad replied.

"Aw, shucks."

"No, there's no way you're getting out of this one, Colonel."

"That's too bad." They both laughed.

"Seriously, though, Zac, as long as I have you on the phone, what have you been doing recently? Have you given much thought to writing your memoirs or teaching at West Point? There's a lot of interest for both."

"Yes, I'm starting to see that," Zac said. She looked up as a group of people came out of a nearby office. To her surprise, she saw Travis Lamont among them. *What could he possibly be doing here?* she wondered.

"Good," Conrad was saying on the other end of the phone. "I meant them both as serious recommendations."

"Well, I've been thinking about it. Who would I talk to at West Point about teaching there?"

"Do you know Major General Steven Grayson?" Conrad asked.

"The Superintendent of the Academy?" Zac said, picturing the tall, African-American general. "I know who he is, of course, but I've never met him."

"He'll be in Washington when you're here to testify. I'd be happy to introduce you."

"That'd be great." When Zac finished the conversation, it was clear that Travis was waiting for her. "What brings you here?" she asked as she stood up.

"I've been getting involved with a number of veterans' organizations, including a new board that was formed to improve the care of injured vets," he said. "The first meeting was here."

"Oh," Zac said, surprised. *That's interesting. I wonder what his anti-war mother thinks of that.*

"Is everything okay with you?" Travis asked.

"Yes, of course," Zac replied, putting her cell phone back in her bag and heading for the door. "Why do you ask?"

Travis followed her. "You looked worried while you were on the phone," he said.

Zac sighed. *Will he really understand it all?* she wondered.

"I read in the paper about the General who was suspected of treason- the article said there was some kind of inquiry going on in Washington. Is that what the call was about?"

Zac nodded as they continued walking towards the door. "Yes." *Better keep it simple.*

"So you have to go up to Washington to testify?" Travis asked. Zac nodded again. "Cool."

"No, it really isn't." *I knew he wouldn't understand. He should have spent time in the Army.* "The reason I have to testify is because I knew him personally, and that isn't making it easy."

"Oh." Travis frowned. "How did you meet him?"

"He was my first commanding officer out of West Point."

"The papers, at least, all praised him as an officer. Many of the people they quoted said he treated them like family and provided them with real leadership examples."

"Yes, that was exactly my experience." Outside, the bright sunshine cascaded down, and Zac squinted as she dug in her bag for her sunglasses.

Travis was already holding his sunglasses and put them on

with a flourish. "Where did you and the General serve together?" he asked.

"In Hawaii," Zac said. "I had both gone to West Point, and then chose a duty station so far away, because I needed to get away from my parents. Victor provided me with the family I was missing."

"Man," Travis said. Then he had another question. "I was reading in the paper that General Rice has long criticized the government for why it entered the Iraq War, and for the fact that we sent so many troops in there without real supplies. Do you think the Army is, like, making a scapegoat out of him or something?"

Zac nodded. *Maybe he does understand it after all,* she thought. "I am concerned about that," she admitted. "But supposedly, Special Forces also captured him behind enemy lines, so…"

"So he may have committed treason."

"As much as I hate to think so, it's certainly a possibility."

"Did you experience anything of what he was complaining about- the lack of supplies, the corruption among the contractors?"

Zac swallowed, contemplating how to answer that as she and Travis walked towards the parking lot. *Be honest,* she thought, even as she felt a wave of guilt rise within her. *It's just Travis.* "It was hard not to see it," she said finally. "It was everywhere. Sometimes, my men's families were sending them supplies they'd bought with their own money. I myself bought a few things with my own money."

Travis looked horrified. "Maybe that should be a part of your testimony," he said.

"My therapist suggested that too," Zac admitted.

"I think you should tell the truth."

Zac nodded. "At the same time, though, I'm also looking into getting a position teaching at West Point. I can't imagine that would happen if I bashed the Army's shortcomings. If I wanted to say something about the wars' inadequacies, I'd have to…." Her voice trailed off as she tried find a good way of phrasing what she was thinking.

"You'd have to walk the line," Travis said.

"Yes, exactly." *Maybe he does get it after all, or is starting to.*

"That's tough," Travis sympathized. "When are you testifying?"

"August 28th."

"Well, I hope it works out, whatever path you end up taking."

CHAPTER 10

A few days later, Alex surprised Zac with a question about her family. "Are you in touch with them at all?" she asked. "Your parents? Your siblings?"

"Barely," Zac said. "My little brother- Ben- helped me move in and has come to visit for a couple of weekends. I talk to him regularly but I haven't really spoken to the rest of them." *They all suck, except for Ben.*

"What's Ben doing professionally?"

"He just finished his freshman year at U Arkansas, and he's been spending the summer working at an office on campus."

"So he drives over from Little Rock?"

Zac nodded. "He usually drives over on a Friday night after work and stays until Sunday afternoon. I think he's visited me more often than he's gone to our parents'," she added. "Maybe he's going the way me and Clive went, after all."

"So you haven't been in touch with your parents or older siblings at all?" Alex said.

"No. My older brother still thinks he's better than me, especially now that I'm disabled, and both he and my sister went the way of our parents- dirt poor with a lot of kids. We really haven't spoken at all recently."

"Maybe there's room for change there," Alex said. "Little

Rock isn't that far a drive."

"It's far enough," Zac replied. "Even when Ben comes in, it takes him at least four hours, and my parents are decently outside the city."

"What about that good friend you grew up with- Harvey?" Alex asked. "Are you in touch with him at all?"

Zac shook her head. "He enlisted pretty early in the war, and he got killed after only a few months of fighting."

"I'm sorry to hear that," Alex said.

"I was too," Zac replied. "I knew the lieutenant who went to inform his mother when he died- he said she attacked him when he came with the news."

Alex shook her head sympathetically. "It's never easy to get that kind of information."

"Especially for that family," Zac agreed. "They were pretty tight-knit. They couldn't have been much better off than my family was, and yet Harvey always seemed to have more food and clothing than we did. His mother was good about feeding us too when we went over there- it's why Clive and I spent so much time over there."

"Did you speak to Harvey's mother after he was killed?"

"I did, actually. I was in Afghanistan when it happened, but I called her." Zac took a deep breath as she remembered the crackling on the phone line that almost obscured parts of the conversation.

"Did she appreciate hearing from you?" Alex asked.

"I think so," Zac replied. "We got into a long conversation- longer than I was expecting. When I first called, I didn't even know what to say besides, 'I'm sorry.' I mean, Harvey was a really good friend of mine." She swallowed.

"I'm impressed that he enlisted," Alex said. "He'd already graduated from college, right? That could have been his ticket out of the area's poverty."

Zac thought about it, kicking one foot back and forth across the carpeting as she tried to form her thoughts. "His enlistment wasn't about getting away from Bearden like my going to West Point was," she said finally. "He enlisted because he felt like it was his duty to do something for the country after we were attacked." She stopped talking and clenched her hands together in her lap.

"What is it?" Alex asked, sensing Zac's frustration and anger.

"Harvey's death was just one more reason I don't really have ties to this area anymore," Zac said. "I really do feel like I'm only back here by chance, because it happens to be where my grandpa had a house, and because he happened to leave it to me."

"So you'd really like your next act to be somewhere else?"

"Yes, I really would."

*   *   *

Zac stood in a phone booth, listening to the phone ring. *Come on Clive, pick up,* she thought. *I don't want to talk to Ma or Pa.* Her yearling year at West Point was nearly over, and Zac needed to know where her brother had decided to go to college.

Finally, Clive answered the phone, and Zac was glad to hear his voice. "I was wondering when you'd call," he said.

"When I have more than two minutes to do it," Zac said.

"I figured," Clive replied. "Listen, Zac, I've decided to go to the Naval Academy."

"Really?" Zac asked. "I thought you were going to come here."

"That was my original plan," Clive admitted. "But I really liked Annapolis."

"But how are you going to feel when the Army beats the Navy at football every year?" Zac needed to know.

Clive snorted. "When has Army *ever* beaten Navy?" he asked.

"We won last year."

"It'll be the last time!" They both laughed. Then Clive

became serious again. "I want to be a Marine," he said. "That's the main reason I chose Navy."

"The Marines," Zac said. "That's a tough road."

"I know," Clive said. "But I really want to give it a shot."

"Well, good luck then. I want you to succeed."

"Thanks. If I don't make it, I can always transfer to West Point." They both laughed again.

* * *

Within a month of starting at Schofield Barracks, Zac had met Colonel Rice's family- his wife and eight children. Zac had to work at remembering everyone's names, but she was drawn to his wife Mary immediately. *She's a sweet, warm, woman, and she's gone out of her way to make me feel welcome,* Zac thought. *But she's also been a military wife for all of her adult life. Her whole life has been spent supporting Colonel Rice and raising their children. I'm not sure I could handle that.*

As Christmas approached, Clive made plans to visit her rather than go home for the holidays, and Zac was only too happy to see him. As his flight landed, she waited at the airport with anticipation, watching as his plane taxied to the gate. As she looked from the plane to the people around her, she saw plenty of people looking back at her. *It must be the uniform,* she thought. *Well, whatever. These people can stare all they want- I don't care as long as Clive makes it here.*

As Clive deplaned in his dress uniform, Zac grinned and waved. "Clive!" she yelled, and he came over with a grin. As they hugged each other, Zac remembered when she had been the one coming home from West Point, and Clive had been the one meeting her. "How was your flight?" she asked when they'd parted.

"It was fine," Clive said as they moved towards the baggage claim. He glanced behind them as they walked. "Everyone's looking at us."

153

Zac grinned. "I was just noticing that before you landed." They both laughed, and Zac put her arm around her brother. "It is so good to see you."

"I'm looking forward to meeting Colonel Rice," Clive said as they drove away from the airport. "I've been looking forward to it since you told me about when you first met him." They both laughed again.

"He's a character," Zac agreed. "I was pretty terrified of him for awhile."

"I'm not surprised," Clive said. "He's got quite a reputation for being a bully if you don't get along with him, but being great if you do hit it off. But you said you'd met his family too?"

Zac nodded. "He has eight kids, and he treats me like I'm his ninth. I mean, his oldest is only a few years younger than I am, so maybe it's not much of a stretch for him, but…" She took a deep breath and stared at the road in front of her. "It's been a big deal for me."

Clive nodded. "It's certainly different from what we had growing up."

"Tell me about it," Zac said, relieved that her brother understood what she was saying. "This is one of the few times I've seen what a functional, decent family looks like."

"I'm not surprised," Clive said as he lowered the window next to him and inhaled the warm, humid air that flowed through it. "Sometimes I think Ma and Pa would have been better at their lives if they'd been single people growing up in a city."

"But it didn't have to be like that. I mean, Colonel Rice's youngest child has a disability, and still his family holds it together and are decent people. I don't know how he does it."

"Well, his wife is a housewife," Clive said. "She probably runs the household."

"She does, but even so. They have eight kids. It's a lot. Ma and Pa couldn't hold it together with five, or even four."

"What's the matter with the youngest one?"

"I'm not sure, exactly- they don't ever talk about it. But I

154

think he has Down's Syndrome, and he definitely gets seizures-I've heard about that for sure."

Clive sighed. "That's rough," he said. He stared out at the palm trees around them.

"What are you thinking?" Zac asked after awhile.

"We're really lucky we didn't turn out that way," Clive said. "Especially Ben- I mean, given how much Ma and Pa drink and everything." He shifted uncomfortably in his seat.

Zac tugged at her seatbelt, feeling as uncomfortable as her brother did. "I know," she said. "Frankly, I'm amazed that Ben's turned out as well as he has. He's a good kid. It's the only reason I wish I weren't so far away- I wish I could keep a closer eye on him."

"You've done okay," Clive said. "He always enjoys the phone calls and the video chats."

"Even if he has to do the chats from school because Ma and Pa can't afford internet access or a computer." Zac rolled her eyes.

Clive shrugged. "At least he's able to do them from somewhere. We can only work with what we're given."

When they arrived at the base, Clive hauled himself out of his seat and examined the car for a minute before getting his bags. "This is a pretty good ride," he said.

Zac nodded. "It's cheap and functional," she said as they walked towards her living quarters. "Exactly what I was looking for."

"Still, it's a new car, not a broken down piece of farm equipment. You're really moving up in the world."

He was smiling, but Zac could tell he was serious, and she nodded seriously as well. "It's what I wanted when I went to West Point."

"I know," Clive said. "Meanwhile, Melanie's pregnant with her fourth kid, and Abe just had his fourth as well."

Zac shuddered. "I'm so glad I escaped that."

"Me too. No marriage or kids for you at all, though?"

Zac spent a minute unlocking the door to her quarters as she thought about it. "Maybe eventually," she said. "But definitely not right away." *And maybe not ever- I've never had one guy I've been interested in be interested back.*

*   *   *

For days now, Zac had been eyeing the square cutout in the ceiling over the hallway in the second floor, knowing that it was the entrance to the house's tiny attic space. *It's more of a crawlspace,* she thought, even if she could not remember ever having been up there. *Grandpa and Grandma used it as a storage space. It's the last part of the house I haven't fixed up yet, or even touched.* She looked up at it, frowning.

But finally, she steeled herself and dragged her ladder out of the corner, opened it, and began her ascent. Towards the top of the ladder, with two steps left, she put both hands out and found that she could comfortably reach the trapdoor above her. She pushed, and was immediately rewarded with a cloud of dust that covered her hands and head.

Zac coughed and her eyes watered, but she pushed harder on the door until it opened fully and she could prop it open on a nearby hook. With the door firmly open, Zac climbed the last two steps on the ladder and stuck her head into the space above her. "Whoa," she said as she looked around.

The crawlspace was filled with boxes upon boxes, many stacked up as high as the roof. *Oh man,* Zac thought. The thought of having to get all the boxes down the ladder and going through each and every one of them made her eyes water again. *Am I really up for this?* she wondered as she continued looking around the space in front of her.

Then her eyes fell on a number of large glass jars that lined the one part of the floor not covered with boxes. Zac looked closer. Each jar was completely filled with- *are those pennies?* Zac hoisted herself up into to the crawlspace to get a better look. *Yes, those are all pennies. Oh my God, there must be thousands, if not millions, of pennies in those jars.*

As she thought about it, Zac vaguely remembered Ben saying something about their grandfather collecting pennies, *but that was years ago- even before the wars started, I think. Maybe Grandpa kept at it. That would certainly explain why there are so many of them.*

Taking a deep breath, Zac looked around again, taking in both the number of boxes and the jars of pennies, trying to decide what to do. She found her gaze going back to the pennies more than once. *Okay,* she thought. *It's most obvious what to do with those, because they have the most immediate value. But God, there are so many jars of them.*

Bracing herself, Zac lifted one jar and carefully carried it down her ladder and into one of the spare bedrooms on the second floor. After carrying two more jars down, though, she'd had enough. *That's it for now,* she decided. *It's plenty to put into rolls for now- I can always bring the other jars down later.*

"God, what is all this?" Max asked a week later when he visited and saw rolls of pennies stacked up on the floor, as well as two empty jars sitting next to them.

"Apparently, Grandpa collected pennies," Zac replied. "I've been putting them into rolls and will eventually deposit them into my bank account."

"Looks like you're almost done," Max said, gesturing at the two empty jars.

"No, I've got at least another seven or eight full jars up in the crawlspace, maybe more."

"Oh God," Max said, groaning.

"Tell me about it," Zac said. "I only started with the pennies because I thought I could handle that better than the five million boxes of my grandparents' stuff that are up there."

"Man," Max said. "I'm happy to help you bring everything down from there, though."

"Are you sure?" Zac asked. "There's no staircase- it's just my ladder."

"If it's a rickety old ladder, you're out of luck," Max said with a grin.

"No, it's a nice new one," Zac replied with a smile. "I just bought it."

A few minutes later they were taking turns hauling both jars of pennies and boxes out of the attic. "Are any of those pennies special enough to be worth anything?" Max asked as they worked.

"I haven't seen any yet that are old enough or unusual enough that I can picture them being worth more than one cent," Zac admitted. "But I think I may have started with my grandfather's most recent jars- all the pennies I've seen have been from the last few years."

"I can't believe you have the patience to put all of them into rolls like that," Max said.

Zac shrugged. "I've been enjoying it," she said. "It's actually been relaxing. Besides, at least they have some monetary value, so it's easy to see it being worth it to do, at least until I find some full time gig."

It was not until they were finished lugging all the boxes down that Zac saw Max remove the hook that covered his stump and massage his arm. "Are you alright?" she asked.

"It does sometimes hurt after heavier work like that," Max admitted.

"Do you want something for the pain? What works? Ice? Heat? I also have leftover pain meds from my surgeries."

Max was quiet as he contemplated the question. "If you have a heating pad, I'll start with that," he said finally. "I don't like having to take anything as heavy duty as the meds, but if it gets worse, I might."

In her kitchen a few minutes later, Zac wrapped the warm heating pad around Max's wrist. "Let me know if that works," she said.

Max reached out with his good arm and took her hand. Zac started to pull away, and Max gripped her hand tighter. "What's your problem?" he asked. "You know I was interested in you even back at West Point?"

"I know," Zac said.

"So what's your problem?"

Zac stared away from him as she thought about it. "It's always been tough to juggle the military with a romantic life," she said. "Besides, I've spent the last ten years in three deployments, thinking I would be killed in each of them. It didn't seem worth the effort to pursue someone romantically." *Even when Eric was writing his last email to me, suggesting marriage, he was thinking of getting out of the Army first, then having a relationship second.*

"Well, the wars are over, and you're alive," Max said. "You're also out of the military now. You can live your life differently."

"I know."

After a minute of silence, Max put his good arm around Zac and pulled her to his chest. This time, she didn't object.

*   *   *

Clive, in his Naval Academy uniform, watched, smiling, as Zac made one last adjustment to her body armor. "It's fine," he said. "It was fine before that, too."

"I know," Zac said. "But I intend to use every inch of this armor to come home alive."

"Damn straight," Ben said, nodding at his sister. Their grandparents stood behind him, eyeing her nervously.

All around them, all of the soldiers in Zac's unit were getting into their armor and saying goodbye to their families. The United States had been attacked by terrorists nearly a year before, and Zac, now two years out of West Point, had watched many of her classmates' units deploy over the last six months. Now it was Zac's turn to be deployed to Middle East to retaliate. Clive, in the midst of his own preparations for graduation and then deployment, had flown in for the occasion.

"I don't think I'll actually head to the Middle East for at least a month after graduation," Clive said. "And it'll probably be longer than that."

"Be careful," Zac warned him seriously. "I mean it. I want to see you back here alive."

"I want to come back alive too," Clive said, just as seriously.

Zac looked at Ben, still only nine years old. "So Ma and Pa decided not to come?"

Ben shook his head. "It's just Grandma, Grandpa and me again."

"Like at my graduation from West Point," Zac said, smiling at the memory.

"I remember that, too," Ben said. Then he wrapped his arms around his sister, armor and all. "Please come home."

"I will," Zac promised, hugging him back. Suddenly, Zac heard someone calling for her over the din. She looked around and saw Eric Johnson coming towards her. He too was in full armor. "Eric!" she said, surprised.

"I heard you were deploying too and I had to come find you," he said. "Where are you going?"

"Afghanistan."

"I'm off to Iraq. A lot of our classmates are heading to both places."

"Can't say I'm surprised."

"Me neither."

A general announcement was made for Zac's unit to begin boarding the plane, and she looked back at Eric one last time. "I hope you make it home safely," she said.

Eric's face broke into the grin she remembered so well. "I will," he said. "Don't worry. We're going to win this war, Zac. The terrorists attacked us, and we're responding. This is a good war."

Zac smiled. "I hope so," she said.

"Hey, do you have my email address?" Eric asked. He dug into a pocket of his armor, came up with a pen and a small pad of paper, and scribbled something onto it. Then he ripped off the top sheet of paper and handed it to Zac. "Write to me while you're over there," he ordered. "And be careful."

"Yes, sir!" Zac said, smiling now. Eric disappeared into the crowd, and Zac gave her family one last hug before boarding the plane.

The flight to the Middle East seemed interminable. For the first time, Zac started to feel nervous at the prospect of commanding the men and women on the plane with her. *Will they obey my orders?* she wondered. *It makes me glad I'm not a tiny, five-foot-two female. A few of my classmates at West Point fit that profile, and our classmates and professors didn't always take them seriously.*

In Kuwait, Zac's unit spent a nearly a month waiting to be transferred to their station in Afghanistan. *Hurry up and wait,* Zac thought, her frustration rising throughout the four weeks. She spent the time maintaining discipline and morale. Her soldiers were awake at the same time every day for marches or morning runs, and she made it clear that uniforms were to be kept in tip-top shape. At the same time, she made sure the soldiers had access to movies, card games, newspapers and other diversions, and she tried to keep the lines of communications between them and their families back home as open as possible.

When they finally flew to Afghanistan, Zac was relieved. *I need to see some action, and my troops do too,* she thought. As the unit reached the Forward Operating Base, flying in under cover of darkness to maintain their security, Zac was given her first glimpse of the place she would call home for two years. From the air, she could see a few simple buildings in the foothills high above the open terrain. *It's smaller than I thought. It looks like my unit might be one of the few units manning this station.*

The choppers landed three hundred meters from the post, and the soldiers walked through the cold and the dark towards the gate of the outpost. Once inside, Zac finally got a sense of just how small the post actually was. Generators provided the electricity that ran the base, which had a small operations and communications center. Nearby was a mess hall, and the barracks where they would be sleeping was only a short distance away. *This is really basic- no frills whatsoever,* Zac thought. *I just hope it's functional.*

Within a few days, Zac was realizing just how tough the terrain outside the base was. She and her unit climbed through steep mountains, often with close to a hundred pounds of gear on their backs. *This may be the first time in my life I wish I were a six foot four inch, two hundred thirty pound male,* she thought. *This gear would be so much easier to carry if I were.*

Just as quickly, Zac realized that the maps they had were useless, especially for the Air Force pilots that would be giving them support from above. *The mountains and desert all kinda look the same from the air,* she thought. With that in mind, her unit spent its first few weeks in country mapping the caves and hills they searched.

Then, feeling nominally reassured by their maps, Zac was more comfortable when a mission came together to search out some high-level Taliban leaders believed to be hiding in one of the larger caves in the area. That night, however, Zac and her unit did not even make it within a few hundred feet of the cave when they were met with an intense firefight. Several U.S. soldiers went down immediately, and Zac cursed as she fired back at the enemy. All around her, the cold darkness was illuminated by the shooting.

It soon became obvious that the terrorists had a larger fighting force than Zac had anticipated. A hail of bullets came from all directions, and from large guns as well as small. *We're outnumbered here,* Zac realized. *Where is the air power that's supposed to be backing us up?*

As if on cue, Zac could hear the rumbling of the Air Force overhead, and several bombs crashed up against the mountains, close to the caves that Zac and her unit were trying to empty out. *Alright!* Zac thought, but her celebration came too soon- one last bomb fell too close to her own soldiers, and a few were thrown backwards, their limbs coming off and flying away from their torsos. Zac tried not to see that, but it was too late. She kept firing. *Fucking Taliban,* she thought. *Fucking terrorists.*

After a few more shots, she realized that the enemy's fire had lessened, and she signaled her troops to stop firing. All around her, injured American soldiers were groaning, and Zac howled for the Medavacs to come quickly. A few more enemy shots came through as Zac helped load the wounded onto the birds. She prayed silently that the soldiers would survive their wounds. Her healthy troops continued to return fire, protecting their comrades. With her losses as heavy as they were, Zac had no choice but to retreat. On the brutal slog back out of the mountains with all of their equipment, Zac felt every fiber of her body aching.

In the few hours after the firefight, Zac was forced to report to her commanders that her unit had lost nearly a quarter of its soldiers. Twelve of them had been killed, and many more had been badly wounded. After she had finished her report, Zac retreated to one of the only empty spaces on the base and wept for the men that had perished.

Even as firefights and losses like that became the norm, the unit's deployment was extended- first from eight months to thirteen months, then to eighteen months. "I need more men," Zac complained to her commanding officers after she had been deployed for a year and a half and her tour was extended rather than ending. "We've suffered heavy losses."

As the deployment was extended, more and more soldiers were flown in to compensate for the ones who had been injured or killed, and Zac struggled with her troops' morale throughout the whole period. When the news finally came through that the unit was actually going home, it was nearly two years to the day since they had first deployed. Zac ordered the whole unit into the mess hall for the announcement, and when she had everyone's attention, she said, "we've got another set of marching orders, soldiers. We're going home!"

Every last soldier in front of her cheered loudly. Many of them high-fived and hugged each other. *It's the best news they've gotten in awhile,* Zac thought, smiling as she watched the celebration.

Late that night, Zac was checking on the unit's inventory when there was a knock on the office's door. "Come in," she said. Private Alexander Martin entered and saluted. "At ease," she told him.

Private Martin relaxed into position, then said, "I'm glad we're going home, ma'am."

"Me too," Zac said honestly.

"I just came by to thank you, ma'am," Martin continued, and Zac arched her eyebrows. "I came from a military family, ma'am. My father served in Vietnam, my grandfather in World War II, an uncle in Korea. None of them ever had a female commander, and all of them gave me hell for being the first."

Zac looked amused.

"I have to admit, ma'am, that my family's attitude made me want you to fail as an officer, ma'am, but since we've deployed, I think you've done a fine job. I've been most impressed by how you've always come out on patrol with us. You've never hung back at the base like I expected. It's been an honor to serve with you, ma'am."

"Thank you, Private," Zac said sincerely, and walked around her desk to shake his hand.

CHAPTER 11

At their next therapy session, Alex started with a question that Zac was not expecting. "So whatever happened to some of the females you were good friends with at West Point?" she asked. "Like Lucy and Heather?"

Zac swallowed. "We all got deployed in the war, multiple times."

"And?"

"And I don't now, Alex! We fell out of touch."

"Really?" Alex asked. "I find that hard to believe. You guys were so close at such a difficult and seminal time in your lives. What really happened?"

"I don't know, exactly," Zac admitted. "There came a point where they both stopped answering my emails and calls."

"When was this?"

"Uuummmm…" Zac frowned as she thought. "During and after our second deployments. I mean, our deployments didn't all start and end at the same time, but they overlapped. I think I was the last of the three of us to get deployed a second time.

By the time I got home, I realized that I hadn't heard from either of them in awhile, so I tried again. My emails to Lucy bounced back, though, and the phone number I had for her was disconnected. I never managed to figure out her new contact info."

"And Heather?"

"She stopped responding too. I mean, my emails to her never got returned, and I always got her personalized voicemail when I called, but she never called me back. Then I got deployed for a third time, and it kind of fell off my radar, especially after I got injured."

"Well, maybe it's time you tried again," Alex said.

"Maybe," Zac said doubtfully.

"What's stopping you?"

"I don't know," Zac admitted.

"Are you worried they'll be injured beyond recognition?"

"I'm not sure. I… I mean, like I said, for awhile there, I was the one reaching out, and getting nowhere."

"It sounds like something must've happened," Alex said.

"Something really bad," Zac agreed.

"Does that scare you?"

Zac frowned. "I'm not sure 'scared' is the right word. But I'm having trouble picturing what our contact would look like at this point. It's been awhile, and I've been through so much."

"I think that's going to be true for them, too. Perhaps it's worth another shot. Who knows- maybe they want to hear from but aren't sure how to reach out after all this time."

"How hard is it to send an email?" Zac grumbled. "They wouldn't even have to hear my voice or see my face when they sent it."

"You're having your own trouble readjusting to life after the war," Alex reminded her. "Try to be sympathetic."

Zac spent several days kicking around the idea of contacting Heather and Lucy again. *You can send an email just as easily as they can,* she thought, remembering what she had told Alex. *But they could have responded as easily as I can try to contact them again.*

For a second, Zac stared at herself in the mirror in her bedroom. *Why are you so angry at them?* she asked herself. It took her a few minutes to realize, *I'm not angry at Heather and Lucy, I'm just angry.*

Taking a deep breath, Zac sat down at her computer and opened her email. Her missive to Lucy was a short one. *I guess I'm really not expecting anything,* she thought as she wrote a longer message to Heather. By the time she hit "Send" on the message to Heather, her email to Lucy had bounced back into her inbox. *Figured that,* she thought. *But maybe Heather will respond this time.*

Still, when an email from Heather landed in her inbox the next day, Zac was a little surprised. *Maybe Alex was right,* she thought as she opened the email. *I guess I should have reached out again.*

She smiled as she started reading. "Omigod, Zac, you have no idea how much I've been thinking of you recently," the email began. "I'm back in Chicago, and have been since I got back from the war. I, too, was injured, but in the middle of my second deployment. All the emails and voicemails you left me were in the middle of my surgeries and rehab. It's been a horrible road, and there are still many miles left in front of me.

"I finally have a job, working in the administrative offices of a local gym. It's steady employment. Besides, it's part of a chain that has several locations in the city, so if this location ever closed, I could probably get another job at one of the other locations, and that makes me happy. These wars have destroyed my life, Zac, and they almost destroyed my marriage too- Charlie almost left me while I was still in that hospital bed, and the worst part of it is that I wouldn't have blamed him if he had.

"Would you be interested in visiting me here in Chicago? It sounds like we have a lot to catch up on."

She's from Chicago originally, Zac remembered. *Maybe I should go up there,* she thought, her feelings cascading out all at once. *Charlie's a good guy- they always had a solid marriage that I was jealous of. I never thought he would have left her, but he is a civilian. It's hard for them to understand what it's like to be in combat. Plus, Heather never actually said what her injury was- I guess I'll probably have to see her to find out.*

But she's working at an office at a gym? Zac thought. *That's hardly a good use of her skills.* For a minute, Zac stared out the window, watching the flowers in her yard swaying in the breeze. *I guess she needed to get away from the military and everything it sucked us into,* she reasoned. *Maybe that's a smart idea.*

After several email exchanges with Heather, Zac decided to go to Chicago to visit her. *She does have a full time job, and I don't,* she thought. *But can I handle a plane ride there without having a panic attack? Those seats are so tiny, and everyone's so packed in. Maybe I should take the train instead.*

But there was no direct train route from Tulsa to Chicago- *it would take me more than a day to get there on the train,* Zac realized. *There's no way I'm doing that. Damn Amtrak. Plane it is, I guess. I'll just have to book aisle seats so that I can get out of there quickly if I have to.*

To her amazement, Zac made it through the flight to Chicago without any mishaps, but she was more than eager to get off the plane when it landed. *Heather said she'd be waiting for me at the airport,* she thought. *I hope I recognize her.*

On the escalator heading down to the baggage claim, Zac spotted her friend quickly. She grinned and waved. Heather waved back- with her left hand. Immediately, Zac noticed that she was missing her whole right arm. *Oh my fucking God,* she thought, feeling her knees shake.

Zac stepped off the escalator, noticing how hard that little step was with her leg still slightly messed up. Nonetheless, she threw open her arms and grinned broadly at Heather. Heather, too, smiled and hugged her friend back with her remaining arm. "Did you check any bags?" Heather asked.

"Just one," Zac replied. The luggage came quickly, and soon they were in Heather's car and maneuvering out of the airport. Zac watched as Heather drove with one hand. "I'm impressed you can drive like that," she said finally. "I couldn't drive at all until awhile after my leg was out of its cast."

"These damn wars, Zac," Heather said.

"I know," Zac replied. "What happened to you?"

"IED while I was on patrol. I would say that I'm lucky I survived, but I'm not sure."

"Oh, come on, Heather."

"It's been a tough road back. There were days I didn't want to be alive."

"Yeah, that's been true for me too." Zac sighed.

"So what happened to you? I saw a slight limp, and burn scars."

"I was thrown by a grenade and shot several times in the leg- after the Humvee in front of me was completely destroyed by an IED." *I still feel guilty about not being in that vehicle.*

Heather shook her head as they arrived at her house. "And all for what?" she asked. "That whole area is still a mess. I'm not sure what we accomplished."

"Unfortunately, I don't have a good answer for that either."

It was the next day, when Heather, Charlie and Zac were having dinner at a local restaurant, that Zac finally plucked up the courage to ask about the friend who had made up their close trio at West Point. "Have you heard anything from Lucy?" she asked. "None of my emails and voicemails have gotten to her recently."

Both Heather and Charlie stopped eating for a second and stared at her. There was a minute of silence.

"What?" Zac asked.

Charlie's eyes had a stricken look in them, a look that was mirrored on Heather's face. "You didn't hear what happened?" Charlie asked.

"No," Zac said, her chest constricting.

"Oh, man," Heather replied, putting her fork down. She glanced around at the other restaurant patrons around them, and lowered her voice. "We both made it through our first deployments safely," she said. "But before Lucy got deployed a second time, she got put in charge of a different unit, one that was supposed to see more action than she saw during her first deployment." Heather swallowed.

"But it didn't?" Zac asked.

Heather shook her head. "Oh, the action wasn't the issue. It was more that the men in her unit were not happy having a female superior. About halfway through the deployment, they got together and tried to do something about it."

"Are you saying what I think you're saying?" Zac asked, feeling shaken and disgusted.

"Probably," Heather said. "The men raped her repeatedly- a few held her down while the others went at her. It happened several times."

"Didn't she complain?" Zac asked. "I've never known Lucy to back down from anything."

"She did complain. More than once. Her deployment ended early because her CO transferred her back to the States and put a male officer in her place."

Zac clenched her teeth, struggling to keep her tears from flowing. "And she came right back here to the crappy Army hospitals and VA staff."

Heather nodded. "The Army hospital closest to her didn't even have an OB-GYN. Nobody listened to her complaints- to the contrary, she was told that if she pursued it, it wouldn't help her career."

Zac's whole body felt tight. "She took her own life, didn't she?"

Now, both Heather and Charlie were nodding. "I'm sorry you had to hear about it like this," Heather said.

"How come I didn't hear about it when it happened?" Zac demanded.

"You were still in the middle of your second deployment," Heather said. "I was sedated in a hospital bed, going through all those surgeries. I didn't hear about it either until awhile after it happened."

It was only when they were back at Heather's house, and Heather and Zac stood in the back yard alone, that Zac felt slightly more comfortable letting her tears flow. "So many vets have been committing suicide," she said. "It's such a waste. We get through multiple deployments and we can't handle being home."

"The whole system is a goddamn mess," Heather agreed. "But our country has been sending people off to war forever. It's not like the support system hasn't had time to evolve."

On her flight home to Tulsa, Zac's plane was nearly empty and she had a whole row of seats to herself. Gratefully, she moved to the window seat and leaned up against the side of the plane, staring out the small pane of glass next to her. As the plane took off, her tears continued to flow down her face. *I can't believe Lucy committed suicide,* she thought. *What can't you believe?* another part of her brain asked. *You've certainly contemplated it plenty of times.*

I have to say something, she decided finally. *I've been worried about making my testimony at Victor's trial about the war's shortcomings, but I have to do it. Lucy's death is unacceptable. If my testimony does away with any opportunities I have at West Point, so be it.*

When Zac's group therapy ended the next week, she was surprised to find Travis waiting for her. "I had another meeting for the board I'm on," he explained. "I was hoping I would run into you."

"Why is that?" Zac asked. "You like me, don't you?" She was teasing, but Travis' reddened face told her that she might have been right. *Uh oh,* she thought. *If he has a crush on me, that can* not *be good. Max and Drew are all the competition I'm comfortable with. Besides, Travis is fifteen years younger than me. That wouldn't work at all.*

"We've been discussing how to improve the VA and treatment options for vets," Travis said as they headed for the doors. "I was hoping for your input."

"Oh God," Zac said.

"What?" Travis asked, looking worried.

"That's quite an undertaking. You'd probably have to overhaul the whole VA, at least."

"Yeah, that's what I've been hearing," Travis admitted. "But what do you mean, at least?"

"Just what the phrase implies. So many Army officers buy private health insurance and bypass the VA system entirely because they can afford to go to private hospitals to get treatment. The whole thing is a mess."

"How come you didn't do that?" Travis asked. "Colonel is a pretty high rank."

"Oh, I did," Zac said. "My group therapy is through a private practice, not the VA- we only meet here because we pay the VA for their space. We're not all officers, but the people that were enlisted are getting financial help through some of the vets' organizations around here. My individual therapy is through one of the CBOCs because the VA doesn't have the staff for it. But I came close to not getting into either."

"What do you mean?" Travis asked. They were already outside, but Travis stopped searching for his car keys, stopped walking, and looked at her.

He really wants to know, Zac thought. She took a deep breath. *What do I even tell him?* she wondered. *Tell him the truth. You already told him you're in multiple types of therapy- how much worse can it get?* "I mean, the first social worker I saw didn't like me much, and I, too, had to go through IAVA to get into the group therapy."

"Isn't Max coming to the VA for treatment?"

"He is now, but he's been out of the Army for two years and they've only recently made time for him. The lack of funding and the lack of decent doctors, clinicians, staff makes everything impossible. So many vets commit suicide waiting for care- the number is in the hundreds a day. There are one or two vets in my group therapy that I think may have been headed in that direction." Zac thought of Lucy and had to control her tears.

"Man," Travis said, scrunching up his face and scratching

his head. Then he rolled up his sleeves as the sun came out and poured heat over them.

"Do you think there's enough energy to overhaul the system?" Zac asked. "You need political will, you need the right people, you need enough funding."

"I've started on the funding," Travis said. "The proceeds from that concert you went to has gone to the VA, as well as other organizations- the Wounded Warrior Project, a few others."

"All in this area?" Zac asked.

Travis nodded. "My family's from here, so it's where we want to make a difference." He looked at Zac for a minute. "When I saw you in my father's store, you said you'd just moved into the area. Where are you from originally?"

Zac eyed the parking lot in front of them and started walking in that direction. Travis followed. "I grew up outside of Little Rock," Zac said. "But my grandparents lived here and left me their house when they passed away."

"And you're more comfortable here than being closer to your family?"

"Yeah. I mean, I spent a year here, living with my grandparents anyway, and..." *Shit,* Zac thought. *I've said too much. There's no way he needs to know any of this.*

"I'm only asking because I'm interested," Travis said when he saw her hesitation. "Why wouldn't you have lived with your parents?"

"Family shit," Zac said with a shrug, regretting, as an afterthought, using that language in front of him. "Sorry," she said.

"Nothing I haven't heard before," Travis said. "Much to my parents' chagrin."

They both laughed. Then Zac checked her watch. "I should be getting home," she said.

"I didn't mean to keep you," Travis said, pulling his car keys from his pocket.

"It's not a problem," Zac replied.

"So you're finally coming to Little Rock," Ben teased his sister over the phone a few days later. "I thought that would never happen."

"Well, you're the one who's always coming here," Zac said. "It's only fair that I go to you at least once, especially now that Drew is there as well."

"Yeah, you can't keep hiding in your own house," Ben agreed.

A few days later, Zac broke up her drive to Little Rock by stopping for lunch about halfway through the ride. *This ride isn't horrible, but it is a slight haul,* she thought as she stretched out after getting out of her car. *I can't believe Ben does it without stopping, although I'm sure he drives faster than I do. I've really been making an effort to go the speed limit ever since I got pulled over that time on the way to Target.*

After she had gotten to Little Rock and checked into her hotel, Zac drove to the University's campus to meet Ben. *Harvey Rendell went to school here, too,* she remembered. *I wonder if he stayed in any of the same dorms that Ben's lived in.*

A few minutes later, Ben grinned at her as he got out of work to find her waiting for him outside his office. As they walked across the campus together, towards Ben's dorm, Zac saw more than a few people eying her, and she became self-conscious. *I guess my limp is still noticeable,* she thought. *Not what I'd wanted this stage of the game.*

"Relax, Zac," Ben said. "Nobody's judging you. If anything, people are curious- a lot of people on campus know that I have two siblings who fought in those wars."

"Easy for you to say," Zac replied. "I'm used to civilians looking at me because I'm in uniform. I'm less comfortable with it being because I'm wounded."

"It might not be because you're wounded," Ben said. "Around here, it definitely isn't. People are more interested in your combat experience."

Inside Ben's dorm, Zac looked around with interest, both at

Ben's room and at the common areas. "So this is what a regular college dorm looks like," she said. "The ones at West Point were all stone outsides and Spartan insides."

"You've had a different life than I'll ever have, Zac," Ben said. "I'm not going to deny it."

The next night, they went to Drew's house for dinner. "Is that a case of beer?" Ben asked as he eyed the car's backseat.

Zac nodded. "Drew ordered that type with dinner when we were in Oklahoma City," she said. "I picked some up after I checked into my hotel." *That and a bunch of other liquor, but I'm keeping that hidden in my trunk. There's no way I'm letting Ben or Drew see it.*

They rode in silence for awhile before Ben said, "Drew likes you, you know?"

"I know," Zac replied.

"Would you consider marrying him?" Ben asked.

"I don't know," Zac said. "Our relationship isn't anywhere near that yet."

"I think it's cool that he grew up right near us."

"I do too. That's not what the issue is."

Ben looked out the window and did not say anything else. *Thank God,* Zac thought. *I'm really not sure I want to discuss that further. Much as I like Drew, he's tied to his job, and if I had to spend the rest of my life in Little Rock, I'd go out of my mind. Also, much as I hate to sound selfish or uncaring, he does have kids. I really wouldn't want to be put in the middle if anything happened between him and his ex.*

When they arrived at Drew's house, Zac was impressed by how large it was. Drew smiled as he let them in, and the smile broadened into a grin when he saw the beer Ben was carrying. "Thanks," he said. Then he looked at Zac. "Your attention to detail is incredible."

Zac shrugged. "Whatever," she said, with an amused smile. She sat on the couch in the living room as Ben brought the beer into the kitchen. Then she looked at the coffee table in front of her, which had a stack of books sitting on it. A box of books sat on the floor next to it. Looking closer, Zac realized that they were all military books, and she picked one up.

"I was hoping you'd be interested in those," Drew said as he came into the living room.

"What are all of these?" Zac asked.

"Memoirs of servicemen and women of all ranks," Drew said. "Some of them served in the Iraq and Afghanistan wars, others in previous wars." He sat down next to her. "Since you've been thinking of writing about your own experience, I thought these might help you."

Zac looked down at the book she was holding. "I don't know," she said.

"There's a lot of interest out there. I've been looking it up."

"Why would you be looking up interest in my memoirs?"

"Because you were thinking of writing them. And because it's occurred to me to do the same."

"Really?" Zac asked as Ben came into the room and sat down.

Drew nodded. "We fought for over ten years, but only a really tiny percentage of the population is enlisted or are officers. It's something like one percent or less."

"I know," Zac said. "It's why so many of us got deployed multiple times, and why Congress was considering a draft."

"There's an increasing perception that the people that served in Iraq and Afghanistan need to tell their stories," Drew replied. "And I don't disagree."

"I think it's a good idea, Zacster," Ben said, using the nickname that Clive had always used.

"Zacster?" Drew repeated with amusement. "I'm totally using that nickname from now on."

"Drewdy," Zac replied, wishing she had something to throw at him.

"Okay, maybe not," Drew said. They both laughed.

Later that night, as Zac and Ben were leaving, Drew carried out the box of military memoirs. The box was stuffed to the top with books, and Zac wondered whether she would ever manage to read them all. Without thinking about it, Zac popped open her trunk as Ben climbed into the front passenger seat to wait for her. It wasn't until Drew was settling the box of books into her trunk that Zac remembered she'd left the rest of the alcohol she had purchased in there as well. *Shit!* she thought.

"I hope you're not planning in drinking that all at once," Drew said.

"Definitely not," Zac said, hoping he would drop the subject.

Instead, Drew eyed her as she slammed the trunk shut. "I mean it, Zac," he said. "I'd hate to see you go the way of your parents."

"We both would, believe me."

"Would you call me if you were having a problem?"

"Absolutely."

"You mean it?"

"Yes."

"I hope so." Drew opened his arms and Zac hugged him. "It's always good to see you," Drew said.

"Likewise."

"I mean it, Zac. You can call me anytime."

"I know."

*   *   *

Zac smiled with relief as she stepped off the plane into the Hawaii airport she had become so familiar with since she had graduated from West Point. *Survived my second deployment,* she thought. *Still, we've been fighting for nearly seven years, and there's no end in sight.* All around her, American flags hung side-by-side with red, white and blue banners. "Welcome home, troops!" read other banners. It felt good to be standing on solid ground after the long plane ride, and standing on safe ground as well. *Clive is still deployed for the second time, though,* Zac thought. *He didn't deploy until six months ago, so he's got awhile left over there.*

Once she had been out-processed and had settled back into her quarters at Schofield Barracks, Zac picked up the phone.

Eric just got home too after his second deployment. His last email suggested we get together, and I'm going to take him up on that offer.

"Zac!" Eric said boisterously two days later as he opened the door to let her in to his quarters. "Are you as happy to be home as I am?"

"No, I think I'm happier," Zac teased.

"Two deployments and we're still in one piece," Eric agreed as they headed out to the back yard. "I hope you like hamburgers- we've got the grill going already."

"Oh yeah," Zac said, feeling her stomach growl as the smell of the cooking hamburgers hit her nose.

"Want a drink?" Eric asked, holding up a bottle of beer in one hand and a can of Coke in the other.

"I'll take the soda," Zac replied. Eric tossed her the Coke, and she caught it easily, feeling the cool can against her palm.

"Still no alcohol for you, huh?"

Zac shook her head as she opened the can.

"I didn't think so- I made sure I bought soda, just in case. I wish I had your discipline, though."

"It would be easy if you grew up with my parents."

"Oh, boy," Eric said. Then he introduced her to the other members of his unit, some of whom were crowded around the grill, and some of whom were just arriving.

Zac looked around the yard, taking in the warm summer sun and the smell of the fresh-cut grass. *I am so glad to be home safely,* she thought.

As she sat down next to Eric at the table once their food was ready, Eric put a hand at her back. She glanced over at him, eyebrows raised. He arched one eyebrow in return, and Zac felt her heart race. *Could he really be interested in me?* Zac wondered. *He's always had so many women falling all over him, that it never occurred to me that he could like me.*

But once dinner was over and the rest of his unit had left, Eric was indeed steering Zac towards his bedroom, and she did not object. To the contrary, she was disappointed by how quickly it was over. Within just a few minutes, it seemed, Eric was finished and sighing on top of her. "I've wanted that for years," he murmured into her ear.

Yeah, right, Zac thought. "So why didn't you say something?" she whispered back.

Eric thought about it for a second. Then he rolled off her and lay on his side, his head propped up against his hand. "If I'd said anything while we were at the Academy, you would have shot me down," he said finally.

"I don't know about that."

"I do," Eric said, putting his hand on Zac's stomach. "You were a rule-follower."

"How could you not be and still make it through West Point?"

"There are rules to follow and rules to break," Eric said.

"Well, if I'd known you were interested, I might have broken a few," Zac teased.

"I still can't picture that," Eric replied. "Besides...." His voice trailed off.

"What?" Zac asked after a minute.

"Nothing," Eric said. He sat up.

"What is it?" Zac asked. *Now I'm really curious.*

Eric swung his legs off the bed, stood up, and began getting dressed. "There's no way I could have made a move on you and not gotten my head handed to me," he said finally.

Zac frowned as she sat up. "That's not true," she said.

"Yes, it is. Even when you were a plebe, you had upperclassmen looking after you."

"Like who?"

"Like Drew Jamieson."

"He wasn't romantically interested in me."

"Maybe he wasn't, but Max Sheffield certainly was."

The Cadet in the Red Sash, Zac thought. "No way," she said. "He hazed me nonstop."

"Only because he liked your accent. He just wanted to hear you talk."

"I never picked up on that."

"Because he was mostly a rule-follower too."

"I thought he was a good leader," Zac said. She grabbed

her clothing, if only to follow Eric's example. *I'd rather stay the night, but that doesn't look like it's going to happen, and I'm certainly not going to grovel.*

"He was a good leader," Eric was saying. "But he wouldn't have done anything to compromise that- including showing romantic interest in a plebe."

"I don't know," Zac said doubtfully.

"Just calling it like I saw it."

"Did you ever keep in touch with him?"

"Who, Max?" Eric asked. "No way. He thought all gymnasts were fags. I was glad to see him graduate."

Two weeks later, Zac took Eric up on another dinner invitation and found herself looking forward to seeing him again. When she arrived at his house, however, it was quiet, and ringing the bell produced no response. Frowning, Zac went around the back, wondering if Eric simply had not heard the bell. But the back yard was empty, and Zac, now at a loss, went back around to the front of the house. *Is it possible I got the day wrong?* she wondered. *It certainly doesn't look like he's home.*

But a minute later, the front door opened, and Eric stood in the doorway in rumpled clothing. "Sorry about that," he said. "I was just taking a nap."

"Is it a bad time?" Zac asked. "We can reschedule."

"No, not at all," Eric said, opening the door to let her in.

Inside the house, it was quiet, and Zac suddenly felt an uneasiness that she could not explain. "Are you sure it's alright?" she asked.

"I invited you over, didn't I?" Eric said as they walked into the kitchen.

Zac was at a loss for words and searching for something to say when she heard a door open somewhere else in the house. A minute later, a young woman, blond and petite, walked into kitchen, barely dressed.

"Who was at the door, honey?" she said to Eric. Then she

saw Zac. "Oh," she said. "Who's this?"

"Zac, this is Traci," Eric said. "Her brother and I went to school together before I started at West Point. Traci, this is Major Zac Madison. She graduated from the Academy a year after I did."

"Oh, yes, I've heard of you," Jenny said innocently. "It's nice to meet you."

Zac nodded. "Likewise," she lied. She looked at Eric.

Eric looked away, a guilty look on his face. The silence lengthened. "I'm sorry," he said finally.

"Me too," Zac said. Then she walked to the front door and left. As she drove home, tears rolled down her face. *I can't believe he's seeing other women,* she thought. *I can't believe I slept with him. I used to have more dignity than that.*

Two days later, Zac saw an email from Eric appear in her inbox, but she ignored it. *Screw him,* she thought. She let a month go by without replying to that email. Another email, and then a voicemail message, came in, all from Eric, but Zac left them unanswered.

Instead, Zac sank her energy into her training, enjoying how safe she felt back on American soil. One night, just after she had finished eating dinner, Zac was about to sit down with a book when there was a knock at the door. *If that's Eric, he's going to stay outside,* she thought. Instead, she pulled open the door to find a tall Marine lieutenant at her door. His nametag read "Hayes." A chaplain stood next to him.

In a second, Zac could feel her knees start to knock together. "Clive," she whispered. She could tell by the look in the lieutenant's eyes that she was right. "Oh, no," she said.

"May we come in, ma'am?" Lt. Hayes asked.

Zac, her face crumbling, stepped aside to let them in. Then she closed the door behind him. Together, they went into the living room, where Zac collapsed into an overstuffed armchair.

Lt. Hayes carefully took a seat next to her as the chaplain remained standing. "I'm very sorry to have to tell you this, ma'am," he said, "but your brother Clive was killed in action yesterday morning."

Zac's tears poured down her face.

"I'm so sorry," Hayes said. "He was a great Marine. It was my pleasure to serve with him when we were first deployed."

Zac bit her lip as her tears continued to flow. "What happened?" she asked.

"His unit was chasing al-Aalafa."

"The sniper?" Zac asked. "He's been on our 'Most Wanted' list for years."

Hayes nodded. "Clive's unit had been on to him for most of his current deployment, and they were finally closing in on him when they came under heavy enemy fire."

"Did they get al-Aalafa?"

"Yes, they did."

"Very good," Zac said. She stood up and went to the window. The street outside was silent, and the shadows of early evening were just beginning to be cast across the trees and houses. Zac looked back at Lt. Hayes to find him watching her. "What's happening to my brother's body?" she asked.

"It's being taken back to Arkansas," Hayes said. "Clive specified a family burial plot there."

Zac nodded. "I know the place," she said. "I'll book a plane ticket. Have my parents been notified?"

"Yes, someone visited them earlier today."

Zac stared out the window again, trying, and failing, to get her tears to stop.

Hayes stood up and went to stand next to her. "I'm very sorry," he said again. "I can only imagine how difficult this must be."

Two days later, Zac landed at the airport in Little Rock in full uniform. Once more, it was Ben and her maternal grandparents waiting to meet her. She wept as she hugged them all. "Where are Ma and Pa?" she asked as they drove out of the airport.

"At the house," Elaine answered from the front seat.

"Where are you staying?" Zac asked her grandparents.

"At the same hotel you are," Elaine said. "We would have stayed at the house, but your mother didn't want us there. Abe and Melanie are there with their families, though, so there isn't much room for us, either."

Zac looked at Ben. Tears filled his large eyes. "Do you want to stay with me at the hotel?" she asked him.

But Ben shook his head. "I'm sharing my room with Anna, Charlie and Jamie," he said of three of Abe's children. "And maybe a few more, too, in the end."

Zac put her arm around his shoulders. "How have Ma and Pa been?"

Ben shook his head again, and his tears fell from his eyes.

The next day, Zac saw her parents for the first time in years as she and her grandparents arrived at the house for the procession to the cemetery. She had spent the better part of the night polishing her boots again, and they shone in the sunlight. The rest of her dress uniform was perfect as well, but Zac was annoyed with herself at focusing on such details. At the same time, she could not help but notice that even though Ben was wearing his best clothes, they still looked worn out and too small for him. *Time for some new clothes, buddy,* she thought. *I would send him money, but Ma and Pa would just spend it on alcohol. Maybe I should send the money to Grandma and Grandpa instead, and they can take him shopping.*

As the funeral procession made its way to the cemetery, Zac felt removed from her body. Her surroundings felt familiar, but not. Once more, she looked over at Ben, who was sitting in the seat next to her, and took his hand. He sent her a grateful look, then looked back out the window. "You didn't want to ride with Ma and Pa?" Zac asked as their grandparents drove.

Ben looked back at her and shook his head. "I'd rather be with you," he said. "Besides, their car is full because some of Melanie and Abe's kids are going with them."

At the cemetery, Zac got out of the car as Clive's flag-draped casket was removed from the hearse. That was all it took for Zac's pain to reawaken, and tears began to roll down her face again. She stood at attention, saluting, for the entire ceremony, but when the honor guard fired its salute, she couldn't help but shudder along with every shot.

When the flag was removed from the casket and presented to her parents, Zac looked at her mother and father. Their faces contained no emotion. Slowly, Zac's mother raised her hands to take the flag. *You look like a robot, Ma,* Zac thought. *What's the matter with you?*

Back at her parents' farm after the funeral, Zac could think of nothing besides getting on a plane and going back to Hawaii. As she eyed the flag from Clive's coffin, which had been carelessly tossed on to the kitchen table, Ben and Abe joined her. Slowly, Melanie followed. "Tough break," Abe said.

Zac nodded. Her eyes went back to the flag, and she began to think of rearranging it more neatly.

"Do you want the flag?" Abe asked, and his thoughtfulness surprised Zac.

"Yes, I do," Zac said.

"I think you should have it," Ben said. "You're in the armed forces, like Clive was. It makes sense."

Abe and Melanie nodded. "Take it, Zac," Abe said. "Ma and Pa won't miss it."

When she returned home, the news of Clive's death had made its way around the base, and Zac's house quickly filled with condolence callers. *Finally, a real community,* she thought.

To her surprise, Eric Johnson was among her visitors. "I'm sorry," he said. "I know your brother meant a lot to you."

Zac nodded. "Thanks," she replied.

CHAPTER 12

After their group therapy ended for the day, Zac, Gail and Jenny headed for the door. Jimmy was not too far behind them, even as the group's remaining vets stayed back in the meeting room, talking to Annemarie. *Drew is back in Tulsa for work,* Zac thought as she walked. *He's coming over for dinner tonight. I'm looking forward to that already.*

As they neared the door of the VA, however, Zac, Gail and Jenny frowned simultaneously and slowed their pace. Security guards crowded the hall and main exit, many with their hands on the weapons. "What's going on?" Jenny asked.

Zac could hear chanting and shouting outside. "Oh my God," she said. "I think there are protesters outside."

"Anti-war protesters?" Gail asked, her disbelief obvious. "You have to be kidding me."

Zac glanced into some of the rooms they passed, and out those rooms' windows. Outside, she could see protesters holding anti-war signs. "The wars are *over*," she said. "What could these assholes possibly be protesting?"

"We still have troops over there as a police-keeping force," Jenny said. "My husband's brother is still over there."

"So they've come here to protest?" Gail said. "Screw them."

Zac nodded in agreement and started walking again towards the exit. One of the security guards, noticing their approach, held out a hand to stop them. "Stay back," he told them. "It's a pretty good crowd out there."

Jenny shook her head. "My mother is supposed to meet me out front," she said.

"She'll have to wait," the guard replied.

By now, Jimmy had caught up to them, and he was frowning at the guard who was stopping them. "We're going to be held hostage here by a bunch of protesting hippies?" he said. "No way."

"Perhaps these people should see what they're protesting against," Zac agreed. "A bunch of wounded vets."

"Who fought for their right to free speech and protesting, while also trying to establish that same right abroad," Gail said, rolling her eyes.

Zac, Jimmy, Gail and Jenny looked at each other. Then they looked at the guards. "Let us out," Jimmy said, standing up straight and throwing his shoulders back. Zac smiled, seeing the Marine's pride in his service for the first time. Then she looked back at the guard and squared her shoulders too.

The guard looked at them uneasily. "I don't like this one bit," he said. When he looked at the other guards for support, however, he found the rest of the guards eyeing the veterans, small smiles on their faces.

"I agree with them," another guard said, nodding his chin at Zac's group. "Why should those assholes outside be protesting against the people that served? This is like Vietnam all over again. It wasn't right then either."

The guards parted, and opened the front doors. Their hands remained on their weapons as they escorted Zac, Jimmy, Gail and Jenny outside. The protesters immediately doubled the sound of their chants, and Zac was amazed at the force of their anger. With Jimmy, Gail and Jenny surrounding her, however, she found that she also was not afraid. She stared out at the protesters defiantly, looking for someone who could have been leading the protest. To her surprise, she found that she recognized a woman in front, who was chanting the loudest. Zac marched down the stairs of the VA and spoke directly to her. "You're Travis' ma, aren't you?"

Shocked, Diana froze and eyed the blond, blue-eyed woman in front of her, whose Southern accent was obvious. "How would you know that?" she asked. "Who are you?"

"Colonel Zac Madison, United States Army."

Recognizing the name from all the times Travis, Cole and Robby had talked about her, Diana drew back a bit. All around her, the protesters quieted down to hear the confrontation. "I wasn't expecting such a high-ranking officer to be injured in the war," Diana said sarcastically. "Didn't you just sit back and give orders?"

"If you knew anything about me, you'd know that wasn't my style," Zac replied calmly, surprising herself at how cool she felt. "If you knew anything about this war, or the people that fought in it, you wouldn't be protesting here at all."

Diana glared at her. "Were these wars worth anything?" she asked. "Was it worth all the lives we lost?"

"We, ma'am?" Zac asked, glaring back. "How can you include yourself in that question, when you deliberately sent your sons to a different country to avoid the fighting?"

As if on cue, Travis rushed out of the building. In a flash, Zac realized he must have been at the VA for a meeting. "Mom," he said, shaking his head and looking embarrassed.

Diana barely glanced at her son. Under Zac's harsh gaze and words, she swallowed hard, but she stood her ground. "You military people are so sure of yourselves," she snarled. "You can't ever see what you did wrong."

"I am in good company, then," Zac snapped.

Diana shook her head. "I doubt that," she said. "Were you really in combat at all? Did you even lose anyone close to you?"

Finally, Zac's temper flared. "What the hell would you know about combat?" she yelled. "I was deployed three times, and my brother was a Marine who was killed during his second deployment! That's the pain you missed when you sent your sons away!"

"I did what any mother who cared about her children would do!" Diana shouted back. "Your mother must be unfit to call herself that!"

"You are totally out of line!" another woman from behind Zac yelled.

Zac turned to see a woman she did not know come behind up from behind her. The woman planted herself right next to Zac, and glared at Diana. Jenny, using her crutches, managed to maneuver herself onto the woman's other side. *This must be her mother*, Zac thought. *Her name is Michelle*. Michelle put her arm around Jenny's shoulders as she continued glaring at Diana. "This is my daughter," she said. "She's barely two years older than your oldest son, and she was injured in her first deployment."

Diana swallowed. She looked uncomfortable.

"How dare you protest my child's service!" Michelle continued. "Take your garbage somewhere else!"

All around them, the protesters began to back off. Diana stood angrily, not wanting to show that she had been beaten. At that moment, Travis ducked around Zac and grabbed his mother's arm. "Come on, Mom," he said. "This protest is ridiculous."

Diana glared at Travis, but she held her tongue. Zac was disappointed by that. *I would love to see that fight*, she thought.

With Travis dragging his mother away, the protest fell apart. The crowd around them dispersed. Travis shot Zac an apologetic look over his shoulder as he pushed his mother away from the VA and towards their car. Only too glad to see the protest over, Zac, Gail, Jimmy, Jenny and Michelle dispersed quickly as well, heading off in their separate directions.

As soon as Travis and Diana were in the car heading towards their house, Travis' anger exploded. "You didn't tell me you were going to the VA to protest!" he yelled. "I never would have given you a ride there if I'd known that!"

"This is my car, young man!" Diana yelled back. "I would have driven there it myself it weren't for your appointment!"

"You know I'm involved with vets' organizations and yet you're still protesting the wars!" Travis shouted. "Damn hippie liberal! Just protesting everything that comes around without ever stopping to think about the people behind it!"

Diana glared at him. "Are you my son?" she yelled. "Did I raise you to think like that or talk like that?"

"You raised me to be a good Christian who cares about other people- and that includes the wounded and the sick!"

"You're so full of it!" Diana howled.

"I think the same of you," Travis replied as he maneuvered the car into their driveway. "You totally undermine everything I've been working for."

"You're like a little boy, blinded by the fancy uniforms and the decorations!"

"That's bullshit and you know it! You know as well as anyone that I ran to Canada because there was talk of a draft! I was too scared to fight!"

By now, Travis and Diana were in their back yard, screaming at each other. Cole and Robby, hearing their raised voices, came outside. Travis and Diana looked at them. "The protest is already news online," Cole said. "A lot of people were tweeting about it too."

Robby raised his eyebrows at his mother, a smile curling at his lips. "Sounds like you spouted your liberal crap at Zac," he said. "It's too bad I missed her response."

Diana glared at him. "So now you're against me too?" she asked.

"The VA was not an appropriate place to protest, Mom," Travis said, speaking more calmly now. "I agree that the war could have been handled better, but you just misdirected your anger at people who have lost everything because they were fighting over there."

Diana looked back at Travis. "Are you out of your mind?" she asked. "That young woman who lost her leg certainly lost plenty, but Zac seems fine!"

"Did you see her burn scars or her limp?" Travis asked, as Robby and Cole nodded in agreement. "Did you see her discharge papers with an 80 percent disability rating? Did you hear any of what she said to you today, or did you miss the fact that her brother was killed in action? No, all you did was insult her mother for being a poor parent."

Finally, Diana's face showed some remorse. Robby and Cole looked slightly disgusted.

Travis sighed. "I'm glad I missed having to fight over there, and all the pain it caused," he said. "But so many people didn't fight because we have soldiers who willingly signed up to do that work instead. The least I can do is help ease their transition back home."

As she drove home a few minutes after fighting with Diana, Zac struggled to contain her anger. *Some things don't change,* she thought. *I must have been wrong about that family. I thought Travis was gaining some insight into the war and what he ran away from, but his mother certainly hasn't.*

When she got back to her house, Zac was still so angry that she had to walk around her yard several times before she started to feel her anger lessening. *This is not what I wanted to be doing with my morning,* she thought as she stared out over the yard and its flowers, which she had replanted since digging them up during her nightmare. *I actually thought it might be a good day to see if I could get any writing done on my memoirs- to see if I could even start writing something like that.*

After a few more deep breaths, however, Zac started to feel better, and as she pictured her laptop sitting in the kitchen, she started to feel more like writing. Inside, however, as soon as she was sitting at her computer with a blank screen in front of her, Zac felt the same as the screen in front of her: totally blank. *I guess I don't really know where to start,* she thought. *There are a million ways to start this thing: getting my acceptance letter to West Point, the first day of getting to the Academy, or, many years later, getting shipped off to the Middle East at the start of the war.*

Looking away from her computer screen, Zac stared outside again. *Based on what I saw online, people are interested in hearing about my experiences fighting in the war,* she thought as she watched a single leaf fall from a tree in her yard. *And I myself would have restricted myself to writing about that, except for all the stuff Alex has been asking about my childhood and time at West Point. Seeing Max and Drew again has also brought up a lot of West Point memories.*

Zac frowned. *That could be two different books,* she realized. *If there's immediate interest in the war stories, maybe that's the best place to start. If there's more interest, you could then do a second book on your time at the Academy.*

Her mind made up, Zac started taking notes on the structure of the first book, finally adding words to the blank document in front of her. *I still haven't forgotten the day I got my marching orders to head out to the Middle East,* Zac thought. *Clive came to see me off. No one expected the war to last as long as it did, nor claim so many casualties. I, too, would never have guessed then what these last ten years would have wrought.*

Zac swallowed. Looking up from her typing, she stared out the window again, the threat of unshed tears stinging her eyes. *I'm still pretty unhappy with my life right now. I wish I were in fighting shape again, and I really miss Clive.*

Turning back to her computer, Zac continued typing up her outline. When she had cobbled together something she thought she could work with, she turned off her computer. *That's enough for now,* she thought. As she had been typing, however, her memories of being deployed at the start of the war had crept up on her, and she began to wonder if she should just start writing. *I am pretty tired, though,* she thought. *I can keep thinking about it for awhile, and start writing tomorrow morning, when I'm fresher.*

She headed upstairs to take a nap, looking forward to her

bed already. She was also satisfied that she could walk up most of the stairs. *These bars are almost unnecessary now, but I think I'll keep them. Maybe I'll continue using them every once in a while, just to make sure I keep up my upper-body strength.*

No sooner had she fallen asleep than a grenade exploded two feet away. Zac was thrown nearly twenty feet with the force of the explosion. When she landed, her arm had been severed from her body, and Zac stared at her detached limb in horror as blood poured from her open wound. As she used her remaining hand to staunch the bleeding, she saw enemy soldiers rushing at her, holding machine guns.

Zac jerked awake, gasping for breath, her heart pounding. "Goddamn it," she whispered after a minute, when she finally figured out where she was. "This can't go on."

Throwing off her sheets and sitting up in bed, Zac started to wonder whether writing her memoirs was in fact a good idea. *It might just bring up more memories.* She headed downstairs and into her kitchen. As she caught sight of the clock hanging on the wall, she realized that it was four o'clock already. *I was asleep for longer than I realized. It only felt like a few minutes.*

Suddenly, the phone rang, and Zac jumped, her heart racing. *It's just the damn phone,* she told herself, and went closer to get a better look at the caller ID. The familiar number that came up made her hesitate to answer it, though. *That's Ma and Pa's phone number,* she thought. *Why would they be calling?*

Zac turned to walk away as the phone kept ringing. *There's no way I'm dealing with them again,* she thought. *But what if it's Ben?* she wondered. "Hello?" she said into the receiver.

"So I finally got you to pick up the phone," her mother said on the other end.

"To what do I owe the pleasure?" Zac asked sarcastically.

"Oh, come on, Zac," Linda replied, her voice shuddering.

Zac could tell she was crying. "What's going on?" she asked.

"Your father's dead."

"What?" Zac felt shockwaves course through her body. Her blood felt like it was rising in her face.

"Heart attack. The coroner's already pronounced."

"I'm sorry," Zac replied.

"Do you think you could come in?" Linda said. "I could use some help with the funeral arrangements."

"I've been back from Iraq for months now, injured and in pain, and you didn't once call to see how I was doing!" Zac yelled at her mother. "You only call when you need something, huh?"

"That's not fair!" Linda said, and Zac could tell that she was really crying now.

Then Zac could hear someone taking the phone away from Linda, and Ben got on. "Don't worry, Abe and I can make the arrangements," he said. "But I do think you should at least come in for the funeral itself."

"Why?" Zac asked.

"Oh come on, Zac," Ben said. "I know Pa was a pain in the ass, but maybe this gives you a shot at moving on."

"I thought West Point would do that."

"That was a long time ago, and a lot has happened since then. This is definitely a final ending."

"You don't know what it was like, Ben! Ma and Pa lost custody of us for a whole year before you were born!"

"Sounds like West Point didn't fully help you move on from all of it," Ben said. He sighed. "And it wasn't much of a picnic growing up here for me either, especially once you and Clive left the house."

Zac took a deep breath and looked outside to the green grass and bright sunshine in her yard. "You're right," she said finally. "Let me know what the arrangements are, and I'll come in."

Even so, as soon as she hung up, an intense despair washed over her. *I can't do this anymore,* she realized. *I really can't go back and see them all again. I'll never get out of there.* She took a breath, thinking once more of the handgun in her bedroom. *That would certainly end things once and for all.*

Tears rolled down her face. *No, I can't bring myself to do that just yet,* she thought. Instead, she eyed her liquor cabinet, thinking of the bottles within it. *Fine, I'll do that instead,* she thought, ignoring the little voice inside her head that said, *you're going to end up like Pa. If Clive were alive, he'd stop me. Clive isn't alive anymore,* she thought. So, she headed upstairs, bringing several bottles with her because she could not decide what she wanted.

Two hours later, Drew arrived at Zac's house for their prearranged dinner. He parked his car in front of the house, rang the bell and waited. There was no answer. Drew frowned. *That's strange,* he thought. *She has to be here. We just confirmed the time this morning. Besides, her car's still in the driveway.* He went around to the back of the house to see if Zac was in the back yard, but the yard was empty. Looking up at the second story of the house, he saw a light on in one of the rooms upstairs. The window of the same room was open, despite the heat. *So she is home,* he thought, and rang the bell at the back door. Still, Zac did not come down.

Drew felt his stomach clench. *Something's the matter,* he thought, feeling certain about it. *What do I do?* Taking a deep breath, he tried the back door, but it was locked. So was the front door. Drew thought of the all the alcohol he had seen in Zac's trunk, and of the gun he knew she owned. His knees shaking, he sat down on the front stoop. *What do I do now?* he wondered. After a minute, he pulled out his cell phone. *I hate to have to call Max about this,* he thought. *He and Zac have definitely been becoming closer than I've been able to get with her. But I really have no other ideas.*

Max answered after two rings. "Hello?" he said.

"Max, it's Drew."

"Everything alright?"

"I don't think so," Drew said. "Zac and I were supposed to have dinner together, but I'm over at her house, ringing her bell, and she's not answering. But her car's still here, and there are lights on in the house."

"Are you sure she's not out back?"

"Yeah, I already looked."

"Did you just get in from Little Rock?"

"Yeah," Drew said. "What's that have to do with-"

"Those anti-war protestors made a big scene outside the VA today, including the boy-banders' mother," Max interrupted. "Zac got into a fight with her. It made the news."

Drew bit his lip. "That can't help Zac at all. She's really starting to care about those musicians."

"Yes, she does."

"Great."

"And yet, Zac can hold her own in a fight, no matter who it's with."

"I'd be less concerned if she weren't drinking so much."

"What?" Max said, sounding more concerned now. "What do you mean?"

Drew told him about all of the alcohol he had seen in Zac's trunk when she had been in Little Rock.

"How do you even know that was for her?" Max asked. "She could have been going to a party."

"Her parents are major alcoholics," Drew said. "They even lost custody of Zac and her siblings for a year until they dried out."

"Oh man," Max sighed.

"Do you have a key to her house?"

"I do. There's also a spare one buried in the soil of one of the flower pots out front."

Drew shook his head. "I don't think I can do this alone," he said. *Especially not if Zac's made use of her gun.*

"Alright," Max said. "I'll be right over." He pulled on his shoes and looked at his puppy. "Come on, Blackie," he said. "It's not that long a drive out there. Let's see what's going on." Half an hour later, he pulled up outside Zac's house to see Drew still sitting on the front stoop. "Anything new?" he asked as he got out of his truck, Blackie on his heels.

Drew shook his head. He was holding the key he had found in the flowerpot, but he had not been able to bring himself to use it.

Without hesitating, Max pulled his key to Zac's house out of his pocket and went to the front door. Drew followed him. Max stuck the key into the lock and turned the doorknob. He pushed the door open and stepped inside. When both Blackie and Drew were inside with him, Max closed the door behind him. Then he and Drew looked around. It was quiet. "Zac?" Max said.

There was no answer. Quietly, Max went into the living room, and then to the bottom of the stairs that led to the house's second story. Drew followed him silently. There was light coming from the upstairs, obvious in the gathering gloom of the evening. "It's hot in here," Max mouthed to Drew.

Drew nodded in agreement, his face screwed up in doubt.

Taking a deep breath, Max silently crept up the stairs while Drew remained frozen on the first step.

Inside her bedroom, Zac lay on her bed, her chest heavy from all the alcohol she had consumed. *I'm kind of hungry, but I don't feel like moving enough to get up and have dinner,* she thought. Instead, she twirled her handgun around her fingers. *This is no way to live,* she realized. *I really ought to end this once and for all.* She removed the safety lock on the gun. Then she heard a sound from outside the room.

"Zac?" Max said from the top of the stairs.

Someone's in the house, Zac realized, her heart racing, her breath coming in gasps. She swung her legs over the side of her bed and crept towards the doorway, gun cocked. In the semi-darkness of the hallway, she saw a person on the stairs and aimed without hesitation.

Max threw himself down. Drew, still at the bottom of the stairs, ducked and threw his hands over his head. "Don't shoot!" Max yelped.

Blackie raced up to Zac, stood on his hind legs, and put his front paws on her knees.

Zac lowered the gun. "Blackie!" she said. "Max! I almost killed you! What are you doing here? I thought you were an intruder." She turned on a lamp in the hallway. Then she saw Drew. "Oh my God, Drew! We were supposed to have dinner together! I totally forgot!"

Finally able to see more clearly in the light of the lamp, Max willed his heart rate to slow down. "Drew called me when he couldn't get a hold of you," he said, pulling himself to his feet. He eyed the gun. Then he eyed Zac. Behind him, Drew had finally made his way up the stairs and was also looking at Zac uncomfortably.

"Don't worry," Zac said. "I'm not going to shoot you."

"You almost did," Max said.

"Yeah, well, you're in my house unannounced. I'd have been well within my rights to shoot you, and if you were anyone else, you'd be dead right now." She went back to her room and started putting the gun away.

Only when he could hear a drawer closing, presumably with the gun inside, did Max creep forward to the doorway of her bedroom. Drew followed him, and they looked around. Drew inhaled sharply, and Max swallowed hard, when they saw various liquor bottles around- a bottle of whiskey, a bottle of bourbon, and a few others. Most were empty or close to it. When they looked at Zac, her face was bright red and heat seemed to emanate from her.

Zac saw them looking at her. "What?" she asked.

His anger flaring, Max raced towards her and grabbed her.

"Stop!" Zac yelled. "What are you doing?"

Hooking his hand under her armpit and forcefully closing his fingers around her upper arm, Max dragged Zac into the nearest bathroom.

"Max," Drew said, holding up his hand. Max ignored him.

Zac struggled. "Stop!" she yelled again. "You're hurting me!"

Ignoring her protests, Max turned on the cold water in the shower on to full blast and pushed Zac under it. He held her there until she was soaking wet and shivering. Blackie whined in the doorway. Drew stood behind the dog, watching with horror. Max, seeing an empty glass next to the sink, grabbed it, filled it with water, and put it aside. He pulled Zac, who was no longer struggling, from the shower and handed her the cup.

"Drink this!" he said.

Zac gulped it down.

"Slowly!" Max ordered. He took the glass from her, refilled it at the sink, and handed it back to her.

Zac took the glass, but instead of drinking from it again, she stood staring at him, soaking wet and shivering. "What the hell was that about?" she demanded.

"You have to sober up," he said.

"And if I don't?" she asked.

"You will." Max left the bathroom.

Zac put down the glass of water and grabbed a small towel before following him. Drew stepped aside to let her through. By then, Max was on his way downstairs. "Where are you going?" Zac asked Max.

"To the kitchen to make dinner," he said. "I haven't had any yet."

Hearing his anger, Zac let him go. Drew went into the bathroom and pulled a huge towel from the closet. "Here," he said, handing it to Zac. He eyed her as she took it. Then he looked back into her bedroom at all of the empty liquor bottles.

Zac looked unhappy. "Why don't you go to the kitchen with Max?" she suggested. "I need to change my clothes."

For a moment, Drew hesitated, and Zac worried that he was going to stand there and watch her undress. His eyes remained on her face, shooting bullets of sadness in her direction. Then he turned and went downstairs.

With Blackie sitting in the doorway and staring at her with large, wet eyes, Zac dried off and changed her clothes. Then she brushed her hair out. When she looked down, Blackie was still waiting for her in the doorway. "Hi, cutie," she said, bending down to pet him. "I'm sorry about all of this."

"Woof!" the dog responded.

Just then, Zac smelled something good coming from the kitchen. *Could they have started cooking something so quickly?* she wondered. As if reading her mind, Blackie raced for the stairs, and Zac followed him. By the time they got to the kitchen, Zac had identified the smell as belonging to the beef stew she had made the day before. *Max must have found the leftovers and is heating them up,* she thought.

Max and Drew looked at her as she walked into the kitchen. "Better?" Max asked.

"A little." Zac went to the sink and filled another glass with water, not wanting to acknowledge how far away she still was from sobriety. "I think I'm still going to have to lie down again, though."

Max glared at her. Drew's sad eyes remained fixed on her as well.

"I'm sorry," she said finally.

"Why didn't you call us to say that something was wrong?" Max asked.

"You were at work," Zac said to Max. She looked at Drew. "And you were travelling. Besides, I forgot that you were coming over."

"You're more important than our jobs," Drew said.

"That's not true."

"Yes, it is," Max said emphatically.

Zac looked away uncomfortably. When she looked back at Max, he was still looking at her, his gaze unwavering. "How did you even know to come here?" she asked finally.

"Drew called me. He thought something was the matter."

Zac looked back at Drew. "I'm sorry that I forgot about dinner," she said.

"I wish you'd called me," Drew said.

"I *forgot,*" Zac said.

"I heard about your fight with the anti-war protestors this morning," Drew said.

Zac rolled her eyes. "That woman's sons may get it, but she sure doesn't."

"Still, I've never seen you stay that angry that long," Max said. "Did something else happen after that?"

Zac sighed. "My mom called. Pa died."

Max's eyebrows jumped. Drew frowned. "I'm sorry," they both said.

"I'm not. He was an ass."

Drew heaved a breath. "I knew your family," he said. "I know what it was like for you growing up. Maybe this will be a relief for you eventually, but it's still gotta be painful for you now."

Zac clenched her teeth.

"When's the funeral?" Max asked.

"Saturday. My brothers are making all the arrangements, thankfully, so I don't have to do anything. My mom only called me before because she wanted me to arrange everything- even though she hasn't called me once since I got home from the hospital."

"We didn't say it wasn't dysfunctional, Zac," Drew said. "But if going to the funeral would help put your whole family situation behind you, maybe it's worth it."

"That's what Ben said."

"Maybe he's right," Max said. "What's happening to your mother now that your dad's gone?"

"I have no idea," Zac said. "All of this just happened this afternoon."

"Well, maybe going back would help you and your siblings get her squared away too," Max replied. "Then you really would have less to worry about."

Zac shrugged, and both men could tell she was unconvinced.

"Would it help if I went to the funeral?" Drew asked. "I was thinking of going anyway."

Zac shrugged again. "Up to you."

"Well, I need to be back in Little Rock on Thursday, but I could easily be in Bearden on Saturday."

"Do you want me to drive to Bearden from here with you?" Max asked.

"And see all the shit I put up with growing up?" Zac answered. "No way!"

"We wouldn't have to stay at your parents' place," Max said. "We could stay at a hotel. If the funeral's on Saturday, we could leave on Friday after I get off from work- the same thing

Ben does when he visits here."

Zac shrugged. "Maybe," she said.

"Well, think about it," Max said. He stirred the stew again and watched as it bubbled. "This is almost ready. You feel like eating?"

"Not really."

"Well, it looks pretty good. Maybe you should make some room."

Zac put out three place settings at the table. "It was good when I made it yesterday," she said. "It was one of the few things my mother cooked well- and only because it was based off my grandmother's recipe."

"The grandmother that lived here?" Max asked as they sat down to eat.

Zac nodded. "My mother was from here originally before she ran off to Little Rock, where she met my dad. Luckily, my grandparents actually had their shit together- it's why we lived with them for a year when my parents lost custody of us."

The next morning, Zac awoke lying on her side with Max lying behind her, his arm curled around her stomach. Instantly she thought of the hook he wore. *It's on his other hand,* she realized, but she had to think about it to be certain. Swallowing her feelings of guilt, Zac sat up and swung her legs over the side of the bed.

"Ah, you're finally awake," Max said from behind her. Zac turned around to look at him and realized that he must have gotten up earlier and returned to bed- he was already dressed in his regular clothes.

"No work today?" she asked.

Max shook his head as he sat up. "I called in sick." Zac started to object, but Max stopped her. "It's fine," he said.

"Where's Drew?"

"He slept in the next room, but he had a business meeting he had to go to, so he left already."

"That meeting was the only reason he was in the area," Zac said. She shook her head. "I've made such a mess of things."

"No, you haven't," Max said firmly. "And Drew comes here partially to see you, too."

Still feeling guilty, Zac stood up. Then she realized that Blackie was curled up at the end of the bed, still asleep. Zac looked at the puppy and her lower slip curled out in sympathy.

"He likes you," Max said. "He spent the whole night sleeping there."

"Awwww," Zac said.

Downstairs, as they ate breakfast, Max stared out over the open land in front of them. "Do you still like it out here in the 'burbs?" Zac teased.

"Oh, this is past the 'burbs," Max said. "This is totally rural farmland."

Zac made a face at him.

"I am right, though," Max said.

"Unfortunately, my grandfather did use this place as a farm."

"No unfortunately about it. This place looks very different from the urban blight of my childhood, and not in a bad way."

"It's still not what I would've chosen for myself," Zac said. "I never thought I'd end up back here."

Max looked at her. "Sometimes, you gotta be grateful for what you have," he said. "This is an incredible place, and your grandfather just left it to you."

"I am grateful for it," Zac said. "It's just not where I wanted to be at this point in my life." She stared out the window again, pushing her fork around her empty plate unconsciously as she did so. "Grandpa and Grandma were always supportive of me." She looked back at Max. "Did you know they came to my graduation from West Point instead of my parents?"

"No, I didn't," Max replied.

Zac nodded. "Clive came too, driving up from the Naval Academy in his dress uniform." She smiled at the memory. "I had to fight some of the West Point cadets off of him." She and Max laughed.

"I remember Clive coming to visit a couple of times before I graduated," Max said. "He was a good kid. You always sent him home with a few bags of food."

"Because there was never enough food at home," Zac said.

Max sighed. "I wish you hadn't had it so rough," he said. "My family was poor, but at least they were they for me."

"Yeah, I remember your family came down when you graduated."

"Did you know that my mom remembered meeting you too?" Max asked. "I spoke to her a few days after we first met up again. She remembered meeting you at graduation and one other time my family visited."

"Really?" Zac asked.

Max nodded. "You must have made an impression on her."

They were silent for awhile as they cleaned up the dishes and pots. Finally, Zac broke the silence by saying, "I'm really sorry about last night."

"Drinking is not the answer," Max told her.

"I know that."

"How long has that been going on?"

"Since I moved here."

Max shook his head. "You need to get help for that."

Zac groaned. "More meetings? More therapy?"

"Whatever it takes," Max replied. "I went through that stage myself. It's not fun. The sooner you get through it, the sooner you can move on with your life. Talk to Alex about it. I'm sure she has some recommendations."

Zac grimaced. There was another silence as they continued cleaning up the kitchen. Then Max said, "so, Zac, there was something else I wanted to discuss with you."

Zac eyed him, wondering what was coming next.

"When I moved down here, I signed a six-month lease on my apartment because I didn't think I'd be there longer than that- my job wasn't extended until after I'd started. But anyway, my lease ends at the end of August."

"Right when we have to testify at Victor Rice's trial."

Max nodded. "I'm hoping to have new housing arrangements set up before we fly out to Washington."

"Do you want to stay here?" Zac asked.

"Are you willing to have me?" Max replied. "Blackie is part of the deal."

"I know that," Zac said. "I wouldn't be offering if I weren't willing to have you both."

"Well, thanks. I appreciate that."

CHAPTER 13

Six months after Clive's death, Eric Johnson's unit was deployed back to Afghanistan. Six months after that, Zac's unit was deployed back to Iraq. *Our third deployments,* Zac thought. *Unbelievable.*

By then, she and Eric were back on speaking terms- he had apologized profusely, but Zac still was not sure she trusted him. *I still like him,* she thought, almost smiling as she thought back to the crush she had had on him back at West Point. *But I don't know that I could ever go back to feeling the way I felt about him when we were at the Academy.*

Nearly two years later, Zac was still in Iraq and had just gotten back from patrol when an Army helicopter landed on base. General Jim Conrad and several junior officers exited from the chopper, and Zac stood at attention as they entered the base. Lt. Colonel Matt Edwards stood next to her, also at attention. "At ease," Conrad said. Then he looked at Zac. "Colonel Madison, I need a report from your patrol, and I also have some news for you."

"Yes, sir," Zac replied, and together they went into the base.

Inside the small makeshift office she had been using, Conrad closed the door behind them, making Zac slightly nervous. "How was your patrol?" he asked. "What have you been learning?"

He spoke normally, and Zac relaxed ever so slightly. "The patrol was fine- no harassment or anything," she said. "We've been gathering intelligence on the terrorist network here, and we think they're based in one or more of the abandoned factories two miles from here."

"So the factories may not be that abandoned."

"No, we think that clearing out the workers for their own safety was just a cover so that the terrorists could have a meeting spot."

"When you're sure, gather your best men together and hit those factories as hard as you can," Conrad ordered.

"My thoughts exactly, sir," Zac said with a smile.

Conrad eyed her for a second. He did not smile back.

Zac became nervous again, and the walls of the small office seemed to close in on her. Taking her eyes off Conrad, she turned on the small lamp on her desk. "So, what was the news you said you had?"

Conrad looked unhappy. "Listen, Zac, I'm sorry to have to tell you this, but there was an attack on our base in Kabul three days ago."

"Kabul?" Zac said, her heart rate doubling. "Eric Johnson is stationed there! Is he alright?"

Conrad swallowed. "No, unfortunately, he was killed."

"Fuck!" Zac slammed her fists down on the desk in front of her.

"I'm so sorry. I know you guys were close."

"What happened?" Zac asked, as her eyes stung with tears.

"One of the Afghani policemen we were training walked into the mess hall with a bomb strapped to his torso."

Zac shook her head as her tears ran down her face. "We can't trust the local population. I've been feeling that way for awhile. They don't want us there- or here." She wiped her face with the back of her hand.

"I'm sorry," Conrad said again, and Zac heard the helplessness in his voice. "I, too, have wondered about our progress in both places."

Zac clenched her teeth as she looked at him. *That's not a vote of confidence.* "Has Eric's family been informed? What's happening with… his body?"

"Yes, his family's been informed. His body is being returned home for burial." Conrad took a deep breath. "Listen, Zac, there's one more thing. Our computer techs went through Eric's emails, to see if he'd gotten any threats or anything."

Great, Zac thought, remembering all of the intimate emails they had exchanged. *Now the whole Army knows we slept together.*

"There was an unsent email in his Drafts folder that I thought you should have." Conrad put the folder he was carrying on the desk and extracted a sheet of paper, which he held out to Zac.

Zac hesitated, then took it.

"I'm sorry to bring you this type of news, Zac, especially given that I now have to get back to Kabul."

"I understand, sir," Zac said, feeling like the words were emanating from a robot rather than from her body. "I'll walk you back to the chopper."

"Make sure you read that," Conrad told her.

"I will, sir," Zac promised. Even so, it was several hours later, closer to dinnertime, before she plucked up the courage to go back into her office and read the missive that Conrad had given her.

"Dear Zac," the email began. "Our deployments are almost over and I am looking forward to getting home and getting on with my life. After nearly twenty years in the military and three deployments in two wars that we cannot win, I've begun thinking of separating from the military once my time here in Kabul ends. I only have two months left in this deployment, and lately I've been counting down the days until that plane comes to take me home.

"I've also begun thinking about what my life might look like after my service is over. My siblings have all married and started families, even the ones who are younger than me. The same is true of so many of our comrades, especially the ones we went to the Academy with- many of our classmates were

207

married by the time we graduated or very soon thereafter. I feel like I've fallen behind.

"For years now, I've told myself that I wasn't marriage material, or that training for the Olympics or for the Army precluded family life. Then I told myself that repeated deployments were not conducive to that either. Yet, when I look around, everyone else is juggling the two in some way or another. As I've thought about it, I've realized that I've been interested in you since we attended West Point together- I've just been avoiding admitting it. I mean that honestly, even if you don't believe me.

"I know how much I hurt you the last time we saw each other, but I'm hoping that we've done some work in moving past that. If we both survive this deployment, please give me another chance when we get home."

Zac put down the piece of paper, glad that the door in front of her was closed, despite the fact that the walls of the small room seemed to close in around her. Tears rolled down her face, and Zac felt powerless to stop them. *What a waste*, she thought. *What a waste of a good life, and the possibility of a good future. That's what 16 years of not being able to communicate with each other will do.*

She flipped over the piece of paper and stared at the blank white of its back. Then she stared at the blank white of the walls around her. *I wish I could've escorted Eric's body back,* she thought. *It's too bad I'm not in his unit.* She clenched her teeth. *There's also so much work to be done here. Jim was right- we're not winning this war.*

*   *   *

Inside the small office with the flowered wallpaper, Alex watched as Zac sat down on the other side of her desk. "So," Alex said. "I hear you're having alcohol trouble."

"How'd you hear that?"

208

"Max called me," Alex said honestly, seeing no reason not to cut to the chase.

"Damn him!" Zac exclaimed.

"What were you expecting?" Alex replied. "Were you expecting him to do nothing?"

"I guess."

"He also told me about your father. I'm sorry about that."

"I'm not."

Alex eyed her. "Perhaps it would be better if you were. Are you going to the funeral?"

"I haven't decided."

"You should go. It may offer you some closure."

"That's what Max, Drew and Ben said."

"Perhaps you should listen." There was a silence that Alex broke by saying, "Max and Drew care about you, Zac."

"I know that. Like I told you, we go way back, to a different time in our lives."

"It's more than that, Zac. If you'd been in the same class at West Point, your lives would have run more parallel, rather than just intersecting now."

"Like I said, fraternization among cadets was frowned upon."

"Are you even listening to me?" Alex asked.

"I am," Zac said with a sigh. "It sounds like my life could have been very different."

Alex nodded. "It sounds like your interest in Max, at least, was reciprocated, even way back when you were at the Academy. And Drew has always kept an eye on you."

Zac sighed and looked away. "So why now?" she asked. "Max was married pretty soon after he graduated. So was Drew."

"Max, at least, divorced pretty quickly," Alex said. "And Drew is divorced now too. Sometimes, these things happen for a reason. You're lucky they were there when you needed them."

Zac shook her head. "I think Drew was too scared to come in by himself."

"What do you mean?" Alex asked, and Zac could tell she genuinely had not heard the full story.

"I was supposed to have Drew over for dinner, but I forgot about it. He came to my house and thought something was wrong. He called Max and they both came in to find me."

"Hhhmm," Alex said. "Max didn't tell me that part. That's interesting. For awhile now, I've thought that both men were romantically interested in you."

Zac crossed her arms and stared sullenly at the floor. Tears gathered in her eyes. *I really don't deserve either of them,* she thought.

"What are you thinking?" Alex asked. Zac said nothing. "I really want you to pull through this, Zac, and I'm not the only one."

They stared at each other for a minute. Then Zac looked away as tears started running down her face. Alex came around from behind her desk and handed Zac a box of tissues. Then she sat in the empty chair next to her. There was a moment of silence.

"Are you still keeping a journal for your group therapy?" Alex said.

"I was for awhile, but I filled up all the notebooks I had, and I didn't feel like buying more."

Alex got up and went to one of the cabinets in her office. She pulled out two notebooks and a couple of pens- a purple and a blue one- and handed them all to Zac.

Zac took them. "What should I write?" she asked. "That I'm a hopeless loser who doesn't deserve to live through this shit?"

"Do you really feel that way?" Alex asked, sitting back down next to Zac.

"Sometimes," Zac admitted.

"Sometimes?"

"Most of the time."

"I think nothing could be further from the truth," Alex said.

Zac shrugged and looked away.

"I know the group therapy usually has you start slowly with what you write, because having the trauma come back all at once is not healthy," Alex said. "But eventually, dealing with the heavy stuff helps you heal."

"I've written about some of the heavy stuff already," Zac admitted.

"Maybe continuing with that would help."

"Alright," Zac said finally. "I'll give it a shot."

That night, Drew called Zac while he was on his way back to Little Rock. "I'm doing better," she said. "How was your meeting?"

"The meeting was fine," Drew said. "That's not what I'm concerned about. Are you going to be alright alone in your house?"

"I'm not alone. Max is here." There was a silence on the other end, and Zac frowned. *Maybe I shouldn't have said that,* she thought. *I think Alex is right and he is interested in me. It can't be easy for him to have Max here instead of him.*

"Well, I'm glad someone is keeping an eye on you," Drew said finally. "It really isn't possible to get through all this stuff alone."

"I've never felt completely alone," Zac said. "Ben has always checked in on me, and my psychologist and group therapy are here."

"I know," Drew said. "But it's not the same as having family living with you or right nearby." He paused for a moment. "Have you ever thought of moving to Little Rock, closer to Ben, at least? You would be welcome here."

"I know," Zac said. "And having you and Ben there would make it easier. But I just don't want to be in this area anymore."

A few minutes later, Max watched with approval as Zac emptied the contents of her liquor cabinet, first pouring the contents of the bottles into the kitchen sink, and then tossing the empty bottles into a large plastic garbage bag. "Way to go," he said.

"I don't know," Zac replied. "All I can think about right now is how much money I spent buying all this stuff, and that I'm just pouring it down the drain."

"You're doing the right thing," Max reassured her as she tied up the garbage bag.

"This from the guy who called my therapist to tell her what happened," Zac said. She rolled her eyes as she hauled the garbage bag out the front door and out to her large green garbage cans outside.

"That was the right thing too," Max said, following her.

Outside, Zac pulled the lid off of one of the garbage cans and tossed the bag inside. "I sure hope so," she replied as she walked back to the house.

Back in the kitchen, Max put his arm around her. "You'll feel better about it as time goes on," he said.

"If I can keep it up," Zac said.

"You will," Max said.

Zac ducked away from him and walked over to the window. For a minute, she stared outside, into the deepening twilight. Then she looked back at Max. "I really do appreciate all you've done for me," she said. "You've been an anchor when I've been floundering."

"It hasn't been a burden," Max said. "I always thought you had a straight inner compass."

"Not recently," Zac admitted. "I've gone off course. I've gotten lost."

"Well, I'm glad to be here for you," Max replied. He opened his arms, and this time, Zac felt comfortable returning his hug.

Slowly, Zac came awake, thinking it was the middle of the night and wondering what had woken her. She looked at her clock. *Oh, it's 0500 already,* she realized. *Definitely not the middle of the night like it usually is when I wake up.*

Rolling over and looking at the window, she could see the gray light that heralded the approaching dawn, even through the closed blinds. The sound of a couple of birds singing reached her ears. *It's almost daytime, and I actually got a decent night's sleep,* she realized.

Then she heard the toilet flush in the nearest bathroom and realized that Max must have gotten up. *Maybe that's what woke me,* she thought as he came back into the room.

"I didn't mean to wake you up," Max whispered when he saw that her eyes were open.

"I'm not sure you did," Zac replied.

Max looked over at the clock as he curled up next to her and put his arm around her. "I might go out for a run before I go to work," he said. "But you should go back to sleep."

"You're so lucky," she said. *I wish I could still run.*

"Don't worry, you'll get there soon enough," Max said, as if he had read her mind. "Just keep up with the physical therapy. The swimming is helping too, isn't it?"

Zac nodded. "It's still not the same, though."

"I know," Max replied. After a few minutes, he did indeed get up and reach for his running clothes. By then, Zac was drifting off to sleep again.

The following Friday night, Zac met Max at the factory after work, and they headed towards Bearden. Max took over the driving after it got dark. Zac had hoped to sleep as he drove, but instead she found herself leaning up against the car door, staring wakefully at the scenery around them.

"You okay over there?" Max asked.

"I don't know," Zac said. "I just want this to be over."

The next morning, Drew followed Zac and Max to the cemetery. They arrived a few minutes early and stood outside Drew's car, talking. When the rest of Zac's family followed the hearse in, Max eyed their cars with interest. Ben was driving a small sedan with their mother in front. Behind them, Abe and Melanie were driving beat up vans with their spouses in the front seats next to them and their kids in the back.

Drew watched Melanie as she parked her van. "How many kids does Melanie have now?" he asked.

"Seven," Zac replied.

"Wow," Drew said.

"Abe has five," Zac added as her siblings and their families poured out of their respective vehicles. She watched Drew as he watched Melanie, seeing her for the first time in nearly twenty years, seeing how much heavier she had become, how much older she looked. *Seven kids and countless bottles of alcohol will age you pretty decently,* Zac thought.

In front of Melanie and Abe, Ben was getting out of his car, but their mother remained seated in the passenger seat, not moving. "Oh, come on, Ma," Zac said under her breath, and went to open the car door for her mother.

When Linda looked up at Zac through the open door, her eyes were red and tears were running down her face. Even with the door open, she sat for a minute without moving before finally swinging her legs over the side of the car and getting up unsteadily. Her hands shook, and Zac surmised that her eyes were red from more than her tears. *She couldn't have started drinking already,* Zac thought. *It's only ten in the morning.* Then she shook her head at herself. *That's what it was like at home, she thought. You've just been trying to forget. If Ma and Pa weren't drunk by noon, it was a miracle.* She glanced back at her older siblings. *They don't look like they've started drinking yet, but from what Ben has told me, they're as good at it as Ma and Pa are.*

After Zac had introduced Max around, she, Ben, Drew and Max dropped back as Abe and Linda went inside the funeral home to finish the necessary paperwork. "So Ma said it was a heart attack?" Zac said to Ben.

"Yeah, the autopsy confirmed it," Ben said. "Heart attack from heavy duty drinking over the course of so many years. If it hadn't been the heart attack, though, his liver would have gone out in a couple of months anyway."

Zac shook her head. "I gotta not go out like that," she said.

When the funeral itself started, Linda sobbed loudly, and Ben put his arm around her. Zac felt the sting of unshed tears against her eyes, *but I'm not sure it's for the life that just ended,* she thought. *There is some relief that it's over. I think I'm just pained that my own life is such a goddamned mess right now.* It was only Max's comforting hand at her back, and Drew's tight clutch around her hand, that made her tears overflow at all. *It's the kindness that undoes me,* she realized. *I'm better at being stoic through the pain.*

As the service ended, Zac glanced over at her older siblings. They, too, had been crying and were being comforted by their families. Once more, Zac felt the hole that Clive's death had left. *There should have been at least one more person here, if not a whole other family,* she thought. *Victor Rice was right in protesting the wars and all the useless deaths they caused.*

When the funeral was over, the family went back to Linda's farm, and Max was given his first glimpse of the place Zac had once called home. The house itself was run down, and Max could see the broken windows and caving-in roof with just a glance. A second look showed how unsteady the placed looked as a whole. *A few of the house's support beams must be rotting,* Max thought. *I wouldn't be surprised if the whole house collapses at some point.*

Inside, Melanie helped her mother get into bed, and Zac and her siblings gathered around the kitchen table as her nieces and nephews played outside. Max and Drew each took seats next to Zac, and they sat quietly. Zac, Ben, Max and Drew drank sodas, but Melanie and Abe had few qualms about digging into alcoholic beverages with gusto, despite the early hour. Abe favored a cheap whiskey, and Melanie enjoyed a large box of white wine. Max and Drew watched as Abe and Melanie went through one drink, and then another, as the siblings sat around in silence. Abe's wife June sat next to him, playing with some food without really eating it.

"I'm surprised you would make it out here for the funeral, Drewdy," Melanie said finally.

Zac was surprised to hear her use the nickname she had

only ever heard Drew's mother use. *They definitely slept together,* she decided, remembering how evasive Drew had been when she had asked him.

"We go back a long way, Mel," Drew replied. "Our families have known each other for a long time."

"Did you come because Zac's here?" Melanie asked him.

She's jealous, Zac thought disbelievingly. *But I guess Drew's interest in me is obvious. I can't quite give up on Max, though.*

"I came because of both of you," Drew said. "I knew your parents while we were growing up too. There's a lot of history there."

At least he's diplomatic, Zac thought. There was another silence. "Ma doesn't seem to be doing too well," Zac said finally.

"Welcome to Earth, Zac," Abe said. "I know you've been off fighting, but we've had a different battle here at home."

"I can't believe Ma was crying as much as she was," Melanie added as she drained her wine glass again. "She wanted Pa dead most of the time, and now she finally got it."

"Mel," Ben said reproachfully.

"It's true," Melanie said.

"Ma always drank as much as Pa did," Zac said, "and now that he's gone, I don't see how she can run this place without him."

"We've been discussing what to about that for some time now," Abe admitted. "They haven't been able to run this place well for years. June and I have been thinking of selling our own farm and buying this one instead."

"Really?" Zac asked.

Abe nodded. "It's a bigger farm with more crops growing on it."

"Are the blueberry bushes still on the edge of the property?" Zac asked.

"Yes," Abe said with a smile. "You interested in coming back and managing them?"

"No way."

"Aw, come on Zac, you're unemployed."

"Not that unemployed," Zac said, bristling slightly. Both Max and Drew bit their lips. Ben also looked uncomfortable.

"You don't think you could pick berries with your leg like that?" Abe said. "Or are you just too good for it now?"

"Shut up," Zac said.

"We may have to rebuild this house before we could move onto the property," June said, trying to change the subject, "but we think it would be worth it."

"What about Ma?" Zac asked.

Abe and Melanie looked at each other, and Zac could tell they had discussed that too. "She'd stay here," Melanie said. "We can't see her being willing to move. But if she is, she could also stay with my family."

"You'd be willing to have her around your kids?" Zac asked.

"What are you saying?" Abe said. "She raised all of us."

"Poorly," Zac replied.

Abe and Melanie glared at their sister. "You really do think you're better than us," Abe said.

"No, I don't," Zac said. "It's just not something I would choose for my kids."

"You're too fucked up to have kids," Melanie said.

"Screw you," Zac replied, her eyes flashing. "You're not winning any mother of the year awards."

"If you're willing to put Ma in some kind of old age home, then you're welcome to pay for it," Abe cut in. "You sure must be rich enough."

"That's crap and you know it," Zac replied. "I haven't been able to work in months."

"But the government's paying your way, right?" Melanie said bitterly. "Just like it paid for your West Point education."

"Mel," Drew said uncomfortably. "It's not like that."

"Seriously," Zac added. "The paperwork and bureaucracy involved with getting my benefits have been a fucking nightmare."

"That's certainly true," Max said.

"Whatever," Abe said, sounding just as bitter as Melanie

had. "While you've been living on the government dole, we've had to actually work to raise our kids."

"Not true!" Zac yelled. "Not true! I deployed three times! We got shot at or were near a suicide bomber almost every day, each of those three times. Don't tell me what it's like to work for a living!"

"You can't possibly know what it's like to go to war," Max agreed.

"It's a nightmare," Drew added.

"A bunch of high-ranking officers?" Melanie said. "You guys probably just hid in the back."

Zac sprang up and whacked her sister across the face. "Do you know how tired I am of hearing that!" she yelled. "We didn't get injured by hiding behind our troops! You never even asked what happened the night my convoy was hit!"

Behind Zac, Max and Drew were already standing, and Ben was slowly getting to his feet, looking nervous. Abe remained seated, looking amused.

Melanie got to her feet unsteadily. When she was standing, she swung at Zac, aiming more at her midsection than her face. Zac grabbed her sister's arm and used it to twist her whole body around. In a second, Melanie was on the floor and howling with pain.

That was enough for Abe. He jumped to his feet and sent his fist into Zac's nose. Blood poured down her face. In an instant, Drew was grabbing Abe and pulling him away. Zac swung back at her older brother's face, and her fist connected with a satisfying crack. Melanie remained on the floor, whimpering. Zac gave Melanie an extra kick, and when Abe swung his arm at her, she grabbed his hand and twisted his fingers. They, too, cracked, and Abe yanked his hand back, howling in pain.

"What the fuck's the matter with you?" Abe yelled as Drew pulled him away from his sister. "You should have died in that convoy, not your underlings!"

Zac lunged at her brother, but Max pulled her away, all the way to the other side of the room. Abe howled in pain as Drew held him tightly and squeezed his broken fingers. Ben grabbed some paper towels and applied them to Zac's nose to stop the bleeding as Max got her some ice. Then both Max and Drew kept an eye on Zac as they stood in between her and her siblings. Abe glared at both of them.

"Don't even think about coming after her again," Max told him.

The next morning, Drew came over to Zac's hotel room early enough to make sure he saw her before she left for Tulsa. He did not look happy to see that she and Max were sharing the room, and Zac stepped out into the hall to talk to him. "I'm sorry about yesterday," she said as they walked outside. "I really appreciate it that you came to the funeral. I just wish you didn't have to see the rest of it."

Drew sighed. "I had a sense of what that looked like, even when we were growing up," he said. "It's why I was recruiting at our high school all those years ago, and why I kept an eye on you when you got to West Point. I wanted to make sure you survived."

Zac looked at him, then back towards her hotel. She wanted to apologize again, but she did not know what to say. *He's a good guy,* she thought. *I would be interested in being with him if it didn't mean staying in Little Rock and never having an opportunity to move on.*

Drew seemed to guess what she was thinking. "It's okay," he reassured her. "I realized I probably wasn't the right guy for you when I couldn't bring myself to go inside and find you by myself the other night."

"I'm sorry about that too," Zac said. "I wouldn't have wanted you to find me with my head blown off either."

Drew put his arms around her and hugged her to his chest. "That's what I was afraid of," he said. He let go of her. "How close were you to actually using that gun, though?"

"I was close," Zac admitted. "For all the times that I was

too scared to go through with it, that was really the one time I might have done it if I hadn't heard you guys on the stairs."

Drew pulled her to his chest again. "I'm so sorry," he said.

"I'm not," Zac said. "Now that I'm still here, I'm glad to be alive."

Zac did not even look in the rearview mirror as she and Max drove back to Tulsa. Ben was her only sibling to see them off, and he had been the only one to talk to either of them since the previous night. "I'm so glad we're leaving," Zac said.

"I don't blame you," Max said. "That was some fight you guys got into."

"It was everything I was expecting," Zac said. "It's why I've never been to see any of them, or even spoken to any of them, except Ben. I'm just sorry you had to see it all."

"Don't worry about it," Max said. "It's why I'm here, remember?"

"Yeeeaahh," Zac said, slowly drawing the word out as she stared at the greenery outside the passenger window.

"But I understand why you've been avoiding your family all this time, more so than I did before," Max said. "Your mother's a mess and your older siblings definitely have your parents' alcohol problems."

"Is it obvious?" Zac asked.

She was being sarcastic, but Max answered her seriously. "Yes," he said. "I feel bad for their kids." There was a silence. "I was hoping that the funeral would make you somewhat able to move past your family's shit, though, I have to admit."

"It did," Zac said. "I do feel like there's been a major weight taken off. And at least Abe and Melanie have some solution as to how to deal with Ma. That alone was more than I was hoping for."

"All that's good stuff. Still, though, I would take some of what they said with a grain of salt."

Finally, Zac took her eyes off of the trees around them and

looked at Max. "What do you mean?"

Max took his eyes off the road for a second to look at Zac. "You can't really believe what Abe said about how you should have been killed by that IED."

Zac clenched her jaw and stared back out the window. Tears stung at her eyes. When the silence lengthened, Max gave her a poke. When she looked back at him, her tears started rolling down her face. "I have felt that way ever since I got injured," she said. "It was just luck that I was in the second Humvee instead of the first one."

Max shook his head vehemently, his eyes now on the road. "That wasn't luck, it was military strategy!" he said. "Never put the commanding officer in the first vehicle! Come on Zac, you know your stuff- why are you doubting yourself?"

"Matt was one of my best officers," Zac replied. "Why should he have been killed instead of me?"

"It was *war*, Zac. Do you know how many close calls I had that happened just that way? We were on patrol once, and one of my enlistees twisted his ankle and needed medical attention, so the whole unit waited. A quarter mile ahead of us, a building was blown to bits as we waited. If it hadn't been for my guy's two left feet, the whole unit would have been right in front of that building when it blew up- and we all would have been killed."

Zac wiped the tears off her face as she looked at Max. "You never told me that."

"There were a million other incidents just like it," Max replied. "You can't keep beating yourself up because you survived. I don't care what your siblings said, or what your parents would have said. Your parents are the reason your siblings are such a mess."

"You don't have to remind me," Zac said. "I went into the military to get away from that, remember?"

"And the military has turned you into a fine officer. It's worth living for."

"Even as a civilian, you think that's worth living for?"

"You have some incredible skills, Zac. Talk to the people at

West Point- it would be a waste for you not to convey what you know to the next generation of officers."

"I have an appointment with the Superintendent of the Academy after we testify in Washington," Zac admitted.

"Good," Max replied. "Make sure you keep that appointment."

When Max dropped Zac off at her house later that afternoon, she found a delivery of flowers on her front stoop. *I wonder who this could be from,* she thought, frowning as she picked them up and unlocked her door. Inside the house, Zac put the flowers on a table in her living room and read the card that was attached to it. "With deepest sympathy," it read. "From Jenny Nichols and Gail Murphy."

"Awww," Zac said aloud, even though the house was empty. "That was really sweet of them." She looked at the flowers. "That bouquet is really pretty too, even if they are supposed to be sympathy flowers." She picked up her phone and dialed Gail's number first. The call went to voicemail, and Zac left a message thanking her profusely.

At Jenny's house, a middle-aged woman answered the phone, and Zac's stomach tightened as she wondered whether it was Michelle. "Good afternoon, is Jenny there?" she asked politely.

"Who is this?" the woman replied, and Zac could tell she was curious.

"My name's Zac Madison-" she began.

"Ah, yes," Michelle said. "I remember you, of course."

Zac could tell she was smiling, and even though she wanted to talk to Jenny, she took a deep breath. "As long as I have you on the phone, Michelle, I wanted to thank you for standing up for me and Jenny in front of those protesters. I think you really diffused the situation."

"I was happy to," Michelle replied. "That woman was just a bunch of nonsense. Don't let anything she says bother you."

"It hasn't, don't worry."

They both laughed, and Michelle said, "let me get Jenny."

"Thanks so much for the flowers," Zac said when Jenny got on the phone. "They're really nice."

"You're welcome," Jenny said. "I know your family's been kind of tough on you, but it's still not an easy thing to go through."

"Maybe not," Zac admitted. "But my siblings did step up to the plate, in terms of taking care of my dad and the end and now my mom too."

"At least that's a relief."

"Yes, it is." Zac wasn't sure what else to say. "I guess I'll see you next week, then?"

"Definitely."

CHAPTER 14

Travis Lamont looked out the window from the front seat of the old pickup truck that he and his brothers had borrowed from their parents. Cole was driving, and Robby sat in the middle. Travis did not want to say anything to his brothers, but he felt like he was squeezed up against the door.

Even despite his silence, Robby seemed to read his brother's mind. "It's a tighter fit in here than the last time we were home," he said.

Both Travis and Cole nodded. "The truck also seems a lot older," Travis said. "Maybe we should buy Mom and Dad a new one before we move out."

"Not a bad idea," Cole replied. "So what do you guys think of the houses we've seen so far today?"

"That first one was nice," Travis said. "The second one was kind of a dump, though."

"Yeah, no kidding," Cole said. "And I really don't feel like doing the amount of work that it would take to fix it up."

"Me neither," Travis and Robby said at the same time.

"None of the ones we've seen this week have been as nice as the first one we saw," Cole added.

"The one you guys saw without me?" Travis asked. His brothers nodded. "Can we get an appointment to see that one again?"

Robby looked at his watch. "Looks like we'll be a little

early to see the one we're heading to right now," he said. "I can give the real estate agent a call to see when she's free."

"That would be a good idea," Travis said. "Hopefully they haven't gotten an offer yet."

The next day, after seeing three more houses, Travis, Cole and Robby went back to the house that Robby and Cole had seen by themselves. Travis swallowed as they pulled up at the house. It stood three stories high, and he could see basement windows protruding from the ground as well. *Cole and Robby are sure this house is the best one they've seen,* he thought. *I hope I think that too. I'm ready to be done searching.*

The real estate agent that Robby and Cole had met the first time stood in front of the house, waiting to meet them again. "Megan," Cole said, "it's good to see you again. Thanks for letting see the place a second time."

"My pleasure," Megan replied. She looked at Travis. "I take it this is the third brother?"

"Yes, I am," Travis said. "I'm Travis. Thanks for meeting with us again."

It was nearly two hours later when the three brothers finally exited the house, and when Travis got out to the street, he felt like his head was going to explode. *Robby and Cole were right, though,* he thought. *This is the nicest place we've seen so far. I'd be happy to make an offer on it and get away from Mom and Dad already. Mostly Mom.*

Behind him, Cole and Robby continued talking to Megan. Travis could only look at the street in front of his as the warm breeze ruffled his hair. *I'm sick of summer and how hot it is,* he thought suddenly. *I'm ready for fall.*

He looked up the street and saw a girl with dark hair walking her dog. As she got closer, Travis could see how green her eyes were. "Hi," she said. "Are you Travis?"

"I am," Travis replied wondering how she had known that.

"I'm Amber," she said. "I live up the block. I met your brothers when they saw the house the last time."

"Nice to meet you," Travis replied.

It was not until Zac was sitting inside the VA Center, waiting for her next group therapy session to begin, that she was finally able to start writing in one of the empty notebooks Alex had given her. Using a red pen that she had found in her ruck, Zac started forming letters on the paper, then words. Not all of them formed complete sentences, but Zac did not care. When the therapy session started, Zac looked around the group. Jenny was still writing in her notebook, and Daniel was holding his notebook on his lap. *Guess I'm not the only one who's kept up with the writing,* she thought.

"It looks like a few of you have continued writing in your journals," Annemarie said to begin the session a minute later. "Does anyone want to share what they've written most recently?"

There was a silence. Everyone in the group looked at each other.

"Zac, I saw you writing out in the hallway before the session began," Annemarie said. "Are you comfortable sharing?"

Not really, Zac thought. She shrugged. "I guess I could read a bit," she said, surprised at her own words. She was just as surprised when the rest of the group nodded, encouraging her. She took a deep breath and opened her notebook.

"The silent desert curved around me, and the stars twinkled above me," she read. "Third deployment, four weeks left before freedom. Then 0300, and our convoy left the base, hunting the enemy. A loud boom broke the silence, and ended the lives of four of my men. Training is an eternity- the end of a life, a second. My best officer flew home, silent, as I was flown to the hospital, injured. Red sand against a black sky, red blood against white stars."

When Zac finished reading, the whole group was looking at her. "Wow," Annemarie said. "That was intense."

Immediately, the rest of the group started talking, and the

words poured out. "You wouldn't believe some of the stuff we saw over there," Jimmy said. "We shot at dogs and kids because they might have had bombs strapped to them."

"I don't regret anything we did over there," Daniel said. "Those guys were the enemy. Anyone walking towards us could have killed us. We reacted how we were trained to react. The worst of it is that people here at home don't have a clue what that's like." He shook his head. "People here judge us all the time for what we might have done, including killing people. I hate it. It's the worst when civilians judge us. Like they have a clue what happened over there."

Zac nodded in agreement. It was also the most she had ever heard Daniel say.

The meeting broke up more than an hour later, and only then because another group needed the room. "Damn civilians," Daniel continued to grumble as he and Zac made their way towards the doors of the VA. "Those fucking protesters were the worst of it."

Zac almost felt amused as she remembered her confrontation with Diana. "That sucked," she agreed. "But there are civilians who are helping us, too. All of our therapists are civilians. That protester I fought with- her own son is actually funding some of the treatment studies here at the VA."

"That sounds like a happy household," Daniel said sarcastically as they got to their cars.

Zac laughed. "Luckily for us, it's their problem, not ours."

That weekend, Diana knocked on Travis' door. "What do you want?" he asked.

"You've been away a lot, looking at houses and spending time in the studio. I haven't had a chance to talk to you much."

"Didn't realize you were interested."

"Oh, come on, Travis," Diana said.

Finally, Travis looked at her. "What do you want?" he repeated.

"Have you heard from Zac at all since the protest?"

"No," Travis said shortly. He continued looking at his mother, still trying to figure out what she was thinking.

Diana's next words surprised him. "I was thinking of going to Zac's house to apologize," she said. "Do you want to come with me? I know I upset you the day of the protest, so I wanted to apologize- to both of you."

Travis shrugged again. His face had a masked expression on it that Diana had never seen before.

Now Diana eyed her son, trying to figure out what he was thinking. There was a silence. "What are you thinking?" Diana finally asked.

"I can come with you if you go over there," Travis said. "Whether we make any progress with Zac depends on how pissed off she is."

A few minutes later, Travis tried to ignore how fast his heart was beating as Diana knocked at Zac's front door. *This is the same fear and anxiety I felt the first several times I dealt with Zac and other vets*, he thought. *I've spent the whole summer trying to change that, but I'm not sure anything is different.* When Zac came to the door, Travis wanted to shrink into nothingness, especially when he saw how Zac glared at his mother.

"I came to apologize," Diana said, and Travis was glad she got that out first, before Zac yelled at them or shut the door in their faces. "I don't know what I was thinking when I organized that protest. I just wanted to let someone know what I thought about the wars."

Zac looked at them in silence for a moment before opening the door and letting them in. "Let me show you something," she said as she led them into the living room.

Max stood in the corner of the living room, trying to remain the background. By the way Diana eyed him, though, Zac was sure that Travis had told her about him- especially when Diana glanced down at Max's hands, expecting to see the hook that covered the stump of his left hand. Blackie sat at Max's feet, eyeing Travis and Diana.

As Zac led him and his mother into the living room,

Travis wondered if she intended to give them a tour of the house. Confused, he followed wordlessly. Zac stopped at a small wooden table that held a number of photographs. She selected one and handed it to Diana. "That's me and my brother Clive as kids," she said as Diana looked at a picture of a much younger Zac with a smaller boy on a red bike.

Then Zac took the picture away and handed Diana another one. "Me and Clive again, about ten years ago, not too long before we both deployed." Again, Diana looked at a picture of two people, but these two people were both grown and wore military uniforms- Zac in the uniform of the Army, Clive in his dress Marines uniform. Clive looked very much like his older sister, even imitating the way she stood and her expression. The similarities made Diana smile.

When Diana looked up at Zac, expecting another, more recent, picture, Zac took the photograph she was holding, but instead of replacing it with another one, she said, "Clive was killed in combat seven months into his second deployment. And we still continued fighting, for three years after that, Mrs. Lamont."

They continued walking. Max continued to hover in the background, listening but not interfering. Zac led them into a different room, still on the first floor- a room which Travis thought was either Zac's bedroom or a spare bedroom. An armoire stood in the corner of the room, and it was to this piece of furniture that Zac walked, opening it and taking out a uniform. Travis and Diana realized it was Zac's own uniform, complete with its decorations.

Zac laid the uniform on the bed, and, pointing to the decorations, said, "This is a purple heart, which I got when I had to take early retirement. It's a disability retirement because of the wounds that I sustained. That first wound was from an exploding grenade. I had burns on more than fifty percent of my body. The second wound, a more permanent injury, came from a round of machine gun fire to my leg." She pointed again. "This is a silver star, awarded for gallantry, because my rifle's bullets happened to hit men wearing a different uniform.

I have never forgotten the fact that the life of someone else's brother or son can be translated into something as simple as this star, and only because that man was on the opposite side."

Zac pointed to a different decoration. "This is a bronze star for my 'meritorious service' to my country. That means that my unit was instrumental in cutting through enemy forces." She gestured again. "That there is the Congressional Medal Of Honor, which is awarded to almost all the men and women who serve in combat. Same with this Presidential Medal Of Honor, except that it's awarded by the President. These decorations here"- and Zac gestured again- "show my rank- Colonel. It's a high rank, but I got there quickly because of my education at West Point and how often I was out in the field with my troops during both wars."

Then Zac looked back at Travis and Diana, her penetrating gaze boring into them. "Do you think the wars are over?" she asked. "Maybe we have stopped fighting, declared victory, but the war is not over. Thousands of people have left behind nothing but their memories. And in the neverending quest for the truth, a general is now on trial for treason. Everyone he ever dealt with has to live through their memories all over again."

Zac frowned. "And that is only the most obvious remainder of the bloodshed," she continued. "Those of us lucky enough to have survived still have to work through our PTSD, nightmares, and fear. So many vets find they can't handle it and kill themselves. A best friend of mine from West Point took that route. Perhaps you can now see, Mrs. Lamont, a little bit of what actually lies behind 'us military people that are so sure of ourselves'."

"So is anything still happening between you and Drew?" Alex asked the next time Zac met with her.

Zac sighed. "I don't think so," she said. "He went back to Little Rock after my father's funeral, and we've talked a few times, but…" She swallowed. "We obviously won't be getting together romantically, which is what he wanted."

"How do you feel about that?"

"I've always been interested in Max, and even more so now that I know it's reciprocated. I think it's probably the right choice, but I still feel bad about it. Drew's a good guy."

"And what about Max? What does he think he'll do if his current job doesn't get extended?"

"He's not sure yet, but he still wants to work with vets. He's real connected to the veteran community, both through West Point and locally." Zac eyed her therapist. "Why do you ask?"

"Well, you mentioned that you're looking into teaching at West Point, and it got me thinking- one of my classmates from my Ph.D. program has been teaching in the CUNY system for a few years now."

"That's the city university up in New York, right?" Zac asked, remembering the term from her years at West Point.

Alex nodded. "With all the veterans that have been returning from the wars, my friend has been looking into designing a course at CUNY's Graduate School of Public Health, that focuses on the health issues of returning veterans."

"Max would really be interested in that," Zac said. "But what would he do there?"

"My colleague had a few things in mind. He could consult on the development of the course, as well as spend a session of the class itself talking to the students. His connections to other veterans would help a lot as well."

"I'll talk to him about it," Zac said. "If I do end up at West Point, it would be great if he could find something in the city."

Alex nodded. "I don't think this is the only thing that CUNY's doing that would be up his alley," she said. "Some of their colleges' history departments are looking into more classes on military history and tactics."

"I didn't know they offered military classes at all."

"These wars have changed things, Zac," Alex said. "Including public perception of and interest in the armed forces. Plenty of high school students- and younger kids even- are expressing interest in learning about this stuff now, even if they don't think that enlisting is the right path for them."

There was a pause. Alex took a deep breath and eyed her patient.

"What?" Zac asked.

"I'm sorry it's been a tough road for you, but I'm glad to see that things are changing for the better."

"No need to apologize," Zac replied. "Up until my discharge from the Army, there is absolutely nothing that I change about my life."

"Who has the grocery list?" Travis asked his brothers as they pulled into the grocery store's parking lot.

"I do," Robby said. "Milk, eggs, vegetables... The usual." He grinned, and his brothers did too. They had just made an offer on the house that they had liked the best- the one Amber lived up the block from- and Travis could tell they were all glad their search was over.

I think our offer will be accepted, Travis thought. *And I'm looking forward to spending more time with Amber.* As they piled out of the truck, Travis looked at the store in front of them. *This might be one of the last times we buy food for the whole family,* he realized. *Mom and Dad will be on their own again, but at least they'll have three less mouths to feed.*

Inside the store, the brothers grabbed a couple of carts and dispersed in different directions. Travis had already spotted a familiar figure in the vegetable section, and he headed over there. "Hey, Zac!" he called.

Zac looked up from where she stood, looking at the rows of carrots. She looked slightly startled. "Oh, hi, Travis," she said.

"Thanks for giving my Mom and me the short walk

through of military life the other day."

"You needed it."

"I can't disagree," Travis said. "It really affected my mom."

"Oh yeah?" Zac asked. "I wasn't sure."

Travis nodded. "I think she's gotten good at hiding her feelings. I don't remember her being like that before the war, but I think she was so worried about everything that was going on, and whether my brothers and I would be swept up in it, that she got better at putting up a wall around herself."

There was a pause as Travis, thinking about what he had just said, wondered what Zac's parents had thought of having two of their children actually fighting in the war, rather than safely hiding in another country. He examined the vegetables in front of him as a way of hiding his confusion. "So what's up?" he said finally. "You didn't look like you were actually examining the carrots."

"Nah, I pretty much know what I need."

The silence grew. "So?" Travis prompted.

"I'm still thinking about what about what to say when I testify at Victor Rice's trial."

"I have to admit that I've been thinking about that myself," Travis said. "Either the guy committed treason or he didn't."

"True, but at the same time, the guy has a family who depends on his salary, and they wouldn't see his pension if he's convicted of treason." Zac stopped to pull a carton of milk from a refrigerator as Travis pulled a carton from the adjacent one. "Besides, Victor has always been a vocal opponent of the war, and the more I learn, the more I agree with him." Zac took a breath as she thought about Lucy and Clive. "But the more that this stuff gets published in the papers, the more I think the Pentagon and the White House are looking to cover their own asses for the mistakes they made, and more and more, I've been thinking that this trial is a part of that."

Travis sighed. "When I first moved back from Canada, I wondered whether I'd made a mistake not coming back and fighting for the country. So many people had the courage to do that, and I ran away. But the more I've gotten involved with veterans' issues, the more I've realized that I wouldn't have made it in any branch of the service."

Zac eyed him as they stopped to examine the supermarket's cereal selections. "It's not the right fit for everybody," she finally admitted. "That's something that I'm just beginning to understand."

That night, Zac sat at her kitchen table, staring out the large windows in front of her. A pen and a pad of paper with several pages of her small handwriting sat on the table, but she was no longer concentrating on it. Having written about the subject at hand as much as possible, indeed, more than she would have thought conceivable, Zac was now willing to put all of it aside for now.

It's about time, too, she thought as she stood up. *I've kicked this issue around so much, it probably has more wear and tear than the soccer ball Clive's high school team used during the whole time he played there. And just in time, too- I have to testify next week.* Relieved, Zac put the pen and pad of paper next to the computer in the first floor bedroom. Then, feeling a surge of energy flow through her, she turned on the computer, sat down and started typing up what she had written.

"The United States has just been through ten long years of fighting two wars in different countries," she began. "Victor Rice opposed those wars, and after a decade of combat, I can understand why. Our troops were sent to fight an ever-changing mission against an elusive foe. We had no clear objectives and no definitive exit strategy.

"To make matters worse, many of the suppliers were in business simply to line their own pockets with lucrative military contracts. Supplies were delivered late and haphazardly, if they were delivered at all. Our troops were often sent into battle without proper guns, ammunition or armor. I personally know of many troops and officers whose families purchased armor and ammunition at their own expense to provide their loved ones with the tools of combat that the Army couldn't.

"Many of our vehicles also broke down in the desert, squarely in the middle of enemy territory- and our enemy was unforgiving. I also know officers and troops who were killed when they were stranded like that right in front of our enemy, because our suppliers couldn't be bothered to provide functional vehicles, or vehicles with any armor on them. And yet, many of our suppliers were rewarded with multiple contracts throughout the wars, even as their failures came to light.

"Furthermore, even troops, like myself, who were lucky enough to come home in one piece, have found a different war at home. We face an underfunded and understaffed network of Veterans' Affairs and Army hospitals that are overwhelmed with the needs of injured soldiers. Increasingly, our combat wounds have compromised our mental health as well as our physical health, but the medicine treating us has not kept up with our invisible wounds as well as it has healed our bullet holes. The long wait that troops and veterans have faced for basic care has resulted in the denial of care, as many have committed suicide because of PTSD and the many other mental health issues that have plagued them.

"And that's not all. One of my best friends from West Point was raped repeatedly by the men in her unit, soldiers that were under her command. Her complaints led to the end of her deployment, and were met with silence here in the States. Women have formed an increasing number of our soldiers in Iraq and Afghanistan, and yet their health needs are even more overlooked than the needs of their male counterparts. My friend's death was very painful for me, especially because it was unnecessary. It was a major reason I decided to spend so much time today on these topics.

"However, despite my extensive knowledge of America's operations in Iraq and Afghanistan, I can say little as to the circumstances surrounding Victor's actions in combat, or about his arrest. Victor was my first Commanding Officer out of West Point, and I served under him for two years. During that time, he was a brilliant strategist and a strong mentor. Since that time, I have been fortunate to have risen through the ranks, and was given my own command through multiple deployments in Iraq and Afghanistan. During the time of the alleged actions that lead to Victor's arrest, I was leading my own unit in combat, far from Victor's command. As such, I cannot shed light on the actions that have brought him here today. However, I am happy to take questions from the floor."

When Zac finally finished typing, her hands were shaking, but she was finished. She saved her work and shut down her computer. Then she headed outside to water her flowers. *Thank God,* she thought. *Now I don't have to wrestle with that anymore.*

Zac's phone rang as she waited for Max and his friends to get out of work. "Hello?" she said. She had parked in the parking lot of the factory where Max worked, and she kept an eye on the door as she spoke.

"Zac, it's Ben," her brother said on the other end.

"Hi Ben," Zac said. "How's work going?"

"Fine. I just got out office, and I'm heading back to the dorm."

"Good, I'm glad to hear it."

"Yeah. So, is Max still planning on moving into your house this coming weekend?"

"Yes, he is," Zac replied. "Why do you ask?"

"I thought I might come out for the weekend and help him move, if that's okay with y'all."

Zac smiled. For the first time, she was aware of how strong her brother's accent was. *That must have been what I sounded like when I went off to West Point,* she thought. "That would be great," she said. "Max's family is coming in too, so you'll get to meet them."

"Are they staying at your place?" Ben asked.

"No, they're staying at a hotel nearby. But you can stay at our place."

"Okay, good. Who from his family is coming?"

"His parents and his sister," Zac said. "That's actually the whole family. He's only got one sibling."

"I can't even picture that," Ben said, and he and Zac laughed.

In front of her, Zac could see Max and bunch of other people coming out the door of the factory. "When do you think you'll come over?" she asked Ben.

"I figured I'd do my usual," Ben said. "Leave here after work on Friday, get to your place later that night."

"That sounds good," Zac said as Max and the other guys joining them for dinner got closer to her.

Ben, hearing the chatter in the background, asked, "what's going on with you?"

"I'm meeting Max and a bunch of people for dinner."

"Well, don't let me stop you."

"You weren't," Zac reassured him as she got back into her car. Max was already in the passenger seat.

"Who was that?" Max asked as she hung up.

"It was Ben," Zac replied. "He's coming in this weekend to help you move."

"How nice of him!" Max replied. "He can meet my family."

"I tried to warn him about that," Zac teased as she drove out of the parking lot, following the cars of the people they were joining. "Unfortunately, it didn't deter him."

"Oh, shut up," Max said, but he was laughing. "How is your family recovering after your father's funeral?"

"I think they're doing okay," Zac said. "I didn't ask specifically. I really do need to get past it."

A few minutes later, they pulled up at an Italian restaurant. As they got out of the car and joined the rest of the group, Max introduced Zac to the people she had not met.

"So this is Zac," said Ron Byrd, a former Lance Corporal

in the Marines whose wife Clare stood at his side. "It's nice to finally meet you."

"Yeah, we thought Max had made you up," joked Al Green, another former Marine whose girlfriend Betty had also joined them. The group laughed as they went inside the restaurant.

"I'm sorry to disprove that," Zac quipped.

"I'm not sorry," said Matthew Bates, a former Air Force pilot. "You have quite the combat reputation. I'd love to hear your stories."

"She is writing her memoirs," Max said as they all got seated around a large circular table in the middle of the restaurant.

The rest of the group looked at Zac with interest. "Oh yeah?" Matthew said.

"I've only just started on it," Zac said. "Everything is still in the beginning stages."

"Then we'll have to hear your stories before you finish writing," Jeff said.

The group laughed again, and Zac felt herself relaxing. A little while later, an order of hot garlic bread and a round of drinks came for the table. Zac stuck with soda, but she did not care. *This is so nice,* she thought.

That weekend, Ben helped Max haul some of his furniture into the U-Haul he had rented. Behind them, Max's sister Alana carried some of Max's smaller belongings into the truck. Zac spoke to Max's parents, Marilyn and James. She played with Blackie as they talked, mostly so that the puppy would not get in the way of the moving.

"He's getting big," James said about Blackie.

"He really is," Zac agreed.

"He was tiny when Max first got him," James added. "Really tiny. Runt of the litter."

"You were a plebe during Max's firstie year at West Point,

right?" Marilyn asked Zac. "I remember meeting you even back then."

"Max told me," Zac said with a laugh. "I didn't realize I'd made such an impression."

Marilyn nodded. "I thought your Southern accent was fabulous. I think you've lost a lot of it, though, unfortunately."

Zac laughed harder. "Max said the same thing."

"I'm real sorry to hear about your father," James added.

"Thanks," Zac said.

They all watched as Alana, Max and Ben loaded more stuff into the truck. "How old's your brother?" Marilyn asked.

"Nineteen," Zac said. "He's the baby of the family." She looked back at Marilyn and James. "I don't think there's too much more stuff to load," she said. "I'm going to start bringing the last of it out." She headed inside the nearly-empty apartment and came back down with a crate of books.

"I really didn't have a lot of stuff to move," Max said.

"Yeah, I've acquired more stuff in the time since I got home from the war than in the fifteen years before that," Zac agreed.

"It's from moving around all the time," Max said. "Who knew where we'd be stationed next, or when we'd be deployed next? It never made sense to acquire a lot of stuff."

"Do you guys think you'll miss that lifestyle?" Ben asked as they all brought down the last of Max's belongings.

Zac and Max looked at each other. "After three deployments, it's been nice to have one place to live for awhile," Zac said. "But I think I'm still getting used to it."

Max nodded. "And we may end up moving up to New York if we both get jobs up there," he said.

"Are you hoping that will happen?" Marilyn asked.

Max and Zac looked at each other again. "I kind of am," Zac replied. "I really do want to be back at West Point."

It was August 26th. Zac put her suitcase into the trunk of

her car and closed the trunk. Then she looked at her watch.

"We're pretty early," Max said. "Do you want to stop at Travis' on the way out, to say goodbye?"

"That would be nice," Zac said. "I think we might catch him before he and his brothers head off to the recording studio."

Max nodded. "Okay," he said. "I'll drive."

Travis and Cole were outside their house when Zac and Max pulled up. Zac got out of the car to talk to them, and Max rolled down his window.

"Hi Zac," Travis said, and Cole smiled and her and Max as Robby came out of house and joined them. "You heading off to Washington?"

"Yes, we're on our way to the airport now. I just wanted to say goodbye before we left."

"That was nice," Travis said, smiling. "Thanks."

"Are you guys busy recording?" Zac asked.

Travis nodded. "We were just discussing our schedule. We have a few tracks laid down already, and we're trying to figure out what work we need to do on the other songs we have before we start recording those too."

"Zac, what's your schedule in Washington look like?" Robby asked from behind his brothers.

"Max testifies tomorrow, and I take the stand the day after that. Then I'll spend some time with the Superintendent of West Point, discussing whether I'd be a good fit teaching there."

"Let us know how that goes," Travis said.

"I definitely will."

"And I'll let you know when we're moving and when our new album comes out." Travis looked at Zac. "Deal?"

"Deal," Zac replied. Then she got back into the car and looked at Max.

"Ready?" Max asked.

"Ready," Zac said. She looked out the windshield as Max pulled away from the Lamonts' house and drove to the airport.

THE LAST BATTLE

ABOUT THE AUTHOR

Tamar Anolic is a writer and lawyer based in the Washington, D.C. area. She started her writing career with feature articles published in her college's newspaper. She also freelanced professionally and had articles published in Newsday and Financial History Quarterly. Her first book, "The Russian Riddle," was the first published biography of the Grand Duke Sergei Alexandrovich of Russia. "The Last Battle" is her first novel.

Made in the USA
Middletown, DE
29 March 2017